The NPR Curious Listener's Guide to

Opera

The NPR Curious Listener's Guide to

Opera

WILLIAM BERGER

A Grand Central Press Book
A Perigee Boo

A Perigee Book
Published by The Berkley Publishing Group
A division of Penguin Putnam Inc.
375 Hudson Street
New York, New York 10014

PRODUCED BY GRAND CENTRAL PRESS
Paul Fargis, Director
Judy Pray, Executive Editor
Nick Viorst, Series Editor

NATIONAL PUBLIC RADIO
Murray Horwitz, Vice-President, Cultural Programming
Andy Trudeau, Executive Producer, Cultural Programming
Bruce Scott, Music Producer (Opera), Cultural Programming
Barbara A. Vierow, Project Manager, Business Development
Kate Elliott, Project Manager, Business Development

First Perigee edition: February 2002

Published simultaneously in Canada.

Visit our website at
www.penguinputnam.com

Library of Congress Cataloging-in-Publication Data

Berger, William, 1961–
The NPR curious listener's guide to opera / William Berger.
    p.   cm.
Includes discography, bibliographical references, and index.
ISBN 0-399-52743-5
1. Opera.   I. National Public Radio (U.S.)   II. Title.

ML1700 B33   2002
782.1—dc21
2001036849

Printed in the United States of America

10 9 8 7 6 5 4 3 2 1

Contents

Acknowledgments — vii

Foreword — ix

Introduction — xi

1. What Is Opera? — 1
2. The Story of Opera — 9
3. Varieties of Opera — 49
4. Opera Deconstructed — 61
5. The Composers — 85
6. The Performers — 119
7. The Operas — 141
8. Opera on CD — 163
9. The Total Opera Experience — 179
10. The Language of Opera — 189

Resources for Curious Listeners — 205

Index — 215

Acknowledgments

The author is deeply indebted to a large number of people, both professional and amateur, whose generosity in sharing their knowledge, insight, and passion for opera has made this project possible. Also, I am grateful to friends and colleagues who have been equally generous with time and support. Among both these groups are some who must be thanked by name: Adam Abramowitz, Frances Berger, Aronnora Morgan, Rich Lynn, Lou Ruffalo, Martin Majchrowicz, Al Zuckerman, Bruce Scott, Lou Santacroce, Mark Mobley, Anya Grundmann, Stephen Miller, and a special thanks to Nick Viorst for his tireless commitment to this project.

Foreword

by Plácido Domingo

Music is both my work and my hobby. Sharing it with others is my passion. And introducing more people to the marvelous, vivid world of opera has been a long-standing dream of mine—from both sides of the stage. On the performing side, developing the next generation of talent has led to our worldwide Operalia competition for young singers, and to the Young Artists Training Program we've established at the Washington Opera. To my mind, programs like these are vital to making sure this artform flourishes in the twenty-first century.

But what of the audiences that will hear these great young artists? There is marvelous talent in our concert halls and opera houses. But something as important and beautiful and timeless as opera should not be only for specialists! It should be for everybody—a cornerstone of musical knowledge and basic education.

But I'm constantly surprised and disappointed that there is not more music education in our schools. There are simply too many missing pages in our young people's knowledge of music. Those blank pages have been filled in by the pervasive beat of pop music, pushing nearly everything else aside. And that is a shame, because opera is so approachable. We simply need to give everyone the opportunity to learn it. I'm convinced that if I take two of my young artists into a school for a week and they teach kids to sing a beautiful, simple aria like "La ci darem la mano" from Mozart's *Don Giovanni*, I'm on the way to making some opera fans for life.

Musical education, of course, isn't just for schoolchildren. And that's why I'm delighted that NPR has published this book. It's clever and concise, entertaining and educational. Whether the world of opera is a new discovery or an old friend, this NPR Guide is a marvelous way to fill in any of your own missing pages. And maybe make YOU a lifetime fan.

Introduction

Any American who first approaches the world of opera today would be in the position of a newcomer approaching baseball. The two institutions, after all, have quite a bit in common. Both opera and baseball claim legions of insanely loyal fans who believe the subjects of their passion to be uniquely eloquent, powerful, and even spiritual in some sense. They are also both equally mystifying to those who are not fans, people who cannot grasp what all the fuss is about and who suspect the fans to be delusional in their passion. Both opera and baseball receive the same criticisms from detractors. Both are called slow, plodding, old-fashioned, and hopelessly out of touch with today's fast-paced world and its less genteel modes of expression. Many "true" athletes decry baseball's lack of pure athleticism and many "true" musicians denounce opera's impure musicality. Both opera and baseball are imbued with rituals and postures that apparently have nothing to do with the supposed tasks at hand, yet that are, inexplicably, accepted and even celebrated by their respective devotees. Both thrive on mythic elements from the past, and both have always been said to be in a state of decline today compared to the Golden Ages (real or imagined), of yesterday.

The simile can be stretched further. Even those who have no interest in baseball or opera accept the fact that an American city must have a baseball stadium and an opera house if it is to be considered a major urban center. In this way, these venues fulfill a function not unlike cathedrals in medieval French towns, except that most residents of the modern American city never actually enter these "cathedrals." Still, they are happy to know that such places exist, and cheerfully accept the status they confer on their hometowns. They might even get curious to know what goes on in these places. Here the newcomers to baseball and opera find themselves in very analogous situations. Asking fans about their passions is hazardous. First, one must endure a long discourse on the beauty of the pastime in question. Then, assuming the newcomer has the fearlessness to pursue the discussion on to the detail level, he or she is flooded by a completely incomprehensible jargon that has no apparent relationship to any other sport or art form. More confused than before, the newcomer can be excused for dismissing the whole subject as irrelevant to his or her own life.

All this is true for both baseball and opera, but it must be admitted that opera has its own unique barriers in addition to those already mentioned. While opera is a palpable and growing presence in America, no one outside of the asylums would (yet) call it The American Pastime. Although a distinctly European art form in origin, opera belongs to the world at this point in history. The notion that opera is not exclusively American permits some to perceive it as distinctly un-American. There are language issues beyond the jargon enjoyed by fans. Most (although not all) operas are written in languages other than English. We in America are given famously little incentive to tolerate foreign languages in our lives, yet the perpetrators of opera would ask us to sit for long hours through performances in languages we neither understand nor particularly respect. The dominant languages of opera—Italian, German, French, and Russian (in that order)—are portrayed in our culture as comical, effete, or downright hostile to our values. If one can penetrate the language, there is the issue of what is being said on the operatic stage. Everyone seems to know that opera plots are emblematically silly, and no amount of explaining them or apologizing for them will remove this notion.

Then there is the music itself. Opera is a form of drama, rather than a form of music, and many different styles of music can be heard in operas. There is, however, a certain style of singing that has been found to be very effective in telling a dramatic story through music, the celebrated (and maligned) "operatic voice." In women, this involves a generous use of the somewhat unnatural instrument called a "head voice," which is inherently piercing and can penetrate layers of other sound even when produced with only moderate strength. The head voice is a problem for many people today. It sounds shrill and extravagantly emotional compared to the earthier "chest voice" preferred in popular music. Anyone who wants to parody the opera need only produce a whooping sound to get across the message that opera is unacceptably weird. The men in opera do not fare much better, although it is the opposite situation that unnerves people. While the male use of the head voice has been standard in popular music from the minstrels to Johnny Mathis to virtually every rock singer, the unamplified chest voice is the hallmark of male operatic overkill. The voices in opera (or at least in the vast majority of operas that have survived) should not alienate audiences because they are atypical, but this seems to be a problem for many people today. Music, despite what Madonna recently sang, does not bring the people together. In fact, it is uniquely divisive. And opera remains on the far side of the divide for most Americans.

The situation is far from dire, however. The perceived foreignness of opera does not carry the weight it once did, and our world continues to shrink to the point where the issue is almost irrelevant. Once upon a time Americans were xenophobic in matters of cuisine, but eventually we found that we can consume cappuccinos and sushi and still have something of a national identity. As our culinary horizons have mercifully expanded, so have our artistic possibilities. One opera-advocacy organization counts sixty-three full-time opera companies in the United States, while a less formal reckoning lists over two hundred professional companies performing opera (compare this to a half-century ago, when there were fewer than a dozen). Every record store has at least a smattering of opera recordings, and the larger ones list hundreds if not thousands of titles. Even the local video store is likely to have recorded performances available. Millions of people who would never attend an opera can watch it on public television or hear it on radio. Opera, contrary to all sensible predictions of the past, is alive in America.

Why? There are many possible answers, but the paradoxical answer seems to lie in the uniqueness of opera; that is, in the very aspects that makes it appear difficult and remote. It is not quite like other forms of entertainment, and this may be its greatest blessing. It requires a greater commitment of time and attention than most art forms, and if this can sometimes be a strain, it can also confer greater rewards. All drama, whether live, on film, or on television, presents human situations in conflict. Opera alone, by its use of music, has the ability to penetrate those places in our subconscious that are off-limits to words and visual impressions. Conversely, all music can make an emotional impact, but opera makes music the actual language of life rather than something that exists outside of normal discourse. In opera, the unreal is the only reality, and Americans are finding in this an antidote to much of the prepackaged nature of our present reality. Opera, as an institution, has its faults, but it is rarely a superficial experience.

This current hunger for opera, of course, doesn't make it any easier to explore. To revisit the baseball metaphor, one does not automatically become enthused about it simply because one comes across it while channel surfing the television. Even attending an actual event might leave a newcomer as befuddled as before. There are a few things one needs to know, plain and simple, in order to unpack the riches of the sport or the art form. People who believe in instant gratification do not appreciate this fact; yet life is full of such examples, and there's no need to dismiss opera just because its appreciation has need of the guidebooks written about it.

This book is intended to provide a sensible framework for exploring opera. It is meant to be an appropriate and useful tool for a newcomer into this rewarding world, and also to fill in many missing gaps in the available literature for people who already have some knowledge of opera. The aim is not to promote any personal agenda about opera (and every opera lover has, to put it mildly, opinions). The goal is to provide a tool for people to use in their own explorations of the subject and perhaps, someday, to develop passionate opinions of their own.

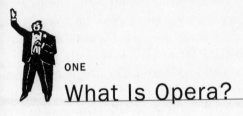

ONE

What Is Opera?

The short answer is easy: Opera is a form of drama that uses vocal and instrumental music to tell its story.

Such a definition is of course a bit naïve. Many stories are told with music, one way or another, yet the word *opera* carries with it a load of baggage. Any man on the street can give a more elaborate definition. Opera is generally understood to be an old-fashioned and rarified art form devised by effete and extinct European cultures. Furthermore, it uses outrageous extremes of the human voice for the sheer display of emotional extravagance. Its main appeal is for rich, old people, and it can hardly be expected to carry any import for the fast-paced, sophisticated American of today.

As obnoxious as such a summary may be, it well represents many people's views on opera and encapsulates much of how we see opera used symbolically in mass media today. Yet opera has been growing on American soil with an inexorable push since its introduction to these shores. This baffles many people, fans as well as detractors. The marketing departments of opera companies and their colleagues in the recording industry have been working overtime to counteract the negative view of opera. They have stressed the timelessness of the art form, the power, and the greatness. At times, they have gone a bit overboard. Opera is said to be "good for you," like a cultural form of cod-liver oil. Children are packed off to special operatic performances, especially of works such as Mozart's *The Magic Flute* and Engelbert Humperdinck's *Hansel and Gretel* that are, despite their difficult music, believed to be especially appropriate for the youngsters. The whole elitist aspect of the art form is down-played. This has all had a positive effect, but many of the prejudices against the form continue.

Perhaps there is just barely enough truth in the negative summary of opera mentioned above to require addressing these accusations, rather than avoiding them. The fact is that opera did originate in an elitist setting rather than arising out of a popular movement. It was "invented" by intellectuals in late-Renaissance Florence who were trying to emulate techniques of Ancient Greek drama. Its next phase, within two years of its invention, was as court entertainment. The public as we know it did not enter into the picture until two generations later. All this took place in Italy, a country whose social structure of four centuries ago is as distant from us as prehistory. Nor did the Italians of the seventeenth century have our supposedly broader view of the world and all its people. They wrote operas for themselves in their own language and with their own conventions, addressing issues that interested them.

Something strange happened. The format that these Italians devised, wherein characters of a story sang their lines rather than spoke them, had possibilities beyond the issues of the day. It moved across Europe and across language barriers. As new music techniques were invented, composers and dramatists alike discovered that there were certain things that could only be represented within an opera. Mannerisms crept in, to be sure, but each of these mannerisms served a purpose at first. A distinct style of singing developed. It included the ability to sing at great length without breathing, to ornament with trills, rapid notes, and so forth. Of course, everyone all over the world likes to sing or at least hear someone singing. Interesting techniques have developed everywhere. But certain techniques only seemed to make sense within the context of telling a dramatic story; in other words, in opera. European singers had for years been training their voices to reach higher, perfecting techniques of the head voice in order to make an impression in both genteel salons and churches, but the tradition of opera unleashed a new monster. Voices learned to go higher and louder and to move about the musical scale with more agility than they ever had in any other setting. A distinctly "operatic" sound developed, and this sound has come to define the genre, erroneously, for most people. As for the type of music associated with opera, it is assumed to be a primarily romantic medium. The large orchestra with lush strings and the occasional brass summarizes opera music in the popular imagination. Small wonder opera is considered remote and outdated.

The fact is that the greatest number of successful operas was written in Italy, Germany, and France from the middle of the nineteenth century to the beginning of the twentieth. Almost every opera company will be laden with works from this period, and these works, too, represent their own time of origin. Not all opera is of this variety, but again it must be admitted that the natural possibilities of telling a story through music found an explosive expression with the techniques and tastes of that time and those places. In other words, there is much more to opera than the works of Verdi, Wagner, and Puccini, but those works are monumental and worthy of attention from audiences today. Shakespeare's language makes him remote from today's audiences, but the core of his art becomes more vital every year.

Then there is the charge that opera is designed for rich people and specialized scholars. Again, this cannot be as easily dismissed as some of our marketing people might wish it to be.

Opera is notoriously expensive to produce. Either ticket prices must be high, or there must be someone (traditionally a king or some such person) willing to pay for it all. Beyond Venice and a few other box office–driven cities, opera was for many years a form of entertainment provided to select audiences by the royal or near-royal courts to demonstrate their wealth and to keep their troublesome courtiers in one place in the evenings. By the nineteenth century, box offices everywhere had opened to anyone with enough cash to scrounge up a ticket. But even then, kings and queens were expected to show their faces at the opera with exhausting frequency. They were also expected to foot a large part of the production bill. (In most countries in Europe, the state still subsidizes the art form with a generosity that makes most Americans gasp in wonder.) Traditionally, people dressed for the opera. They tended to dress up for most social occasions in bygone years, but the opera was the place to go to be seen in one's full finery. In New York, a city always willing to go one step further than Europe on European extravagances, a box at the opera at the turn of the last century was *the* signal that one had arrived. Special clothes evolved that could be worn only at the opera. The opera hat, opera glasses, and opera-length gloves for the ladies (extending above the elbow, with at least twenty-two buttons) are undeniably part of the social history of opera. The archetype dies hard, and people even today imagine they will need to rob a bank and visit a couturiere before going to the opera.

What makes opera so expensive? Some expenses were apparent from the very beginning. To produce a play, one must begin with several actors. That is expensive enough, but singers, being more rare, cost even more. Then there is an orchestra that must be engaged. Many rehearsals are required to get the singers on the stage and the musicians in the pit to work together. Singers must be moved around the stage in some manner that is at least passably convincing as acting, and this can take enormous amounts of time. Sets and costumes and all the other attributes of the stage must be designed and created.

That was only the beginning. Composers found their works flowed better when soloists were accompanied or interrupted by choruses, and a new expense was incurred. Choristers also must be outfitted, directed, and rehearsed. More money. Singers' fees rose astronomically. As much as the public claimed to want new, young singers, houses only sold out when the stars came to town. Singing stars came from all over Europe and eventually beyond. Language barriers made for longer rehearsals, and trade unions made their presence felt. Audiences responded to magnificent settings and spectacular special effects. Experts arose in each aspect of production. Lighting became an issue. Opera, originally outrageously expensive, has steadily climbed in cost to today's almost incomprehensible levels. Several million dollars for a single production is not unheard of.

Clearly, opera as we know it is more than an outrageous style of singing. In fact, it is in some sense the amalgamation and the culmination of all the performing arts. It has evolved into such an elaborate art form that it requires the greatest expertise in singing, orchestral playing, conducting, dancing, stage designing, applying makeup, costuming, wig making, lighting, and diction coaching, to mention only some aspects of live production. It also requires a high level of marketing, fundraising, educational programming, and labor negotiating. Richard Wagner, perhaps opera's most colossal and problematic figure, came closest to realizing the full potential of opera. He dreamed of a "Total Work of Art," a *Gesamtkunstwerk*, that would represent the best of all the arts combined into a single music drama. When he finally presented his *Gesamtkunstwerk* at a specially constructed venue in Bayreuth, Germany, in 1876, even he was a bit disappointed. No one person could restructure society to produce what was, after all was said and done, an opera. In trying to do so, however, he left a mark not only on opera composing and production, but on theater design, acoustical engineering, and even urban planning.

After Wagner, it was apparent that opera not only subsumed all the arts, but has had a huge effect on them as well. Architects throughout the twentieth century were obsessed with Wagner's vision of a *Gesamtkunstwerk*, for better and worse. Painters (Marc Chagall, David Hockney) and poets (W. H. Auden, Gertrude Stein) have worked in the field and many others have been affected by it. Movies learned much from the inherent surrealism of opera and the use of music in telling a story. A disproportionate amount of innovation in stage design has come from opera, although few would believe this. Opera at its best is truly extravagant, and its extravagance has pushed the limits for all the other art forms as well.

Such an art form cannot be easily dismissed as remote, elitist, old-fashioned, or Eurocentric. Many of its best examples were created awhile ago, but there are so many variables that every new performance and recording becomes a new revelation. Many of them were created for royalty, but so were many other of our pastimes (e.g., tennis and horse racing). The power of opera to reach all people has been demonstrated over time. It is expensive to produce and can be expensive to attend, but America revels in garish consumerism, and it is unfair to single out opera as emblematic of pricey entertainment. Indeed, it is available for virtually nothing on television and radio, and even opera houses go out of their way (more than any other performing institutions) to provide cheaper tickets and the occasional free performance. Opera is a source of debate for scholars, but an opera succeeds first as entertainment or it fails, and its primary appeal is emotional rather than intellectual. Because it utilizes music, it has the ability to transcend limitations of language and is in this way less elitist than most spoken or written art. Opera comes from Europe and is steeped in that continent's traditions, but it has provided a format for telling a story that is steadily and increasingly utilized by people all over the world, who have found it adaptable to their own aesthetics and traditions. Contrary from being remote from other art forms, opera has noted and adapted all developments in art and literature and has in turn influenced those genres as well.

With all this mind, it is perhaps possible to devise a definition of opera that is neither reductive nor prejudiced. The key lies in the beginning of the first definition. We must always remember that opera is a form of drama rather than a form of music. All styles of music can be used to create good opera, although time has shown that some work particularly well while others have inherent problems within this context. The core, however, remains drama.

Opera, therefore, is a form of drama told through music and all other aspects of the performing arts. It is derived from specific traditions, but it has a marvelous adaptability to a huge diversity of styles and aesthetics. It is called the culmination of all performing arts, and it has a unique ability to present most issues of human emotion and psychology in a vital and direct manner that can reach all people willing to take the journey.

The Story of Opera

Opera differs from most art forms in that it did not evolve out of a long tradition, finally reaching a point when it became recognizable in its present form. Instead, it was invented in a given moment in history. Since then, however, it has evolved ceaselessly, reflecting all imaginable fluctuations in public tastes and technological developments even while exercising its own influence on the world. It is a remarkable history, full of colorful people and situations appropriate to this most vibrant of art forms. A look at opera's own story is helpful in understanding how opera has become the very peculiar institution it is today.

The Opera Problem

The basic problem is this: How do you tell a dramatic story through music? Songs, of course, usually tell a story of one sort or another, and songs can be strung along to tell a more elaborate story, but what is the best way to apply music to drama? The ancient Greeks seem to have known the secret to this and to so many things, but they didn't write down their music, and we have no way of knowing what it sounded like. We do know that their dramas were perhaps more often sung than spoken. The lines were also accompanied by instruments such as drums and finger cymbals and perhaps others. These works must have been extremely powerful. The theaters of Greece were more than just places of entertainment; the dramas presented involved religion, art, and political analyses. Even today, translated and stripped of music and cultural context, the Greek dramas speak with authority and fascination. What must their effect have been in their own time, two and a half thousand years ago? And couldn't this achievement be, if not retrieved from antiquity, then at least re-created for our own times? Isn't there a way to combine the respective powers of music and drama?

This question was debated by a group of scholars and learned amateurs in Florence in the 1590s. They called themselves the *Camerata*, and their number included musicians, poets, and, not least, Galileo's philosopher father. For years, most people credited the *Camerata* with the invention of opera. In fact, it was a group of men who were growing tired of the endless debates of the *Camerata* who actually created the first opera out of the issues they had been studying for so long. The poet Rinuccini supplied a drama, *Dafne*, based on the Greek myth but written in contemporary Italian. This was crucial. From the start, this experiment was seeking the spirit, rather than the exact form, of the Greek model. The musician Jacopo Peri added music to the drama very carefully. The words were to remain supreme, and the music was meant to emphasize the meaning of each word. This was not to be another exercise in extravagant song, but something entirely different. Only a few instruments (we do not know the precise number) were to accompany the actor-singers. Peri and Rinuccini did not quite know what to call their creation, so it was simply called *opera in musica*, a "work in music." It was presented to a sophisticated audience in a Florentine palazzo in 1597.

No account of the initial reaction to the opera has been discovered, but the libretto (i.e., "little book," the written drama without the music) was reprinted within two years. Thus we know some interest in *Dafne* had been generated. One part of the work remains. It is an aria, (i.e., "air," as in a "song") from the opera. Greek drama was loaded with monologues—solo speeches given by actors who are, in a sense, thinking out loud. These monologues are among the most potent devices of Greek drama since they allow a character to reveal true feelings rather than filtering them through the conventions of interactive speech. In an opera, a monologue became an aria. Rinuccini and other purists did not want this project to result in a string of crowd-pleasing songs, but it is significant that the only part of *Dafne* to survive was exactly one of these.

By 1600, others were creating these operas. A composer named Caccini wrote one that must have appalled the original scholars who debated the nature of Greek drama. Caccini's daughter Francesca was a great singer, and it was said that he had diluted the original intention of the opera by giving her florid music to sing. How could anyone understand the words when the young lady was caroling to her heart's content? In fact, Francesca was more than a flashy singer. She was also a gifted composer in her own right. She and her father had discovered that music had the ability to say many things that words alone could not. None of the works from this period have survived, but accounts of them have. Operas were given as part of the festivities surrounding royal weddings in Italy at this time, which testifies to the fact that they must have been considered luxuries that cost a lot of money to produce.

Opera was embroiled in debate before one had ever been written. It was intended from the very start to be unique, important, and edifying. It had a conservative provenance (being based on Greek models from centuries before), but it scandalized conservative people with the sensuality of its music. It involved the diverse and often opposing talents of many different people, and it was expensive to produce. Every composer had a point to make with an opera and none ever appeared to be entirely satisfied with the results. And the public had a nasty habit of making up their own minds about what they liked without letting experts tell them what was best. This was the situation in opera in 1600. It is the same situation today. Every generation since then has thought it has found the answers, only to realize they had just provided another set of questions for those who came after them. Fortunately, no solution to the problem of opera has yet been discovered. Continued puzzling over the same basic questions, however, has left us with an ever-evolving art form that can claim many of the most profound, moving, and insightful creations of Western civilization among its accomplishments.

Monteverdi

Opera split down two opposing paths after its initial appearance in Florence. Royal and aristocratic courts (of which there was no shortage in the fragmented Italy of the time) were quick to absorb the new art form as yet another type of spectacle to glorify themselves. These early baroque court operas grew quite elaborate, often including fireworks, horse ballets, and even, in one recorded instance, a mock naval battle with choral accompaniment. There was very little difference between these extravaganzas and any of the other balls, "masques," court ballets, or typical court entertainments except that there may have been a bit more singing. The other direction of operatic development was less spectacular, but more substantial. Claudio Monteverdi, an accomplished composer of madrigals and church music, produced *La favola d'Orfeo* for the court of Mantua in 1607. There was such a manageable balance between musical speech and aria that the story seemed to unfold on a separate plane of reality that was neither all musical nor limited to the patterns of speech. In the hands of a brilliant composer (which Monteverdi clearly was), and one with a sense of theater, the music and words would be enough. There would be no need for horse ballets. *Orfeo* still exists, and is still performed. It is an intimate work, not ideally suited for the larger modern theaters, but in the right context it is absolutely fresh and involving.

The Venetian Public Theaters

Operas had originally been produced as a project of an academic society. Next, they were used as entertainment for royal and aristocratic courts. Of course, those courts were, in a sense, open to the public, but the spectacles were primarily meant to impress people with the importance, refinement, and wealth of the local potentates. Public opinion, as we understand it, was not an issue. This changed in 1637, when the Tron family opened a public theater, the San Cassiano. Tickets were to be sold, and an opera that did not sell tickets would be quickly packed away and forgotten. Fortunately for posterity, Monteverdi found the arrangement agreeable. He happened to be living in Venice at this time, composing music for the basilica of San Marco. He wrote dozens of operas over the next three decades, and many of the other talented composers who lived in Venice followed him. Venice had twenty public opera houses by 1650. Most were small and rather humble, but clearly a nerve had been hit.

What exactly was it that Monteverdi and his colleagues created? They created an art form of unique properties and capabilities. Music is more immediately engaging and demands more attention than plain speech. Music does not reflect time in the same way that spoken drama must parallel real time, so this opera could tell stories that wouldn't make any sense in the spoken theater. Characters could be delineated and explored before they opened their mouths by means of the orchestra. Confrontations between characters could be intensified in a new way: actors who scream at the top of their voices all tend to sound about the same, while a singer can rattle the chandeliers in any number of emotional "colors." Dramatic excitement could build in a new way. Most of all, the opera was cosmopolitan. A spoken drama in Italy of that time either had to be in one of the many local dialects of the peninsula or sound distant and academic if it was in standard Italian, not like real speech, to the people in the audience. In opera, the music bridged this gap. All Italians could feel a direct connection to the happenings on stage.

So could foreigners. Tourists in Venice, almost as ubiquitous in the seventeenth century as today, flocked to the opera houses. No trip to Venice was complete without a trip to the opera, whether or not one spoke Italian. This bewildered the purists, who still insisted on opera as a deeper exploration of the words of a drama. It continues to bewilder people today.

Beyond Italy

The sophisticated courts of Europe were accustomed to importing art from Italy, so it should not surprise us to find operas being given in Italian at royal festivities throughout Europe in the early seventeenth century. The Germans were the first to attempt operas in their own language, in the 1630s. Contrary to all expectation, the public yawned, and lined up to see the Italian operas. The French also rankled. While they were happy to import art from Italy, they liked to make it as French as they possibly could in the process, and opera was proving difficult to adapt. Besides, they had their beloved drama, which reached its apex in the seventeenth century, and their ballet. The great tradition of royal ballets, which included performances by none other than the Sun King himself Louis XIV, had likewise originated in Italy but had no linguistic limitations. But what to make of this very Italian thing called opera? They resolved the problem with superb Gallic reason. The court hired an Italian, Giambattista Lulli, as music master, changed his name to Lully, and ordered him to teach the French to compose operas in their own language. Meanwhile, a separate Italian theater was founded with instructions to sink or swim on its own ticket sales. This situation remained the standard in Paris

The Birth of the Box Office

After the first experiments in Florence, operas were given as court festivities to celebrate events and glorify the local lord. Monteverdi's success with the idea of a dramatic story independent of any event was instrumental in separating the form from the courts. In Venice, a republic without a royal court, the Tron family opened the first public theater, the San Cassiano, in 1637. The Trons engaged an "impresario" to hire the singers and instrumentalists and everyone else. The idea was a success. Boxes were rented to noble families for the season, while the general public bought tickets for nights they wished to attend. (With minor adjustments, this became the setup for Italian theaters into recent memory.) Many thought the notion of a public theater would pass, but it caught on, and throughout the century Venice had seventeen theaters giving operas throughout the year. Monteverdi moved to Venice early in the century and wrote for the theaters. In order to sell tickets, the works given had to be interesting rather than merely spectacular. Had Venice not been the city it was, opera never would have developed into the art form we know today.

for two hundred years, until the Théâtre des Italiens finally closed in the 1870s. Louis XIV never learned to love opera, but courtiers at Versailles adored it. They might have had other than artistic reasons for their enthusiasm: Apart from meals or high-stakes card games, the only time they were permitted to sit was during performances.

In Madrid, there was Italian opera given at court while the native Spanish form of musical-dance theater, the *zarzuela*, (in which there was spoken dialogue broken up by songs and dances), became more and more like Italian opera in tone and structure. In Russia, aristocrats and those who wished to imitate them imported everything, including technology, language, and manners. Nobody in Moscow three hundred years ago would have thought it strange to attend an opera performance in a language that was virtually nonexistent in the rest of the country.

England, as always, presented a different situation than did the European continent. Opera was considered too ridiculous for reasonable English tastes throughout the seventeenth century. While Englishmen were content to let music flourish equally in their churches and taverns, the theater was entirely dominated by the great dramatic tradition of the land. After 1660, the restoration of the monarchy even permitted an exciting novelty—women on the English stage! Who needed any Italians warbling incoherently? But all that was about to change, in England and (almost) everywhere in Europe. Once again, the change would be dictated by events in Italy.

The Castrati and the Divas

A century after its invention, opera had come to a full if not precise circle. Originally demanding a great deal of attention from the audience to hang on to each note of the singer, opera had briefly become merely another spectacle for the royal and aristocratic courts. The Venetian public theaters had shifted the focus back to the individual singer. By the end of the century, singers had become more interesting. They were doing things singers had never done before. With hours of time to fill in the opera houses, a public bent on novelty, and freed from the restrictions of church music, singers were developing their abilities, techniques, and mannerisms in bold, even extravagant ways. More important, things were being done to singers that had never been done before. The phenomenon of the castrati created the cult of the singer.

Castrati were men who, as boys, showed great promise as singers and were castrated to preserve their prepubescent voices. Actually, in most cases, a single duct was severed and the testicles were left attached, though they tended to shrivel into near nonexistence. The practice arose from a church prohibition, enforced to varying degrees in different places, against women

A Vintage Year

As Napoleon's armies retreated west across Europe, the main force traveled across Germany. And during the so-called Battle of the Nations around Leipzig in May 1813, Richard Wagner was born in that town. Another force later swept back through Italy, pursued by the allies. While endless skirmishes raged through the province of Parma in October, Giuseppe Verdi was born in the village of Le Roncole. The local people still tell how his mother was forced to hide with the days-old infant in the bell tower of the village church where he would become the organist nine years later, and a plaque commemorates the event. Both Wagner and Verdi were born amid the sounds of gunfire.

Until recently, these two composers were regarded as the opposite poles of the opera experience, but the benefit of time has shown that they had more in common than their tumultuous births. They transcended, in fact destroyed, all the conventions of the form. Each had his own path, but their achievements were much more similar than anybody in their own time could have imagined.

singing during Mass. In the 1500s, a group of Spanish singers had mastered and zealously guarded a technique of singing in "falsetto," the "hooty" upper range of a male voice. The Spanish falsettists reigned supreme in the Sistine Chapel and elsewhere until somebody discovered (probably through an accident) that a boy whose voice did not change at puberty could sing with much greater strength and agility than a falsettist. Everyone knew it was immoral, even barbaric, to mutilate a boy in this fashion. It was always illegal, and the Catholic Church pronounced punishments in the next life for the crime even while combing the conservatories for such unfortunates. People who made a study of the practice noted that no one could be found who knew where the operation was performed, but all suspected it was done "in the next town."

Suddenly, Italy was swept with a wave of "accidents" of a very specific nature.

Whatever the moral considerations, we know from the music written for the castrati and from contemporary accounts that they were without any doubt the greatest singers who ever lived. Undistracted by typical adolescent concerns, they completely devoted themselves to the study of music and the development of their voices during their critical early years. They could sing without breathing for unheard-of lengths, up to, according to one account of the legendary Farinelli, one full minute. Composers, including Handel, wrote the greatest star roles for castrati. Surprisingly, the castrati only rarely appeared in women's roles. In fact, if there was a noble warrior hero to be portrayed on the stage, nothing would do but a castrato. Women in the audience went visibly wild over them.

Women on stage, however, were not ready to surrender stardom to a group of mutilated men. Long denied the right to sing in most churches in Italy (and elsewhere in Europe), many sopranos were enjoying the fame and fortune associated with singing opera. A new breed of soprano, the "diva" ("goddess") appeared to upstage, whenever possible, the castrati. They pushed composers for equally difficult arias to sing, and somehow managed to sing them. Their antics, their vanity, and their tempers became legendary. Handel took advantage of the publicity surrounding two rival divas by importing them both to London to appear on the same stage for the 1727 season. Audiences were not disappointed. The ladies actually fought on stage and tore each other's wigs off. Or so the story goes. . . . The great divas of the era commanded huge fees, sometimes even eclipsing the castrati. In fact, the opera is considered the first place where women were able to make independent fortunes. The crucial role of women in opera history is well documented, but the role of opera in feminist history has yet to be explored fully.

It is all too easy to demean the accomplishments of opera seria, the "serious opera" of the eighteenth century. The pri-

Verdi, Wagner, and War, Again

When the khedive of Egypt decided Cairo needed a world-class opera house, he wanted a new opera by the best composer money could buy to inaugurate the edifice. His first choice was Charles Gounod, but he would also settle for Verdi or Wagner. Neither Gounod nor Wagner ever got a formal offer, but Verdi agreed to compose *Aida* for a princely sum of money. He also insisted that the production be first rate, and in effect coerced the khedive to pay for the subsequent production at La Scala, which Verdi considered much more important anyway. The sets and costumes were to be made to order by the best firms in Paris.

The production was indeed built in Paris, but history had other plans for the premiere. The Prussian prime minister Otto von Bismarck brilliantly provoked the French into declaring war. The French cabinet minister Emile Ollivier, who happened to be Wagner's brother-in-law, made the formal declaration of war in July 1870. The Prussians routed the French, and *Aida* was stuck in Paris throughout the long siege. The Cairo Opera House, complete with shuttered boxes for the ladies of the harem, opened with a performance of *Rigoletto* that year instead of the new opera. The triumphant premiere of *Aida* came several months later. Verdi remained in Milan to bask in the ovations of the Scala audience at the Milan premiere of *Aida* a few days after the world premiere.

macy of the singer meant all other aspects of the drama suffered, and the formalism of the genre was utterly stifling. Yet great operas were created, and we can see in retrospect that the composers and librettists were solving the original problems of lyric drama according to their own best ideas. Perhaps their greatest fault, from our point of view, was their neat division of aria and recitative. Recitative is the "talky" part between arias. In the eighteenth century, it was traditional to have the recitative accompanied only by a harpsichord so the words could be more clearly understood. All the action took place in the recitatives. The arias then commented upon developments and told how the characters felt about them. The recitatives could be dull, but were necessary for the drama. Without recitatives, operas would be strings of songs. It was the same problem that opera had faced since its inception. The eighteenth century used a very artificial format to resolve this, but the era loved artifice in its architecture and gardens and the results are not contemptible for being artificial. It took great skill to balance the narrative movement of recitative with the emotive power of arias. It would take even greater skill, and another century, to remove the distinctions between the two.

Gluck and Mozart

By 1780, many were tired of the old formalism. In landscape architecture throughout Europe, there was a movement away from the formal geometrics of classic French gardening in favor of the "naturalistic," English style of gardening. Naturalism was the new mantra, and the days of the opera seria were numbered. Johann Willibald von Gluck was a composer who attacked the problem directly. He published a preface in a libretto to his opera *Armide* in which he called forthrightly for a reform of opera and a shedding of the restrictive forms of opera seria. Gluck's later works reflected much of what he advocated in writing. The operas, such as *Orfeo ed Eurydice* and *Iphigénie en Tauride*, moved with a more even swiftness in a dramatic sweep, the music building from one section to the next in a masterly fashion. Subtleties such as ironic relationships between words and music were deftly explored.

Another composer at this time approached the issue with less debate but even more effect. Wolfgang Amadeus Mozart began writing operas at the age of ten. By the time he was twenty-five, he had mastered the current style of opera with *Idomeneo* (1782), probably the greatest opera seria. But Mozart transformed every genre in which he composed, be it concertos,

The Great Rivalry

Confrontations between artistic factions, and the attendant hype, are not recent phenomena of the hip-hop world. Opera was born amidst controversy over four hundred years ago, and producers have always known that a bit of bickering makes for good box office. One of the most celebrated rivalries between composers took place in Paris in the 1770s. Two composers with two very different agendas found themselves competing for recognition. The first was Niccolò Piccinni, a composer of pleasant, genial operas who was supported by his most important voice student, Queen Marie Antoinette. The second was Johann Willibald von Gluck, a German whose success and whose stated purpose of "reforming" opera and rescuing it from its mannerisms was causing great resentment in the opera establishment. Factions formed overnight, even among people who had no particular interest in opera, and spread beyond the usual artistic circles. Certain cafés were known to be partisan to one faction or the other, and fights were reported. Vistors to Paris at this time wrote that people talked of little else. It is difficult to unravel the issues at stake in those heady times. Historians have tended to simplify the controversy as one between progressive Germans and conservative Italians battling for the soul of the French, but the facts do not support this (Gluck's librettist was Italian, and Marie Antoinette was Austrian). In any case, the composers themselves claimed to have no problem with each other and in fact expressed admiration for each other's work, but the Paris Opéra saw a gold mine forming. Both composers were commissioned to set the same libretto, *Iphigénie en Tauride*. Gluck's masterpiece premiered in 1779, and is still given today. Piccini's did not see the stage until 1781, by which point Gluck had left for Vienna. It was less of a success, and history in general has judged in favor of Gluck.

The controversy may have created some good box office, but it diverted Parisians from the opportunity to score a real triumph. The twenty-two-year-old Mozart was in Paris at the time, trying in vain to get a job or a commission, but everyone was arguing Gluck versus Piccinni, and no one had any time to invest in the overgrown child prodigy from Salzburg.

symphonies, or sonatas. At last he was ready to transform opera. *The Marriage of Figaro* (1787) had many of the attributes of an opera buffa but treated with the elegance of an opera seria. It was witty but profound, and in this Mozart was superbly aided by a libretto written by the remarkable Lorenzo da Ponte. It was difficult to say which parts were recitatives and which parts arias, since the recitatives were, for a change, fascinating and the arias seemed to grow out of them. Most remarkable were the ensembles, which seemed to evolve organically out of the dramatic situation. The audiences of Vienna were non-plussed (the emperor, according to legend, commented that he thought Mozart's operas contained "too many notes"), but audiences in Prague, less devoted to tradition than those in the imperial capital, were delighted. They commissioned another work, *Don Giovanni*, from Mozart and Da Ponte. Mozart's operas were just about to become popular in Vienna when the composer died at the age of thirty-seven.

Upheaval and Rebirth

Mozart and Gluck represented evolving currents in opera, but the Napoleonic Wars put a definitive end to the eighteenth century traditions. People had little patience with refinement for its own sake. They wanted excitement, novelty, extremes of emotion that would soon be characterized in France and Germany by the Romantic Movement. In Italy, the changes were even more drastic and, in many ways, more disastrous. The conservatories were broke and forced to close or consolidate. The Church was less extravagant and no longer supported music as it had. The castrati themselves had all but disappeared, although the Sistine Chapel continued to support a few and the last did not die until 1922. The public in Italy continued to attend the opera. Indeed, it is said that many spent every night in the opera house because the theaters, unlike their impoverished homes, were at least heated. In this restless atmosphere, a new artist arrived with a new style of opera. Gioacchino Ros-

Don Casanova?

Mozart and da Ponte's magnificent opera *Don Giovanni* was based partially on previous tellings of the legend of Don Juan, the notorious Spanish ladies' man. The opera, however, is so profound and insightful that many have speculated other sources for its inspiration. Many wonder how much the historical figure of Casanova was incorporated into the characterization. Casanova, the Venetian rake, may have known da Ponte in Venice and certainly was on friendly terms with both him and Mozart in Vienna at the time that they were writing *Don Giovanni*. It is even thought that Casanova contributed some lines of "rewrite" to the libretto, although scholars bicker about exactly which lines. The level of Casanova's involvement with Mozart's and da Ponte's lives and works is difficult to ascertain. Casanova's lengthy memoirs skip over the period in question, and da Ponte's memoirs, written years later when he was trying to be assimilated into then-puritanical New York society, downplayed his friendship with the famous libertine. Still, it is tantalizing to ponder the intersection of history's most emblematic lover with the stage's greatest representation of the same archetype.

There are, however, important differences between the psyches of Casanova and Don Giovanni. The Don is indiscriminate and compulsive, or what we would today call a sex addict. Casanova truly believed himself totally and utterly in love with every single one of the hundreds of women with whom he was involved. In fact, he expresses great disapproval of indiscriminate sex-seekers, and is not above a bit of moralizing in his memoirs. The Don's character has no apparent morals. He does, of course, have some good techniques for seducing women, and these may have been "inherited" from Casanova. The Don finds something to praise in all women: the blond's refinement, the brunette's constancy, and the sweetness of the gray-haired. Casanova's famous formula was similar, yet simpler, and more effective: he praised the brains of beautiful women, and the looks of intelligent women.

sini was a bubbly, agreeable man who wrote music everyone could enjoy. It was always lively and never tedious. And it was especially well suited to a new type of dramatic singer, who could inform the florid lines with excitement and fervor. Basses, tenors, and mezzo-sopranos, usually relegated to minor roles, and lower salaries, in the days of the castrati, began to capture the public's attention. Tenor Manuel García and his three magnificent children (one bass and two mezzos) were the new stars of Rossini's vehicles, creating a sensation wherever they went. And they would go to some very exotic places before long.

Opera Comes to America

Having triumphed in Naples, Paris, London, and other European capitals, García decided to attempt the New World. He assembled a company, including son Manuel and daughter María Malibran, and sailed to New York. They performed Rossini's *Barber of Seville*, (in which García Sr. had starred at its Rome premiere in 1816) at the Park Row Theater. More intriguingly, they performed Mozart's *Don Giovanni* with da Ponte, who was also trying his fortunes in the New World (and had even done some time as a greengrocer in Hoboken), in the audience. It was an auspicious beginning for Italian opera in New York; although the art form did not take the New World by storm, a seed had been planted. Not all the trip was to go so well. Moving his company to Mexico City for a season, García was robbed of all his earnings and returned to Europe broke but full of interesting stories.

Paris and the Grand Opéra

Back in Italy, Rossini was finding fame but insufficient fortune. He settled in Paris, first as director of the Italian opera house, but soon conquering the august Paris Opéra itself with a huge, ambitious work, *Guillaume Tell*. The French were enthused but had other priorities. The July Revolution of 1830

A Royal Serenade

Opera fans are famous for excessive devotion to their favorite singers, but King Philip V of Spain must win special honors in this field. By 1737, the country was beginning to despair of its melancholy king, who was so depressed he could barely attend to official business. The greatest singer of the time (and probably of all time), Farinelli, was engaged at the opera in Madrid. Upon hearing the great castrato, the king offered him a huge sum of money to remain in Madrid. The singer's primary job was to sing four songs under the king's window every night. Farinelli's voice had a magnificent effect upon the king, whose change of character was noted with wonder by the court. Farinelli stayed in Madrid for twenty-five years, keeping quite busy producing operas and improving musical life. But every night for twenty-five years he sang the four songs under the window of the king, who never grew tired of it and who credited the singer with his health, sanity, and his very life.

nullified Rossini's contract with the Opéra. He lived until 1868, mostly in Paris, but inexplicably never wrote another opera. Many explanations have been offered, but it seems likely that Rossini felt incapable, or unwilling, to keep pace with changing styles in music.

And music was changing rapidly during that period. Beethoven had unleashed the full sonorities (some thought them vulgarities at the time) of the orchestra and had written an opera, *Fidelio*. Beethoven's only opera not only made tremendous use of the orchestra, but employed a new approach to setting text. Much of the score was based on the cadences of the German language itself, a technique used by Bach in his religious oratorios but scarcely explored in opera. For once, German audiences were able to hear an opera whose music sounded as German as its text rather than as an ill-fitting substitute for Italian. Carl Maria von Weber went a step further, choosing stories that explored the German love for the eerie and supernatural (the "Gothic," as we still say) in his operas *Der Freischütz* and *Oberon*. The French were still eating up Italian opera but were finally beginning to enjoy works in their own language and style. A German Jew named Meyerbeer arrived in Paris and noted the public response to *Guillaume Tell*. He produced his own grand opera, *Robert le Diable*, a huge success in 1831. A format had been discovered that would dictate the way operas were to be performed at Paris's major theater for the rest of the nineteenth century. They were to be sung in French given in five acts, and include as much spectacle as possible among other requirements. If all this sounds a bit pedantic, many at the time would have thought the same. It is important to remember that opera, and indeed many of the arts, had been regarded as issues of state since at least the time of Louis XIV. Repertory choices were debated in legislatures like tax bills. This was the French tradition, and it still is so today.

The Two Giants

Richard Wagner and Giuseppe Verdi were both born in 1813. Neither received much formal training in conservatories and neither looked, on paper, like good candidates to become the prime movers of the opera world for the remainder of the century and beyond. Yet this is precisely what happened. Wagner was imbued, to a much greater extent than he would later admit, in all the styles prevalent in his youth, including Italian bel canto, French Grand Opéra, and the German speech-singing style Beethoven had brought into the opera house. Like most reformers, he had a conservative, even reactionary, core. His goal was to find the perfect marriage of word and music using the ancient Greeks as a model, in fact the very same goal as the Florentines who had invented opera two and a half centuries previously. After 1848, Wagner was so disgusted with the state of opera that he insisted his works be called "music dramas." He began to visualize these works on a vastly different

She Did Not Want to Be Alone

In the movie *Queen Christina*, Greta Garbo converts to Catholicism, re-nounces the throne of Sweden, and leaves for a quiet life of retirement. In historical fact, Christina's noisiest years began with her abdication. She moved to Rome and pursued her greatest passions, including patronizing the arts and causing scandals. At first, the pope was greatly pleased to have such a notable ex-Protestant in his entourage, but successive popes were less amused by her meddling and, not the least, by the men's clothes she insisted on wearing everywhere. Opera was another of Christina's great passions. In 1674, she was the main patron behind the opening of the first public opera house in Rome, but within two years the severe Pope Innocent XI closed all the public theaters of the city. Christina's theater, the Tor di Nona, survived the storm as a semi-private institution. With Alessandro Scarlatti as Christina's choirmaster and Arcangelo Corelli as her orchestral conductor, standards were high. Her palace became the intellectual center of the city. Musicians mingled with scientists, philosophers, and artists, and Christina continued to patronize the arts, stir up controversy, and scan-dalize everyone. She was buried in a fabulous tomb in St. Peter's, partly as a tribute, and partly, insisted the wags, so the Vatican could keep an eye on her.

The Teatro Tor di Nona, after many vicissitudes, became known as the Apollo, and was the site of two of the most important premieres in Italian opera history: *Il trovatore* (1853), and *Un ballo in maschera* (1859), both by Verdi. It was during the days of the *Ballo* premiere that Verdi's very name became a byword (as an acronym for Vittorio Emanuele Re d'Italia) for the unification of Italy and the end of the Papal State. Perhaps Christina's spirit was still hovering over the place. The theater itself, however, was precari-ously close to the Tiber River and was prone to flooding. It was demolished in the later nineteenth century as part of necessary embankment construc-tion. A plaque along the Tiber marks the spot of the theater today, lauding Verdi's contributions to the nation. There is no mention of Christina on the plaque.

level from anything ever seen, even setting out to work on an epic of four operas, *The Ring of the Nibelung*. He didn't stand a chance of getting the *Ring* or anything else produced in the 1850s. His music had alienated the general public, his politics had alienated the authorities, and his unpleasant nature offended everybody else. He was a megalomaniac who never forgave the world for failing to faint dead away at the first signs of his genius, and he wrote pamphlet upon pamphlet that told society in no uncertain terms what ailed it. Famously, he also attacked the entire race of Jews as being against him.

Just as he seemed destined to disappear, he received notice that the new, eighteen-year-old king of Bavaria, Ludwig II, was a great fan and would happily pay off all of Wagner's debts if the composer would come to Munich and compose. Wagner's *Tristan und Isolde* was produced at Munich in 1865, puzzling many with its near atonality and blowing wide open the possibilities of Western music. Wagner managed to get himself kicked out of Munich within two years, but the king kept producing his operas. Eventually, Wagner decided he would not tolerate his beloved *Ring*, on which he had worked for an astounding twenty-eight years, produced in a standard opera house alongside the works of such "trash" composers as Donizetti and "the Jew Meyerbeer." He built (mostly with the king's money) his own theater to his specifications at Bayreuth, far from any existing opera establishment. He called the edifice a *Grossfestspielhaus*, a "Grand Festival House," wanting to distance even the building itself from any existing opera house. The Bayreuth Festival House was a marvel of acoustics and several innovations that have since become standard in modern theaters. These included a raked auditorium without boxes along the sides, and a sunken orchestra pit. The audience was expected to look at the stage and at nothing else, least of all at each other. In any case, the auditorium was entirely darkened during performances. Wagner required an almost religious devotion out of his audience. Composers since have demanded no less. Against all odds, *The Ring* was produced at Bayreuth in

A Disaster of Operatic Proportions

In the movie *San Francisco*, Jeanette MacDonald appears as a diva singing Gounod's *Faust* at the opera house. Later that evening, she goes to an all-night party and sings the rousing theme song of the movie, bringing down the house. Literally. The Great Earthquake strikes just as La MacDonald finishes to tumultuous applause.

In historical fact, *Carmen* was the opera given in San Francisco the night before the earthquake. The tenor was none other than Enrico Caruso, who was staying at the Palace Hotel on Market Street. After the shaking stopped, Caruso's valet dressed the tenor and sent him to wait outside, lest the building collapse. Calmly, the valet packed Caruso's trunks and left the hotel before the fire engulfed it. They walked to the St. Francis Hotel, bags and all. The chef, an opera fan, recognized Caruso and made him a breakfast of ham and eggs. Caruso fell asleep on his trunks in Union Square. Soon the fire was raging. He and his valet managed to find a horse and buggy whose driver agreed to take them to the waterfront, for a hefty fee. There, they caught a boat to Oakland and a train back to New York.

Caruso, a gifted sketcher, made some drawings of what he had witnessed in San Francisco. These were published in the London review *The Theatre* in July 1906, along with his reminiscences. He never returned to California.

1876, and nothing was ever quite the same at the opera after that. Wagner produced his mystical *Parsifal* in 1882, and died in Venice the following year.

Verdi was less interested than Wagner in writing tomes of theory and arguing with everybody in Europe, but his career took much the same route. At base, his overriding goal was to eliminate the distinction between aria and recitative; that is, between dramatic action and song. He was content to write arias until he could transcend the form effectively, but his whole

career was a move toward this end. Along the way, he understood, like no other composer before or since, that people must
be moved on a visceral level at the opera house. Without emotional engagement, there was no point in theorizing. He took
the opera world by storm with his third opera, *Nabucco*, which
premiered in 1842 at La Scala in Milan, Italy's most important
theater. It was loud, unrefined, and unschooled; everything, in
fact, that older people have always complained about in new
music. Whereas Mozart and other composers had used jumps
over two octaves in their soprano arias, they challenged the
singer to make such extremes appear somehow elegant through
technique and good taste. Verdi, on the other hand, seemed to
be daring audiences to gasp. They did. The opening night of
Nabucco caused a sensation that required the intervention of
the (occupying) Austrian police force.

Explicitly in their subject matter and implicitly in their wild
styles, Wagner and Verdi were making the same call as their
contemporary Karl Marx—the total destruction of the old to
make way for the idealized new. In this, they were reflecting
currents in literature and visual arts as well as politics. People
wanted to be shocked, stirred, and offended if necessary. New
styles of singing were adapted. A certain tenor named Mario
(from such a noble family that he never used a last name) is
credited with being the first to sing all the way up the scale to
a high C in full chest voice, rather than using the reedy head
voice that had been traditional in upper ranges. The effect, like
all new music, was freakish, vulgar, and utterly electrifying. Nor
were these developments mere salon chatter. They were rightly
regarded as the harbingers of a modern era. Identity politics
were fought in opera houses. The Brussels premiere of Auber's
Masaniello in 1830 caused a riot that grew and resulted in
Belgian independence. Wagner hobnobbed with the anarchist
Bakunin in Dresden and was exiled from Germany for his role
in the 1848 revolutions. Riots at performances of Verdi operas
throughout Italy were the norm in the 1840s, and protesters hit

A Talking Device

Some inventions take the world by immediate storm. Others evolve over time. The phonograph falls into the second category. Thomas Edison was attempting to create a device that would record telegraph messages and the spoken voice from the emerging medium of telephones. In 1877, Edison created a method of transcribing telephone messages onto indentations in paper, which could then be slowed down to be transmitted by a telegraph operator. The invention was a failure for the immediate purposes, but Edison was startled that a voice could create a distinct and reproduceable sound onto paper. He and other inventors continued to refine this discovery. Tinfoil and wax cylinders replaced paper. Eventually, celluloid disks were chosen, since they could be more easily stored and shipped. The recording industry had begun.

the streets singing choruses from his works. Opera was getting marvelously edgy.

America

Meanwhile, opera was growing in America. People had known first-rate opera ever since the Garcías' trip to New York in 1825. New Orleans had a long tradition of producing various qualities of French opera, but the East Coast cities were now including opera as a major hub of their social season. In New York, opera was performed at the Academy of Music (later the Palladium nightclub and recently demolished) on Fourteenth Street. Boston and Philadelphia also saw high-quality opera. But the truth is that there was an opera-going public throughout the whole country, even in the least civilized parts. Our image of the American West does not usually include Italian opera, but in fact the opera house was a fixture of many a mining camp and emporium town. The bel canto operas, especially Bellini's *La sonnambula*, were particular favorites. The promoter P. T. Barnum engaged the popular European soprano Jenny Lind, "the Swedish Nightingale," for an American tour that went far beyond the luxurious theaters of the Northeast deep into the West. One mining town in California's Gold Country is named after her. San Francisco's great operatic tradition began with the Gold Rush itself, when the city was still mostly tents and beached ships. There are accounts of Verdi operas given in San Francisco as early as 1853, which means scores must have been rushed by ship and then by horse halfway across the world to eager audiences who couldn't hear these works quickly enough.

New York, however, was destined to be the center of the American opera world, thanks to its cosmopolitan population, its love of theater, music, spectacle, and intrigue, and its enormous wealth. Members of the city's old society held a lock on operatic life at the Academy of Music. Because boxes in the theater were a sign of social status, the old guard was not willing to share them with the "newcomers" who wanted to attend the opera. These newcomers, who included bankers, industry magnates, and Jews, had enough money to open their own opera house uptown. The Metropolitan Opera House was opened in 1883 at Broadway and 39th Street with a mandate to import the best singers of the world, no matter the price. Within a few years, the Met had become one of the world's leading opera houses. Europeans no longer had a monopoly on opera. South Americans, too, were making their presence felt, using the "reversal" of seasons to lure singers to Rio de Janeiro, São Paolo, and Buenos Aires during the European summer. Brazilians even boasted their own great composer, Carlos Gomes, whose operas were admired by Verdi. In 1908, the Teatro Colón, possibly the most beautiful opera house in the world, opened in Buenos Aires.

A Much-Loved Woman

Opera audiences were once content to see the same stories, and even the same librettos, set over and over again. Mozart's setting of Metastasio's *La clemenza di Tito* was the seventh time that old warhorse had been used, while others of Metastasio's librettos were set dozens of times. At a certain point, however, the public began to demand novelty in words as well as music. Rossini's *Barber of Seville* was booed off the stage on its opening night mostly because of resentment from fans of composer Giovanni Paisiello, whose own *Barbiere* (1782) was still popular. In fact, Rossini originally called his opera *Almaviva* after the lead character in an effort to stave off criticism. He probably knew this wouldn't help since the opera was and remains subtitled *"ossia la precauzione inutile,"* that is, "or, the useless precaution." After Rossini's death, Verdi faced the same problem with, of all people, Rossini. For a time, Verdi considered titling his great opera *Iago* in deference to Rossini's now-sadly neglected *Otello,* but he decided against it. The opera was about Otello, not Iago, and the name had to reflect this. Verdi commented that it was better people should say he had battled a giant (Rossini) and lost than attempted to hide behind a ruse.

Puccini was a young composer who was just beginning to be noticed when he received an important commission from the Teatro Regio in Turin. His friends and colleagues were aghast when he announced as his choice of subject the novel *Manon Lescaut.* The Abbé Prévost's tale (considered the first French novel) of a worldly young woman was not new to the operatic stage. Composer Daniel Auber had written an opera on the subject in 1856, and, much more significantly, it had been set with astounding success by Jules Massenet in 1882. Massenet's version reigned supreme, especially in Italy, where his operas have always remained popular. Puccini was warned that he was courting disaster, but the young composer rejected all dire predictions. The story fascinated him, and that was what mattered. Besides, he told everyone (including the newspapers), "a woman like Manon must have at least two lovers."

Nationalism

The mid-nineteenth century witnessed a surprising dearth of good new operas from Italy and Germany beyond the exciting works of Wagner and Verdi. It was almost as if these two giants drained the creativity off their fellow countrymen, and the next developments in opera were to come from France and elsewhere. As the Grand Opéra format finally began to creak in Paris, other opportunities arose. Bizet's *Carmen* (1875) caused little stir at its initial run at the Opéra Comique (where dialogue was used instead of recitative), but it soon became an international sensation. The philosopher Nietzsche turned against his mentor, Wagner, and proclaimed *Carmen* nothing less than the format for a new and glorious world order. Tchaikovsky was almost as impressed as Nietzsche. Russians had finally begun to write operas in their own language in the middle of the century as part of a burgeoning sense of national identity, and works such as Mikhail Glinka's *A Life for the Tsar* and *Ruslan and Ludmila* were vast epics. Tchaikovsky, with *Carmen* firmly in mind, introduced a new human intimacy into Russian opera. Suddenly, everybody in Europe wanted to write an opera in his own language. Composing operas had been an issue of national identity for Verdi and Wagner and their followers, and now Danes, Norwegians, Englishmen, and others began to do the same. Even Czechs, Finns, and Catalans (a people without a legal country of their own) postulated their own worth as nations by composing operas in native languages.

The French, particularly, blossomed at this time. Gounod's *Faust* (1859) paved the way. Although composed within the parameters of Grand Opéra, *Faust* took great liberties with the form and achieved its greatest heights in its most intimate moments. It accomplished with charm and grace what Meyerbeer had taken huge choruses and ballets to say. *Faust* was soon popular throughout the world. It opened at the Metropolitan in 1883, and was soon so often performed in that house that one wag nicknamed the place a *Gross Faustspielhaus*. Freed from the constrictions of the Grand Opéra format and reliance on

The First Bayreuth Festival

Wagner had wanted a private theater built to his own specifications ever since he began to conceive of *The Ring of the Nibelung* as a four-day-long culmination of the performing arts. This was partly due to awesome artistic vision, and partly due to his paranoid megalomania, but he eventually got what he wanted. After twenty-eight years of conniving, threatening, fulminating, and begging, Wagner, with the financial help of the devoted King Ludwig II of Bavaria, was finally ready to present *The Ring* in a special Festival House built in the town of Bayreuth in 1876. The new German emperor Kaiser Wilhelm I attended, telling Wagner as he stepped off the train, "I never thought you'd pull this off."

The Festival was the talk of the art world, and newspapers in several countries (including the *New York Times*) carried front-page updates. In certain ways, Wagner found the whole affair disappointing, but in others he had clearly triumphed. His notions for the ideal opera house have become standard, for better or worse, for opera houses and theaters today. The darkened auditorium, the inclined seating floor without boxes along the sides, and even the diagonal opening of the curtain were among the many innovations at Bayreuth that are typical in theater design today.

Italians, the French began to welcome such diverse native talents as the lyrical Massenet, the sentimental Gustave Charpentier, and even the crusty Debussy, whose progressive *Pelléas et Mélisande* was a great success in 1902.

The Italians were not quite dead yet. Verdi's refined and charming final masterpiece, *Falstaff* (1893), proved that Italian art could match any other on an intellectual level and restored a great deal of national pride. The younger generation, however, moved in an entirely different direction. Mascagni, Leoncavallo, and, most of all, Puccini became the core of what was called the verismo school: short, intense operas on gritty, realistic subjects. Some saw more than a hint of *Carmen* in the verismo style, but these composers expressed themselves in a thoroughly Italian manner. Old timers, of course, complained of the grunginess of the new operas, but the public was thrilled.

The Modern Era

All the prosperity and new technology of the dawning twentieth century boded well for the opera world. Stars traveled great distances in trains and steamships to win the acclaim of audiences literally around the world. Newspapers carried reviews of distant performances. One single invention, however, changed the opera world more than any other. Thomas Edison patented his "talking machine" in 1877, a simple roll of tinfoil that held an impression of the human voice. Edison's invention was an accident, and at first he didn't see that it would revolutionize the world. It was originally meant as an office device to aid in the dictation of letters. Some people buzzed about the talking machine, but many, like Edison, did not see its possibilities. Wagner's wife wrote in her diary that she couldn't imagine how the new invention could be of any use to her husband. Edison, however, began tinkering with his device, and refined it. He replaced the tinfoil with wax cylinders and eventually acetate discs. He received over forty patents on refinements to the device for the next forty-five years. Soon there was a recording industry, and its first star was a tenor originally from Naples who would score his greatest successes in New York, Enrico Caruso. The new-style opera, with its short, intense, instantly hummable melodic arias was a gold mine for the new industry, and people who had no interest in actually attending operas were suddenly whistling them in the streets of the world.

Joseph Stalin, Opera Critic

Dmitri Shostakovich, one of the greatest Russian composers ever, produced his second opera in Moscow in 1934. *Lady Macbeth of the Mtsensk District* was a sensation with its bold, innovative music and powerful, ironic drama. Performances in Cleveland and London followed soon after, but not everyone was pleased. A front-page article in a January 1936 edition of the Soviet newspaper *Pravda* ripped the opera and its composer to shreds. The music, astoundingly enough, was accused of both "bourgeois formalism" and "crass vulgarity." Shostakovich's patriotism and even his sanity were questioned. The article was widely assumed to have been written by Stalin himself. Shostakovich was cowed, and never wrote another opera.

Lady Macbeth of the Mtsensk District was soon banned in the Soviet Union. Shortly after Stalin's death, it was revised and produced under the name *Katerina Ismailovna*, but the Shostakovich's original creation survived and eventually prevailed. *Lady Macbeth of the Mtsensk District* now holds its rightful place in the international repertory.

The Golden Age

Opera fans love to look back on the past and imagine the glories of bygone eras, but it is fair to assert that the beginning of the twentieth century was without a doubt a golden age of opera. Beautiful theaters were the center of cities from Cairo to San Francisco. We know from the recordings made in that time, technologically primitive though they may have been, that there was an abundance of extraordinary singers. Those singers had incredible range in terms of repertory, singing the old classics as well as new operas by Puccini, Massenet, and many others, including the remarkable Richard Strauss, who had proved himself Germany's worthy successor to Wagner. Conductors, too, were raising the level of orchestral performances at the opera in a way Wagner could have only dreamed about. The Metropolitan alone boasted both Arturo Toscanini and Gustav Mahler during the seasons from 1908 to 1910. Opera management had become more sophisticated as well. The old system of presenting a single opera until everybody in the city was heartily sick of it faded away in all but some Italian theaters, and houses now presented different operas on alternating nights. Audiences, from the rich in their boxes to the poor in the balconies, debated new currents and opposing styles. It was a brief moment too glorious to last.

War's Aftermath

There must have been some who supposed (and possibly hoped) that opera would cease to exist after the collapse of the European empires in 1918. In a sense it did. The old order had passed and opera would never be the same, but it did not die altogether. It had spread too far to be contained. The new threat to opera came indirectly, from a post–WWI quandary about the purpose of music itself. People sought out forms that carried minimal baggage from the painful past. America gave the world jazz. Russians experimented with electronic music that defied all assumptions about music. In Germany and Austria (or what was left of them at any rate), Arnold Schoenberg and his students went so far as to propose a new system of composing, Serialism. Kurt Weill and others went far in the other direction, deciding that any music not immediately comprehensible by the man on the street was elitist and worse. It would take a long time for all these currents to find their way into the opera house, and then only haphazardly. Opera had always been challenging, but there had been a certain complacency about what one could expect. There would be an orchestra (in a standardized form) and singers on the stage that would be attempting to produce what they considered to be a beautiful sound. By the 1920s, this could no longer be assumed.

Three things happened. The canon of repertory works, long

moving toward stagnation, was basically fossilized. There would be new operas, but only sporadically, and they would be considered curiosities rather than the center of an opera season. For all practical purposes, the era of grand opera (in the larger sense of the term) ended with the posthumous premiere of Puccini's *Turandot* at La Scala in 1926. The second development was that standard works began to be interpreted in more daring and original ways. Germany took the lead in this field during the brief flowering of the arts in the time of the Weimar Republic. Original and even shocking productions of such standards as Offenbach's *Tales of Hoffmann* caused riots in theaters. People did not argue about composers as they had in Wagner's time. Everyone basically agreed that the operas given were good in themselves, or, if they didn't care for them did not see fit to start brawls over them. The productions were the issue. The director had arrived as a new star. The third development was an extreme chasm between composers and the public. Failure at the box office became something of a badge of honor. It meant one was too lofty to be appreciated by one's contemporary public. This pose had always haunted the arts, and not without reason. After the First World War, it became something of a neurosis. These three major developments of the 1920s turned out to be far-reaching. To a large extent, they continue to define opera today.

Opera and politics became directly involved again in the 1930s. The Third Reich made an absolute fetish out of Wagner. The connection was not gratuitous, but Wagner already belonged to the world by this point in history. From an operatic point of view, Hitler shot himself in the foot. Many of Germany's greatest singers and conductors were Jewish, and they and others who could not tolerate the Nazi regime fled the country in the early years of the decade. Even the great conductor Toscanini loudly quit the Bayreuth Festival (by then run by Wagner's heirs, producing only Wagner's works, as is still the case today) with a sly letter to Hitler. American musical life was greatly enriched by this influx of émigrés from Europe

The End of an Era That Had Ended Long Before

Professor Alessandro Moreschi, director of the Sistine Choir, died in Rome in 1922. While the death of such a musical notable would be mourned by the music world in any case, there was an additional reason to take notice of Professor Moreschi's passing. He was the last castrato.

The last opera written for a castrato had been Meyerbeer's *Il croctato in Egitto*, written in 1824 for Velluti. It seemed that Domenico Mustafà, director of the Sistine Choir until as late as 1902, was nearly the last of this strange type of singer. Mustafà kept to his liturgical duties and avoided the operatic stage, although for a time around 1880 Wagner considered writing the role of Klingsor (a eunuch) in his opera *Parsifal* for him. The very last was Moreschi, who had trouble finding anyone who could teach him how to use his voice. Moreschi was engaged for a single recording session, held at the Vatican in 1902.

The Moreschi recordings are not excellent representations of what the castrato voice must have been capable. The recordings are primitive, and Moreschi was considerably past his prime when he made them. Even in his prime, Moreschi probably would not have been much competition for the great castrati of the past. Also, he was rather partial to sobs and other "effects." Still, the recording is extraordinary, giving us a tiny but tantalizing look into this bizarre practice that kept European audiences crying "Evviva il coltello!" ("Long live the knife!") for two hundred years.

in these years, and there was an enlarged audience to appreciate the new quality. Millions of Americans turned to radio as their chief form of entertainment during the Depression. The Metropolitan began broadcasting performances in 1931, and, under the sponsorship of Texaco, initiated regular broadcasts of their Saturday matinees across the country in 1933. Recordings had brought snippets of operatic music into people's homes, but radio brought the entire operatic world home in real time.

La Scala Reborn

Milan's great Teatro alla Scala took a direct hit during the air raids of July 1943. Reconstruction began within days of the war's end, and the venerable theater was ready to reopen by 1946. The event carried great significance beyond the opera world, and was nothing short of a symbol of Italian postwar rebirth. Conductor Arturo Toscanini, who had spent the war years in New York railing against Fascism, led the concert, which included such new Italian singers as Renata Tebaldi. Years before, Toscanini had played in the Scala orchestra at the time of the premiere of Verdi's *Otello*, learning the score partly from the maestro himself. The concert in 1946, therefore, was hugely symbolic. The singing of Verdi's great patriotic and spiritual chorus "Va, pensiero" elicited an emotional response from the audience. It stated clearly that the true Italian soul was not Fascist, and the country was not in ruins, but in fact was poised for a new and better life.

From the Ashes

After the Second World War, the cultural situation was even more dire than it had been in 1919. The wholesale destruction of property was astounding, with the great theaters of Berlin, Vienna, Warsaw, and Milan having been destroyed outright and Naples, London, Moscow, and many others severely damaged. The feeling, however, was different than it had been a generation before. The Allies' plan for reconstruction of occupied (and virtually occupied) countries very much included opera. Although the Nazis had made a fetish out of Wagner and "Holy German Art" (Wagner's phrase), a resurrection of the artistic spirit was seen as a means of granting people a sense of identity that predated the totalitarian extremes. This sense of national identity was necessary as a bulwark against Soviet expansionism, the most urgent issue in Europe after the war. The Italians were the first to get back on their feet with a still-famous concert at La Scala led by Toscanini.

Germany presented other problems. The Bayreuth Festival was reopened, with the Allies' permission, in 1951, still under the aegis of the Wagner family despite their close associations with Hitler. Many were outraged, and many still are. The Vienna State Opera was reopened in 1955. Berlin, however, remained a divided city for another four decades, and the opera house was in the center of the Soviet zone. The Communists themselves could not bear to expunge opera from their midst, although the Soviet government severely limited the scope of works permitted. Still, the state assumed responsibility for their "workers' theaters," and the Warsaw Pact nations all had state-run theaters and conservatories throughout the Soviet era. Another company was quickly formed by the West Germans and the Allies in West Berlin and was magnificently funded. The Komische Oper ("Comic Opera") was in the Eastern, Soviet zone. Despite official monitoring from the Communist authorities, the Komische Oper developed an international reputation for daring and creative productions throughout the 1960s and 1970s. Strangely, both sides in the Cold War used opera to demonstrate their own legitimacy. The irony was profound. Berlin had always wanted to be perceived as a center of European culture and, specifically, opera. All it took to achieve this long-desired goal was the total destruction, division, and occupation of the city.

While Berlin was experiencing operatic mitosis, the rest of the opera world was embarking on another glorious era. Exciting new singing stars, hidden for years by the war, suddenly appeared. The most riveting of all, a shy New Yorker named Maria Callas, was followed like a movie star by millions of fans who would never have considered themselves opera people. Recording technology improved, and in the late 1950s conductor Sir Georg Solti was even able to begin a long-cherished project: a complete recording of Wagner's *Ring*. And a new medium, television, provided yet another vehicle for opera to disseminate.

A Victory for People and Art

Marian Anderson, an African-American contralto, had a remarkable career in concerts throughout the United States and Europe, but the great opera houses remained off limits to her because of her race. She appeared at Carnegie Hall in 1920, and beat out three hundred competitors to sing with the New York Philharmonic in 1926. In Salzburg, Toscanini told her that hers was a voice one hears "once in a century." Yet even after this acclaim, and after the famous incident in Washington when Eleanor Roosevelt resigned her membership in the Daughters of the American Revolution because of their refusal to let Anderson perform at their hall, the contralto still had no offers from the Metropolitan.

The New York City Opera had engaged black singers since its initial seasons in the early 1940s, but the Met maintained a color line. Finally, the Met offered her the role of Ulrica, the fortuneteller, in Verdi's *Un ballo in maschera*. Anderson sang the role in an emotional performance in 1955. She was fifty-eight years old and well past her prime, but for many people the event was as significant as Jackie Robinson's accomplishment in baseball a few years earlier. Opera itself was the biggest winner. Anderson opened the door for a virtual flood of African-American singing talent that would make the United States the primary source of exciting new voices for the next few decades.

On Christmas Eve, 1951, NBC presented a holiday opera by Italian-American Giancarlo Menotti, *Amahl and the Night Visitor*. Opera, contrary to all expectation, was proving itself the most adaptable of all art forms.

There were also new developments within the opera house itself. For the reopening of the Bayreuth Festival House, Wagner's grandson Wieland realized he needed to break with all tradition if his grandfather's operas stood a chance of being seen in a new light. His stark, minimal productions of this era were probably the most important and influential in the history of theatrical (not merely operatic) design. The director and the designer achieved new importance as talent from the film and stage worlds flocked to work on opera, often bringing new insights to old works. In 1955, the Metropolitan engaged its first black singer, Marian Anderson. The smaller New York City Opera had done so twelve years earlier, but the Met's move opened the operatic doors once and for all to an explosion of American talent that had previously been held at bay.

The developments of the 1950s were echoed and expanded in the following three decades. A systematic relationship with television was inaugurated in 1977 with the first *Live from the Met* telecast, a performance of Puccini's ever-popular *La bohème*. It is estimated that more people watched that single performance on television than had seen the opera live since its premiere. American theaters (and others) began to provide in-house translations, providing yet another attempt to solve the issue of understanding what singers are saying, to which audiences have responded enthusiastically. Directors of such talents as Luchino Visconti, Franco Zeffirelli, Patrice Chéreau, and Robert Wilson have made their mark on the opera. Every new style and technology that is supposed to render opera obsolete always gets absorbed by this most unusual art form.

Opera at the New Millennium

There are two ways to assess the state of opera in our present day: the prevalence and popularity of a standard repertory of time-proven, classic operas, and the future of opera in terms of new works that speak to a wide public. To begin with the first case, there is little doubt that opera is performed to a large, enthusiastic, and growing public all over the world. Singing stars now travel to Tokyo, Hong Kong, and Cape Town as well as the more traditional centers in Europe and North and South America, and smaller companies and workshops are to be found at all spots in between. Recordings have a steady clientele in parts of

The Television Era

On Christmas Eve, 1951, NBC presented an opera written especially for the new medium of television. It was called *Amahl and the Night Visitors*, written by the popular and easily appreciated American composer Giancarlo Menotti. The response was favorable and enthusiastic. Ironically, *Amahl* does not appear frequently on television anymore, but holds the record for the most frequently performed live opera, American or otherwise, in the country.

Besides *Amahl*, opera had made smaller "guest appearances" on variety shows and reviews. The full-length opera, however, remained elusive. In 1977, public television inaugurated the *Live from the Met* series. The performance was memorable. Luciano Pavarotti and Renata Scotto appeared in that perennial favorite and classic "best first opera for people to see," Puccini's *La bohéme*. It was estimated that more people saw that broadcast than had seen the opera live in its entire history. People responded well to opera in their living rooms, and also appreciated the subtitles that translated the dialogue. This pushed opera houses toward providing in-house translations, which have in fact increased attendance at opera houses.

The *Live from the Met* series eventually expanded its repertory to include a wider range of operatic genres, and continues to be a leading factor on the national arts scene. Television is often blamed for destroying most of the performing arts, but the marriage of opera and television seems to be uniquely beneficial to both parties.

the world, and performance standards are, all things considered, rather high. Even such a difficult and demanding work as Wagner's *Ring*, once thought to be a white elephant from a bygone era, is given to appreciative audiences in such surprising places as Perth, Australia; Flagstaff, Arizona; and Santiago, Chile. Opera, definitely, is a part of the world's consciousness.

Seen from another point of view, however, there may be more cause for concern. Critics have long complained that the opera presented has a museumlike quality to it. Five major composers (Mozart, Wagner, Verdi, Puccini, and Richard Strauss) continue to dominate the field. Unless new works are presented, opera is sure to be a dead art form.

Yes and no. First of all, opera need not be dead merely because its greatest creators happen to be. A live performance will always tell us more about its own times than those of its composer. Productions, techniques, and tastes change every day. If Shakespeare can always seem new in the hands of intelligent interpreters, then it must be even more true for great operas, with their countless inherent variables. Secondly, new operas are commissioned, written, and performed with probably as much frequency as they were at any time in the past. If we look back over the canon of repertory works, we will find they cover a span of many years. The glory decades that gave us an abundance of exciting new operas in several different styles, such as the first decade of the twentieth century, were few and far between. Only a very few of the many operas written survived the test of time, and only a few ever will. The form itself is too valuable to disappear altogether. Too much can be said in an opera house that cannot be said in a film, a play, or in any other medium.

We cannot be too alarmed about the impending death of opera since it has constantly been declared dead. It can even be said to have been dead before it was born, since it was from the beginning intended to emulate an art form (Greek drama) lost for centuries. It was declared dead after the disappearance of the castrati and the baroque conservatories. It was "killed off" by the supposed excesses of Verdi and Wagner and the coarseness of the verismo composers. It was never expected to survive the holocaust of the Napoleonic Wars, nor the First or Second World Wars. It became irrelevant with recordings, radio, television, and the Internet. Yet people continue to write them. There are huge challenges. The rift between so-called serious and so-called popular music is wider than ever. It appears that today's composers have the choice of being well regarded by critics or selling tickets, yet even this is old news at the opera and many are managing to do both. Academically trained composers such as Tobias Picker and John Adams have discovered that one need not be incomprehensible to be good. And there are promising developments among popular songwriters such as Tom Waits and Lou Reed who are fascinated by the format of opera. Interestingly, the challenges faced by these composers are exactly the same as those faced since before the first opera was written. That is, what is the most effective way to tell a dramatic story through music? Every era will answer this question in its own way, and fortunately, no era will ever get the answer exactly right.

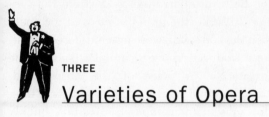

THREE

Varieties of Opera

While most art forms use different categories to help demystify their complexities, opera often seems to be made more complicated by the words people use to explain it. Each category seems to have a general and a particular definition, both of which are used indiscriminately. Everything from the nineteenth century is said to be *Romantic*, while it is impossible to read of a new work without encountering the word *Minimalism*. And then there is the whole thorny issue of *Serialism* and the twelve-tone scale.

Below is an alphabetical survey of common categorizations of opera that are necessary to discuss the art form. It is far from complete, but it is a good start. The important thing to remember is that these categories represent archetypes. Very few operas actually fit neatly under a single heading. Opera is a much too vibrant medium for clear-cut distinctions.

Bel canto: Translated, bel canto simply means "beautiful singing," and should, in theory, apply to all but the most cynical twentieth-century operas. The term, however, generally refers to a specific genre of operas composed by Italians around 1810–1840. The great definer of the form was Rossini, who was, in fact, surrounded by a bevy of exceptionally talented singers, and composed accordingly. Bel canto borrowed freely from the conventions of both the opera seria (the grand *scena*) and the opera buffa (elaborate ensembles). Rossini was not considered a radical innovator, but he introduced many techniques (such as the fully orchestrated recitative in place of the harpsichord-accompanied dialogue of baroque opera) that allowed great freedom of expression for subsequent composers. Rossini's bubbly music was very well suited for comic opera, and his *Barber of Seville* (1816) has been supremely popular since shortly after its disastrous opening night. The music is often said to have laughter written into it. It is only within the last few decades, however, that much attention has been paid to his tragic operas. In bel canto, unlike in eighteenth-century opera, tragic and comic operas use the same forms, styles, and techniques, and this lack of distinction in Rossini's operas confused audiences in the time after his retirement. It was only in recent decades that such masterpieces as *Semiramide* (1823) have commanded respect again. The other popular composers of the bel canto style are Bellini and Donizetti, whose fortunes with critics paralleled Rossini's, but who have never been entirely abandoned by audiences. Besides the "big three" of bel canto, components of the style can be found in many subsequent composers. The early operas of Verdi, many of which languished on the shelves for years, have been more popular lately since conductors and singers have been learning to interpret them as bel canto operas. Even Wagner's *Flying Dutchman* benefits from sensitivity to the precepts of bel canto.

Grand opera: People use "grand opera" to describe any opera that is big in scale, but there is a specific meaning to the term as well. It refers to a format of opera that reigned supreme at the Paris Opéra from about 1830 until around 1900. The requirements were as follows: A historical subject presented in five acts comprised of large choruses, great spectacle, at least five star roles, and a ballet. Rossini unwittingly launched the format with his great success *Guillaume Tell* in 1829, and Meyerbeer solidified it in 1831 with *Robert le Diable*. It sounds like a suffocating set of strictures, and many people of the time thought the same, but the Grand Opéra form had its virtues as well. The Paris Opéra paid the highest fees of the time and drew the best singers. Even Wagner, who railed against the institution after his own *Tannhäuser* bombed there, admitted that the orchestra and chorus had no equals. The rehearsal schedule was the most thorough and exhaustive in Europe. Verdi, in fact, thought productions there to be over-rehearsed and lacking in spontaneity. The structural parameters of the operas also had benefits. The choruses and spectacles traditionally came earlier in the evening, with a ballet in the third act. Each of the lead singers then had their great solo moment in the fourth or fifth act. Wagner may have spewed venom about Grand Opéra, but he himself noted the advantages of this format for his own very long works. An *aria di bravura* at the beginning of an opera will often go unnoticed by a modern audience. Things have changed since Mozart's time, when a less hectic way of life held sway. People who run to the theater from their offices, schools, or housework need to have their ears assaulted for a while before they can focus their attention on the vocal glories of a single aria. It was, of course, in Paris, the most modern city of the nineteenth century, that this discovery was made and originally exploited. These great arias themselves, among which *"O beau pays de la Touraine"* from Meyerbeer's *Les Huguenots* is perhaps the best example, are astoundingly beautiful, and extremely difficult. Some fans of Grand Opéra insist that the form died out not because it was superseded by more effective forms, but because no one could sing it anymore. Still, by the late nineteenth century even the most conservative Parisians had to admit Grand Opéra had become a bit of a dinosaur. Wagnerism and verismo attacked the

Parisian complacency from abroad, while Massenet's simple lyricism and the surprising success of Bizet's "trivial" *Carmen* taught the French they could compose in a different style within their own language and musical vocabulary. Grand Opéra only remained popular in Italy for several decades, and recent attempts to revive it have been sporadic and only partially successful.

Minimalism: This much-used term was originally applied (perhaps with some condescension) to the works of Steve Reich and Philip Glass, composers whose compositions began attracting attention in the 1970s. It derives from the minimal amount of musical material (clusters of notes, a simple vocal progression) that, with many repetitions and subtle modulations, was the basis of their works. Minimalism is a good example of public taste diverging from authoritative scholarship. Few musicologists had anything nice to say about this style for a long time, but audiences found them remarkably enjoyable. Even though musicians complained of the difficulty of counting their way through the scores, the effect on the audience was just the opposite. Minimalist works seemed to grow organically and achieve great swells of sound without resorting to the stridency that has marked so many twentieth-century opera genres, from verismo to Serialism. Reich's and Glass's works have also had an influence on eclectic composers such as John Adams and Tobias Picker, who have used these techniques to build tonal excitement in their own works.

Neo-Romanticism: It was inevitable that many composers would find the polemics of twentieth-century musicologists to be irrelevant and pedantic. While no composers proclaimed themselves Neo-Romantics, the term has been useful in categorizing the accessible and melodic works of Giancarlo Menotti and, to a certain extent, Samuel Barber. More often, Neo-Romanticism is cited as a steadying influence on many modern composers who have found that music need not be atonal to be good.

Opera buffa: Although the name literally means "comic opera," opera buffa's main legacy was not only humor but also a certain naturalism that transformed opera. Opera buffa began in small, often grungy theaters in Naples and other Italian cities. The stories revolved around real people in mundane, contemporary situations, abundant with young love, mean-spirited old men, and conniving servants. The humble parameters of the form meant expensive castrati and great divas were out of the question, so ensemble music became more eminent. Even arias tended to flow more naturally out of the recitative than in the rigid strictures of opera seria. The definitive opera buffa of this era was *La serva padrona*, by Pergolesi (1710–1736), a piece of great charm and casual elegance still given today. Eventually, even the aristocracy became interested in the appealing and increasingly refined form. *Opere buffe* (pl.), generally composed in two acts, were given between the three acts of opere serie. This made for long nights at the theater, and often the whole evening was finished off with a ballet or a ball. It was only a matter of time before the features of the two forms would be combined to create works of great range, power, and dramatic elasticity. Mozart's *Don Giovanni* (1788) has easily identifiable features of both opera seria and opera buffa. It was, however, the opera buffa that cast the longer shadow over future opera development. Even tragic operas of the nineteenth century tended to use opera buffa's format for voices, with young lovers generally assigned to the tenor and soprano, concerned parents being baritones and mezzos, and bad guys sung by the bass. Beyond this, the move toward more realistic situations and naturalistic "speech" in subsequent opera was a legacy of the opera buffa.

Opera seria: The dominant form of opera throughout the eighteenth century, opera seria (literally, serious opera) became a very complex, formalized, and eventually stifling genre. The form consisted of remote historical subjects from classical antiquity, centered on noble figures behaving nobly. The main component of opera seria was the aria, with ensembles and choruses used very sparingly. The aria itself was usually the *da capo* ("from the top") aria, also known as the ABA aria because of its form: a melody, a break, and a repeat of the first melody. On a good night, this avoided becoming tedious solely because of the talents of the great castrati, sopranos, and occasional others who were not only riveting in themselves but who took great liberties in the repeated final section. Another notable feature of the opera seria was the grand *scena*. In this, a character came on stage alone, sang a slow aria, was interrupted by a brief bit of news, and then launched into an explosive aria. For example, a castrato bemoans the death of his sweetheart in a long sad aria, accompanied, say, by the oboe. A messenger arrives, informs him that she is not dead, and quickly exits. The castrato swears to fight all heaven and hell to find her in a *da capo* aria with blaring trumpets. Curtain and applause. The singer, therefore, has been able to display a huge range of emotion, style, and ability, and many singers had contractual clauses for the number of grand *scenas* they expected in each performance.

The chief proponent of the opera seria form was the poet Metastasio, the court poet of Vienna from 1730 until his death in 1782. His highly stylized libretti were set over eight hundred times by seventy different composers, and his single libretto *Artaserse* was set by forty different composers. Gluck bucked against the tradition and created a polemic against it. Mozart, typically, preferred to master the form with his opera *Idomeneo* and then subsequently destroyed the form with *Le nozze di Figaro*.

Opera seria lay dead for a century and a half, but scholarly efforts to revive it were successful from the middle of the twentieth century on. Audiences have discovered that interesting singers can make the form come alive, while directors have noted that the bare, remote stories hold up quite well to new, and occasionally outrageous, interpretations. For years, performances of opere serie (the plural) were typically cut to shreds under the theory that eighteenth-century audiences were not expected to sit still during performances as we are, and that in any case they seemed to have a higher threshold for boredom than we do. This proved to be a mistake. Critic/scholar Will Crutchfield and others have promulgated the notion that cutting these works paradoxically makes them seem longer. The onus of making these works come alive lies with the singers, the director, and ultimately the conductor, and not with the editor.

Operetta: The exact definition of an operetta is elusive and somewhat subjective. An operetta uses spoken dialogue between musical numbers. Of course, so do some operas, the most famous examples being *Carmen* and *The Magic Flute*. The distinction is often made by tradition. Technically speaking, there is no structural difference between an operetta and a Broadway musical. The difference is more one of tone than structure, although there are some works (e.g., *Rose Marie, Showboat*) that could be classified as either. Roughly speaking, an operetta has the same structure as a musical but has the stylistic tone of an opera. The spoken dialogue allowed for more humor to be introduced, and the shorter musical numbers tended to allow for more buoyancy than grand opera, so operettas tended to be comic or at least lighthearted. The operetta format also meant that it could grow along different lines in different places according to local tastes to a much greater extent than grand opera. The Viennese long had a special love for operetta, and Johann Strauss, Jr.'s *Die Fledermaus* (1874) and Franz Lehar's *The Merry Widow* (1905), both still very popular, represent the apex of the form. In France, Jacques Offenbach reigned supreme, his *Orphée aux Enfers* thrilling audiences in its day as it still does with its ubiquitous *Can-Can*. The Spanish *zarzuela,* a venerable tradition of song, dance, and drama, became more like the Viennese and Parisian operetta, with waltzes and love duets and other stock features. In England, Gilbert and Sullivan's witty operettas became national treasures. Bandmasters

and composers in America jostled to compose operettas in a
jaunty and brash style that sought to combine all the refinements of European opera with the energy of American music
John Philip Sousa wrote several popular operettas around the
turn of the last century. The greatest American operetta composer was Victor Herbert, who had once been the principal cel-
list of the Metropolitan Opera. His works, such as *Naughty
Marietta* (1910) and *Sweethearts* (1913) are in fact considered
the direct ancestors of the Broadway musical.

Romanticism: Romanticism was a movement, begun in literature
and picked up in other arts, which celebrated spontaneous expressions of pure emotion. A communal depression settled over
European youth after the disasters and disappointments of the
Napoleonic Wars. All notions of order, good taste, and propriety
appeared tainted. Nature, as opposed to culture, was fetishized,
and the social outcast and outsider became icons. The Middle
Ages held a fascination for Romantics because of their image
as a barbarous, lawless time, and in fact much of what we
assume about medieval life has more to do with Romantic notions of the era than any historical fact. The supernatural, being
inexplicable, was also celebrated, and a fascination with death
became fashionable. Even suicide was often praised as a noble
response to the disappointments of the world (e.g., Goethe's
Sorrows of Young Werther). Musically speaking, this meant that
decorum was to be sacrificed to anything that smacked of emotional truth, even if that truth was expressed somewhat sloppily
according to the notions of the time. Beethoven had shocked
audiences with his loud, crass symphonies. Berlioz and Franz
Liszt would go even further. It was an exciting time, and no
one who grew up in Europe between 1815 and 1840 could fail
to be affected by the winds of Romanticism. As it happened,
the two greatest composers of opera, Wagner and Verdi, were
of this generation.

Scholars explain that Wagner transcended writing Romantic
Opera midway through his career, after completing *Lohengrin*

in 1848. Similarly, Verdi also outgrew his own roots at a certain point and finished his career with masterpieces that are difficult to categorize as Romantic or as anything else. Yet their achievements in the development of opera were similar and both sprang from their roots among the Romantics. They both found methods of uniting music and drama in a seamless fashion in which the melody flowed from the present situation. The eighteenth-century opera seria simply divided action (recitative) and reflection (aria). Wagner and Verdi, having Romantic backgrounds, could never be satisfied with such a neat and arbitrary arrangement. They discovered that action had its own melody. Music was not a stumbling block to dramatic development of a story, but rather the very core of the story being told.

Of course, Romanticism is a very wide and imprecise category, and has come to mean many things. Massenet and Gounod—who set famous operatic versions of Goethe's *Werther* and *Faust*, respectively—and many others are called Romantics simply because of the emotionalism of their work. Even Richard Strauss, who battered at the very walls of tonality itself in *Elektra* (1909), is often categorized as Romantic, and not without reason. Moreover, the word has taken on a negative connotation of sentimentalism. Yet it remains undeniable that there is something in the spirit of the Romantics that has worked supremely well in the format of music-drama we call opera. By its very appeal to the inexplicable primal emotions in humans, there is something Romantic about every successful opera.

Serialism: The actual number of operas composed in a purely serialist form is small, but the influence of the movement has been enormous and it is not possible to speak of twentieth-century music or opera without referring to this style. It is an issue that tends to confuse the general public, and many music experts seem to delight in its remoteness, adding to its obscurity.

Just before the First World War, Arnold Schoenberg experimented with the idea of changing the musical scale as it was commonly understood in Europe and America. The standard scale of Western culture is based on eight notes per octave, with the in-between notes designated as sharp or flat variations on the closest note, a half-step up or down the scale, respectively. Schoenberg thought this system had stultified the possibilities of music. People in India, for example, are able to discern twenty-two notes per octave. In order to break open the mold, Schoenberg formulated an entirely new system. Taking any note as a starting point, he wrote a "series" comprised of all twelve (i.e., including sharps and flats) notes in the octave. Each of the twelve notes had to be used once, and only once, in each series. A note could be of any time duration: half, quarter, or whatever. A note could not be used again until the other eleven notes in the "row" (or series) had been used. After the first series had been completed, the next would follow under the same structure, beginning on whatever note the composer desired. This was also called the "twelve-tone system," which, at first, was synonymous with Serialism. Later, disciples of Schoenberg added variations to the system. Miniature clusters of three or four notes, rather than the individual notes of the twelve-tone scale, could be used once each per series until every variation had been played. Still other composers devised structures based on the time duration of each note instead of, or in addition to, the pitch value. These later more complicated variations are also Serialist, but not, strictly speaking, twelve-tone in its original sense.

All of which leaves most people asking the obvious question: Why? Isn't this all a rather arcane game more suited to mathematicians and puzzle solvers than artists? Yes, it is, if done by pedants. In the hands of a real musician, however, it can be quite powerful, utilizing powerful musical expressions to depict human emotions and situations that simply cannot be explored within the standard scale. The original Serialists were quick to point out that so-called normal music wasn't natural or organic at all, it was merely an old, old habit. Serialism forced composers and audiences alike to question their assumptions about "good" music. Even though the rules were restrictive, the result was often paradoxically quite liberating. At the opera, the most successful twelve-tone opera was *Lulu* (1935) by Alban Berg, a work that is still considered musically shocking despite its popularity. Indirectly, Serialism influenced almost all subsequent composers, and the widespread use of electronic instruments in the late twentieth century made many of the Serialists' discoveries commonplace.

Verismo: The term verismo, meaning "realism," was originally used by authors to describe a new style of narrative around the 1880s. Inspired by Balzac, Zola, and other Frenchmen who wrote in a detached, cool style, Italian authors sought to remove the tedious conventions of storytelling with a plain, direct style. The definitive example is Giovanni Verga's shattering, four-page short story *Cavalleria rusticana*. The story concerns lust, adultery, and murder among simple village people in contemporary Sicily, and is told using the then-revolutionary, all-knowing, third person, Omniscient narrative voice. But how does one translate this into operatic terms? The fact is opera had been moving toward *verismo* for many years: Verdi's *La traviata* (1852) dealt with a prostitute and even showed her trying to balance her checkbook. (Verdi meant it to be presented in modern dress, but tradition and the fact that costume departments didn't own any contemporary outfits prevented this.) However, *verismo* hit the opera full force in 1891 with, predictably, a setting of *Cavalleria rusticana* by Mascagni. Opera audiences accustomed to seeing lords and ladies of ages ago venting vaunted emotions were amazed to see scrubby peasants stabbing and screaming at one another. It was a sensation, and young composers throughout Italy, such as Puccini and Leoncavallo, jostled for similar subject matter. There was a musical facet to *verismo* as well. While veristic authors sought to present only the facts as they happened, composers wrote scores that were directly emotional and unencumbered by musical ornamentation. The concept echoed the authors' in that the goal was to present truth rather than to show off how smart the creator was. However, the result was the exact opposite of what Balzac and Zola had aimed for. Instead of a cool, detached style, operatic *verismo* was frenzied, gushing, and even deliberately crass. Instead of the grand finale arias of previous operas, *verismo* operas packed their punches in short explosions of melody thundered out by the singer and the full orchestra. In truth, opera composers had been moving toward this for years even in such conventional works as Ponchielli's *La gioconda* (1876), but the combination of this musical style with the new dramatic sensibilities was revolutionary. Eventually, operas became defined as *verismo* because they held to this musical style of intense, earthy emotionalism rather than because of any dramatic content. Thus Zandonai's *Francesca da Rimini* (1913) is generally consigned to the *verismo* camp despite its historical/aristocratic subject matter, period costumes, full five acts, and ballet. Composers in other countries attempted to write *verismo* operas, most notably Massenet in France (*La Navarraise*, 1895) and d'Albert in Germany and Bohemia (*Tiefland*, 1903), but the style did not catch on in languages other than Italian. By 1920, the style was dead even in Italy, but its influence is still felt, particularly in film and Broadway scores. In fact, it was so apparent that Andrew Lloyd Webber's *Phantom of the Opera* used not only the *veristic* device of the single melodic motif, but an actual theme from a Puccini opera that Puccini's heirs filed and won a plagiarism suit.

FOUR

Opera Deconstructed

Opera composers have a variety of techniques and devices to use in creating their work. Most of these came about the hard way: by trial and error. Some became conventions of opera, others clichés. Furthermore, opera has become an increasingly discrete world, separated from so-called popular culture in a way that it was not a hundred and fifty years ago. In those times, a composer could send any number of messages to an audience by drawing from the arsenal of conventions. But what exactly were those conventions, and what did they signify? And what of the stories of operas? Where do they come from and how do they evolve? Before we can comprehend the full experience of hearing an opera, let alone seeing one, we can dismantle the features of an opera score piece by piece and come to a fuller appreciation of the sum of the parts.

The Story

It cannot be stressed enough that opera is a form of drama, making its unique statements by the use of music to unfold human confrontations. The first thing one must have when embarking on the creation of an opera is a good story. This can be quite tricky in itself, since a good drama does not necessarily make a good opera, and conversely, it is possible to create a good opera out of a mediocre story. A composer who would write an opera must be able to detect qualities in a story that will work in opera, and discard the others. This may actually be the single most defining aspect of a great opera composer.

Many composers begin by taking a successful drama and adding music to it. This was, in fact, how the first opera was created, and the composer, Peri, had strict orders not to make his music too interesting and thereby interfere with the words. Composers did not waste much time before they began to direct matters a little more, however. Since Monteverdi found that certain forms of arias expressed various emotions more effectively than others, we know he must have told his librettists where to include different poetic forms. The power had shifted from the librettists to the composer, and has remained there ever since. Yet the libretto is still the starting point, the genetic code, so to speak, that will determine both the form and the content of the completed opera.

Developments in librettos paralleled other literary forms for some time, becoming formalized during the eighteenth century and somewhat more unstructured in the Romantic Era. From at least the time of Mozart, it became more common to adapt successful stage plays (such as Beaumarchais's *Marriage of Figaro*) to the operatic stage rather than remain limited to librettos specifically written for operas. The plays still needed revisions by librettists, since opera used specific formulas for poetic verse well into the nineteenth century. But the possibilities of what one might encounter in an opera house expanded exponentially. The turgid "Rescue Dramas" of the Napoleonic

Era found their way into the opera house via Beethoven's *Fidelio*. Soon, plays by such social misfits as Victor Hugo and Antonio García Gutierrez were set as operas by the trouble-maker Verdi, (*Rigoletto* and *Il trovatore*, respectively), after they were "versified" by experienced librettists. Shakespeare, the darling of the Romantics, became a favorite source of operatic dramas at this time, and continues to prove a treasure trove for opera composers.

Wagner, predictably, changed everything. He insisted on writing his own librettos, which were a disaster from the purists' point of view, but clearly magnificent vehicles for creating opera. Since then, many have emulated him in writing their own librettos, with varying success.

The modern opera composer has a wide array of choices when choosing a libretto. A play can be set to music (e.g., André Previn's *A Streetcar Named Desire*) or a librettist with an original drama (William Hoffman's *Ghosts of Versailles*) can be found. Composers and librettists sometimes work very closely together when creating an opera (such as Stravinsky and W. H. Auden on *The Rake's Progress*) while others find a certain distance helps the final result. Richard Strauss and Hugo von Hoffmannsthal corresponded only by mail (their correspondence is published and makes for fascinating reading) and almost seemed to avoid each other's live company.

Occasionally, the composer has music in mind before there is a libretto, and the music must be imposed on the words in some way. Musetta's Waltz in Puccini's *La bohème* seems perfectly appropriate where it is, yet it was originally written without words, to be played by a military band at the launching of a battleship. Likewise, it is inconceivable that all the melodies of Verdi's *Rigoletto* sprang to the composer's mind in the few short weeks he took to score (i.e., set to music) the libretto. It was easier to adapt existing melodies to words in the days when both words and music tended to follow standard forms. Yet adapting existing music to the libretto was never the standard routine, and the libretto, then as now, has always been the source of the finished opera. Whether the opera is to be a traditional narrative drama, (such as Tobias Picker's *Emmeline*, based on Sophocles' *Oedipus the King*) or a drama of poetic sounds with a barely discernible drama (such as Philip Glass's *Satyagraha*) the libretto remains the structure around which the opera is built.

The Vocal Solo

The vocal solo is the basic unit of operatic currency, without which little else can be achieved. For all the grandeur and spectacle of opera, the individual ultimately matters most. Many of the "greatest hits" of opera are in fact arias, vocal solos that are set pieces within a score. This leads many to believe that opera is overly stylized, since an aria usually represents a break in dramatic development. Indeed, many opera composers of the last 150 years have thought the same and sought to avoid set arias. Yet the traditional aria has a great deal of versatility to it and can accomplish many unique things.

Traditional operatic forms of the aria can even be detected in the most form-defying works of modern composers. Arias come in several forms, many of which became standards, or even clichés, of traditional opera. First, we'll examine some of these forms before seeing how they have evolved into other forms.

The Love Aria: It is very difficult for a character in a spoken drama to reveal feelings of love, since so much of love is unspoken and unspeakable. Opera circumvents this problem by blurring the lines between what is actually being said and what unspoken feelings are being revealed. Therefore, opera can show us a character expounding on his or her love in great detail in a way that would sound truly ridiculous if merely spoken. A character can explain, "I'm in love and I'm thrilled about it!" (the tenor Des Grieux in "Donna non vidi mai," from act I of Puccini's *Manon Lescaut*), "I'm in love and it's killing me!" (tenor Don José in "The Flower Song," ("La fleur que tu m'avais jetée") from act II of Bizet's *Carmen*), or "I'm in love and I'm going to do something about it no matter what anybody says!" (baritone di Luna, "Il balen," from act III of Verdi's *Il trova-tore*). Note that the men, and the tenors in particular, get to sing most of the arias of this type. Love plays a huge role in almost any aria, of course, but declaring love outright has been considered a male prerogative throughout history. The tenor voice is especially well suited for these sorts of feelings, conveying urgency and emotion rather than judicious behavior. Women tend to respond to love or, as so often in life, deal with its messy consequences.

The Farewell Aria: It is one thing to say "I'm sad because I must leave" in words, but a singer can linger over the sentiment slowly and with much reflection. The Farewell Aria, therefore, became one of the stocks-in-trade of the operatic composer. The poet Lenski, a tenor in *Eugene Onegin*, assumes he will be killed in a duel with the title character. Alone on stage, he sings the haunting "Kudai ve udallilis" (usually simply called "Lenski's Aria"), bidding farewell to both his own short life and his sweetheart Olga. Aida's great solo moment is "O patria mia," when she bids farewell to the homeland she will never see again. The eponymous heroine of Alfredo Catalani's *La Wally* leaves her home, singing "Ebben, ne andrò lontano" as the curtain falls for act III. The opera has become a rarity, but the aria, familiar from television and especially from the movie *Diva*, has outlived the opera. A good Farewell Aria allows the audience more than empathy with the character in question. It allows us to ponder and taste again all the moments in our own lives when we have had to let go of something important.

The Suicide Aria: An extreme form of the Farewell Aria is the Suicide Aria, wherein a character recounts the events and situations requiring the ultimate sacrifice. Suicide, in order to serve a greater good, was praised by the ancient Romans and can therefore be found in many baroque operas, although admittedly the hero or heroine is often prevented from carrying out the final deed. In the Romantic Era, suicide was a common trope of literature, especially for those forced into it by an unfeeling society. Bel canto opera, which coincided with the initial flush of Romanticism, is rife with suicide finales, as in Bellini's *Norma*. The hero of Donizetti's *Lucia di Lamermoor* gets two arias before he plunges the knife, "Fra poco a me ricovero" and "Tu, che a Dio spiegasti l'ali." *The Sorrows of Young Werther*, by Goethe, was the definitive Romantic novel. Massenet set it as an opera. The hero sings at some length before, and even after, he shoots himself. Puccini's *Madame Butterfly* does the same with a samurai sword. *La gioconda's* heroine makes us certain of her intent in her final aria, unsubtly titled "Suicidio!"

The Mad Scene: One of the most enduring clichés of opera is the great Mad Scene, where the diva screams and yells and goes visibly nuts on the stage. Most of the great Mad Scenes in opera, however, are much more interesting and even more subtle than this. The frightening thing about a good Mad Scene is that they make sense; that is, the music shows us the inner logic of the madness. There is also usually a very disturbing calm middle section to every Mad Scene, just to make sure we follow the insane, subsequent histrionics. The definitive Mad Scene in opera is in act III of Donizetti's *Lucia di Lamermoor*. The heroine, having axed her groom to bits on their wedding night, appears at her wedding banquet in a blood-drenched gown. The visual statement alone is enough to sear the image onto the communal unconscious. If one did not know the opera, one might expect Lucia to launch into fifteen minutes of shrieking and yelling. Actually, Lucia's Mad Scene is delicate and refined, calling for great control and even elegance from the singer. The scene climaxes with roulades (rapid runs up and down the vocal scale) and Lucia's collapse. By the time the music becomes anything we could frankly call "mad," we have been swept up into the melodic flow. There is only the finest of lines between beautiful music and total insanity. Surely this lesson is at the core of Lucia's enduring fascination. Other great Mad Scenes are to be found in Ambroise Thomas's *Hamlet*, Mozart's *Idomeneo*, and Verdi's *Macbeth*. Nor are women the only purveyors of operatic Mad Scenes, although the soprano voice is especially well suited to portray this state. The bass Assur in Rossini's *Semiramide* gets to sing a particularly devilish one, and Vivaldi composed a masterpiece of slightly "off" eerie music for the castrato lead (now usually sung by mezzos) of his *Orlando Furioso*. Verdi, who always toyed with classic forms, has the baritone hero of *Nabucco* go mad in an instant, and instead gives him a "Sane Scene," "Dio di Giuda," later in the opera when his senses are restored.

The Song: There are many opportunities in opera for a character to sing a song; that is, a set piece that would theoretically be a song even if it were not an opera. The song can have any number of interesting relationships to the drama. The Princess Eboli, the femme fatale of Verdi's *Don Carlo*, sings a Moorish "Veil Song" shortly before she becomes involved in a veiled intrigue in a midnight garden. Cherubino, the randy young man (actually sung by a woman) in Mozart's *Marriage of Figaro*, is asked to amuse the ladies with a song in act II. He sings "Voi che sapete," about the sufferings of love shortly before all the characters will experience them. Carmen sings of the magic of gypsy music in act II of her opera. Mascagni's *Cavalleria rusticana* opens on an empty stage, and we hear the hero Turiddu singing of love off stage, a stunning coup that was still considered revolutionary when done fifty years later in Rodgers and Hammerstein's *Oklahoma!* The longest opera in the regular repertory, Wagner's *Die Meistersinger von Nürnberg*, is actually about the composition and performance of a single piece of music for a song contest. The "Prize Song" is sung repeatedly, and the developments of the song define the evolution of the characters throughout the opera. At the end of the evening, the song is heard and repeated in part by the townspeople, who are transformed and visibly improved by its influence. Having a song within an opera is a composer's way of underscoring the mystical and inexplicable power of music over the human soul.

The Drinking Song: One specific type of song that became a commonplace of traditional opera was the Drinking Song, usually an aria with choral accompaniment. Sometimes a Drinking Song can merely create a festive atmosphere (such as the beginning of Verdi's *La traviata*), but often it can have an important plot function as well. Donizetti's *Lucrezia Borgia* sings a lusty Drinking Song as she encourages her victims to imbibe poison. In Verdi's *Macbeth*, Lady Macbeth leads her guests in a rousing Drinking Song as her husband begins to hallucinate Banquo's ghost. In Verdi's *Otello*, the evil Iago gets Cassio drunk with an irresistible Drinking Song, only to disgrace Cassio as a hopeless drunk. The buoyancy of Mozart's so-called Champagne Aria, "Fin c'han del vino," from *Don Giovanni*, classifies it as a Drinking Song, but the pounding insistence of the music lets us know what it is the Don likes to do after he has a few belts.

Heroic Aria: One sure way to get the audience riled up is to have a character sing a heroic "rally the troops" sort of aria. Most traditional operas have this device in one form or another, and so do many newer operas. The classic example must be "Di quella pira" from act III of Verdi's *Il trovatore*, but the trope is much older. Handel used it extensively, while Mozart parodied it in the famous bass-baritone aria "Non più andrai" that ends act I of *The Marriage of Figaro*. Nor are the "heroes who take action" always men. Women can rally themselves and the troops to beating drums and blaring horns. A mezzo-soprano named Preziosilla leads the soldiers in a chorus, "Rataplan!" in act III of Verdi's *La forza del destino*. In Stravinsky's neoclassical romp *The Rake's Progress*, heroine Anne Trulove sets out to find her wayward lover with the aria "No word from Tom" in act II. The martial beats in the orchestra and even the Handelian rhythms seem to signify militaristic determination even to those who have never heard a baroque opera.

We should not assume that arias are all similar because so many of them fit into categories. There is a tremendous amount of information that can be communicated in an aria. Remember that we have all the potential of a human voice, an entire orchestra, and a dramatic situation that can inform an aria. Sometimes the words match the music, other times they are at odds. In Gluck's *Iphigènie en Tauride*, we encounter a superb example of words and music playing off each other in the act II aria "La calme rentre dans mon coeur." The tenor languishes in prison, awaiting execution. He says "My heart is calm," but there are tense ripples in the orchestral strings that are anything but calm. He is whistling in the dark, as we might say. A playwright might suggest this, but an opera composer can illustrate it perfectly. Sometimes the irony is suggested by the dramatic situation; that is, what happens after the aria. In Mozart's *Così fan tutte*, the soprano sings a heroic aria about remaining true to her fiancée despite temptations from another man. All the rushing strings and martial spirit of a Handel hero rallying the troops are present in the aria as she insists she will remain "like a rock," "Come scoglio." A moment after she finishes (to great applause, usually), she agrees to leave with the suitor after all. While she sings, she is totally convincing (and perhaps totally convinced). Yet she changes her mind in an instant. It is Mozart's comment on the transitory nature of human emotions, as well as a reminder that all art is a bit of a lie. Sometimes, even having a character sing at all is a remarkable statement. In John Adams's popular *Nixon in China*, the character of Pat Nixon sings a dreamy aria, "Isn't it prophetic?" about her notions of a utopian world while alone on stage. The opera presumes that people remember the historical character of Mrs. Nixon and her famous reticence, and shows us the unexpected inner depths even a silent person might have.

The examples listed above are archetypes. Many of opera's greatest vocal solos use the forms and details of those arias in very different ways. Composers, at least since Wagner, have fought the formal structure of the classic aria, using more amorphous vocal solos called "narratives." The career goal of Wagner, Verdi, and practically every opera composer since has been to transcend the aria as a structural form. The idea was to find a way to have the drama move seamlessly between action (recitative) and reflection (aria). Even in such a work, however, there would be vocal solos, and for convenience's sake we call these narratives. Narratives, however radical in structure, can still use all the devices of the great arias. Verdi's Rigoletto journeys from angered madman to pleading supplicant in three minutes of solo music in that opera's act II "Corteggiani, vil razza dannata." Few people would call "Corteggiani" an aria, since it has no single overriding musical structure. Verdi, however, understood how music could represent different emotional states, and packed at least six arias together in this brief and devastating solo. Hans Sachs in Wagner's *Die Meistersinger von Nürnberg* unburdens his soul at every conceiveable opportunity whether anyone is on stage to hear him or not. The Marschallin of Richard Strauss's *Der Rosenkavalier* ends act I with a long, self-reflective narrative. The character development is internal, since she does not actually do anything as a result of her musings. Yet we experience her growth. Strauss used a sad ambience reminiscent of a Farewell Aria to let us understand the Marschallin is taking leave of her youth.

George Bernard Shaw pointed out that Wagner's *Ring of the Nibelung*, which was presented as a complete rethinking of the operatic form, in fact ended much like any bel canto opera. The heroine stands at the footlights and sings what is in effect a Suicide Aria. The famous "Immolation Scene" from act III of *Götterdämmerung* (the fourth opera in *The Ring*) is hardly a standard Suicide Aria, yet the signs of the form are clearly discernible in it. Shaw might also have pointed out that Wotan's beautiful Farewell at the end of *Die Walküre* had more in common with a set Farewell Aria like "Ebben, ne andró lontano" than Wagner would have cared to admit. One can even find musical similarities between the two examples, such as descending chord clusters and a heavy use of the cello. Even if no one would ever call Wotan's Farewell an aria, familiarity with the basics of the standard form improves one's appreciation for it. By the same token, the hero of Berg's *Wozzeck* loses his tonal center and sings in an altered key before wandering into the lake and dying at the end of that opera. It is both a Mad Scene and a Suicide Aria, even if it is neither. Wozzeck's death has structural elements that recall both the Mad Scene in *Orlando Furioso* and Norma's suicide, although neither Vivaldi nor Bellini might be able to recognize these if they could experience them.

Some composers have been able to encapsulate all the power of all aria in a single vocal line. This is partly because composers have become savvier about manipulating operatic structures than their forebearers were, but also because audiences became more sophisticated and better able to discern forms of operatic shorthand. (This is also one of the reasons why opera has become increasingly rarefied and remote over the last century and a half from people who are not opera fans.) Thus the heroine of Verdi's *Otello* bids good night to her maid in a single line of melodic outburst, and we can understand it as a Mad Scene, a Farewell Aria, and even a Suicide Aria all in one line. (It has been described as all three of those types.) In that composer's final masterpiece, *Falstaff*, the two young lovers can never be alone with each other amidst the grown-ups' intrigues. They would each like to expound on their love, but they have time only for a single line. Still, these two lines are among the most eloquent "Love Arias" ever penned. The maid Brangäne keeps watch in a tower while the love scene unfolds in *Tristan und Isolde*. Her simple cry of "Be careful! The dawn approaches" encapsulates the ancient tradition of a Morning Song, telling the lovers they must part. Her line is tonally at odds with the lovers' music—frightening, haunting, and eloquent in its simplicity. In Gershwin's *Porgy and Bess*, the heroine recovers from a near-mortal illness while street vendors pass by. One, the Strawberry Woman, simply cries "Fresh strawberries!" from the bottom of the scale up to the highest reaches before she leaves the stage. The opera seems to be suggesting the healing powers of music itself.

Combined Voices

Perhaps the greatest facet of opera is that it can combine characters in a way that simply will not work in spoken drama. Characters can "speak" simultaneously. Besides saving a lot of time, this can show us the relationship between characters as they develop, reflecting the emotional world rather than the literal world.

As with the aria, certain conventions have formed around combined voices, and some have become hackneyed. But even the most radical of operatic reformers were familiar with the conventions they were supposedly discarding or transcending.

The Love Duet: The Love Duet is more of an archetype than an actual reality. Moments of perfect love, where, say, the tenor and soprano sing of their love at the same time, are surprisingly rare in opera. Mozart, Verdi, and Wagner all avoided standard duets to portray two young people in love. Donizetti permitted himself an actual Love Duet in *Lucia di Lamermoor.* The soprano sings a verse, the tenor sings the same, and finally both sing the same verse together. Donizetti did not lack the imagination of the other composers. The perfect symmetry of the Love Duet in *Lucia* is a splendid setup for the subsequent deaths of the two lovers, who will die separately because they are parted from each other. Most operas, however, prefer a more complicated analysis of the love relationship and leave the symmetrical duet to Broadway, where it has been used to death. The most popular Love Duets in opera are not really duets at all. In Puccini's *La bohème*, the tenor sings of his love, the soprano sings of her life (and only mentions love obliquely), and the two sing a reiteration of his aria to let us know they have come to a point of agreement. It is more like a dialog. Wagner was very adamant about not letting lovers sing at the same time. Act I of *Die Walküre* is a protracted love scene (between a brother and sister, no less). Neither sings at the same time. First one sings, then the other, and so forth until they build to an unmistakable and thrilling climax. In fact, many love scenes are more like conflicts than pleasantries. The conventional love duet always eluded Verdi, but he created a unique one in act I of *Otello*. The tenor's music utterly dominates the soprano's, and it is clear that their love will consume her in some sense. He is a more powerful force of nature. The lovers in Wagner's *Tristan und Isolde* appear to consume each other in their love scene, which is almost the entire second act. Puccini died before he was able to finish his opera *Turandot* with a final love duet (which his manuscript notes implied would refer to *Tristan und Isolde* in some way), but the scene he did write for the hero and heroine contains all the hostility that has ever existed between the sexes. Comedian Anna Russell called the final love scene of Wagner's *Siegfried* "Anything you can sing, I can sing louder." In Puccini's *Madame Butterfly*, the tenor is insistent and clearly aroused in a sexual sense, while the soprano sings lyrically of the poetry of the night. Anyone can tell that these two have separate agendas.

It is a mistake, therefore, to assume it is time to "sit back and relax" when encountering a love duet, or a love scene, in an opera. The closer you listen to the dynamics of the two parties, the better you will follow the nuances of the relationship the composer is seeking to portray.

The Oath Duet: It has often been noted that hate is very much a perverted form of love rather than its opposite, and opera can demonstrate this more bluntly than any other art form. One convention of opera is the Oath Duet, wherein two characters swear to do something (usually kill somebody). The perfect union of two voices united in a common evil purpose is a chilling exposé of the inherent attraction of evil. There is a rather melodramatic duet of this type in act II of Wagner's *Lohengrin*, and a magnificent one (the apex of the form) in act II of Verdi's *Otello*. Bel canto opera features several. The most rousing is both an oath duet and a "call to arms," "Suoni la tromba" from act III of Bellini's *I puritani*.

The Comic Duet: Most comic operas include some sort of a rapid duet, often between two men. Few may realize this, but these duets are inherent parodies of Oath Duets, often with the foolish older men plotting to steal the blushing bride or some such situation. These were so common in bel canto operas that a specific category of bass, the *basso buffo* (comic bass), became common at the time. Marvelous examples of comic duets with basses or a bass and a baritone can be found in Donizetti's *Don Pasquale* and Rossini's *La Cenerentola*. Verdi knew his audience was so familiar with the comic bass duet that he was able to parody the parody, so to speak, in *Rigoletto*. The hunchbacked title character has a casual conversation in the street with a hired assassin, who blithely speaks of his honest business practices like any swindler from comic opera. The scene was meant to be funny, or at least humorous, though this often goes unnoticed today. Benjamin Britten was more overt in his parody in his opera *Paul Bunyan*, where two campground cooks vaunt their respective stews with the musical structure of two bel canto bad guys plotting a murder.

Comic duets are not limited to lower-voiced men. The first act of Rossini's *The Barber of Seville* contains a long scene between the tenor and the baritone as they plot and plan an intrigue. It amounts to five or six of the best comic duets ever written, one after another. Donizetti's *L'elisir d'amore* has the charming "Venti scudi" in act II. Women make occasional forays into comic duets. In Mozart's symbolic comedy *The Magic Flute*, the birdman Papageno meets his birdgirl Papagena, and they chatter away about all the "little birds" they will have together.

Multiple Voices

There is something inherently fascinating about several voices singing at once in complicated harmonies, with threads of melody weaving in and out of one another. In fact, it is so compelling that it presents a problem for opera composers. The temptation to spin beautiful melody for its own sake, rather

than to propel the dramatic action, is often too great. The technique, called polyphony (Greek for "many sounds") was developed in the Renaissance, and it immediately caused opposition.
Church authorities declared it inappropriate for religious ser-
vices, although that position has vacillated over the years. The
original creators of opera were no more accommodating. The
Camerata of Florence and their friends were quite clear that
their new art form would have absolutely no polyphony. What
kind of drama could there be if everyone on stage was singing
away to their hearts' content?

They had a point. Not many composers would be able to
write a trio, a quartet, and so forth without having them be
anything more than a sort of madrigal sung in costume. The
baroque composers generally agreed with the *Camerata*, and
baroque opera seria tends to be one solo after another. Only the
occasional duet and the very occasional trio, as well as the
jaunty chorus at the finale, interrupted the parade of solo stars.

Mozart changed that, as he changed so much else. The *Marriage of Figaro* is an early example of a drawing-room comedy,
with slamming doors and suspected lovers hiding in closets and
so forth. In act II, there is a classic comedic scene in which
there are disguises, a furious husband, and a generally confusing
situation. The action progresses from an aria to several duets,
then a trio, a quartet, a quintet, a quartet, and, finally, a septet.
Characters tumble in, and all on stage sing according to the
new situation at hand. It appears to be the most natural thing
in the world. Actually, it is nothing short of a miracle of stage-
craft, not to mention music.

Rossini did not fail to learn from Mozart's triumphant innovation, and his comic operas are loaded with similar situations.
Some of them are less sophisticated than *Figaro*, if hardly less enjoyable. The finale to act I of *L'italiana in Algeri* gets the six
main characters on stage together, hopelessly confused. They
each sing how confused they are, saying things like "I hear
bells!" and "It's like I've been hit over the head with a stick!"
while making appropriate musical noises. It is some of the most
inherently funny music ever written, as well as a bit psychotic.

Comedy, however, can step outside of time more easily than tragedy, and the use of polyphony in "serious" opera was more problematic. Beethoven composed a gorgeous quartet for act I of *Fidelio*. Even though it is very formal in structure, the *Fidelio* quartet does allow us to examine the intersecting lives of the people involved. This idea was taken to new heights by that most dramatic of composers, Verdi. In act IV of *Rigoletto*, a quartet shows us the contrasting emotions of the four characters involved. The miracle of the *Rigoletto* quartet, however, is that there is a single overriding structure to it even while it is composed of four very different vocal lines. As lovely as the *Rigoletto* quartet may be to whistle or even hear in a recital, its true genius is dramatic. It provides a cross-section of human relationships.

Verdi continued to explore this throughout his career. A quintet in act III of *Un ballo in maschera* brings together five characters in the most different emotional states imaginable: joyous anticipation, guilt, and vengeance. Everyone is excited, but is it nervous, happy, or terrified? In fact it is all three. Like Michelangelo's famous statue of the Rondanini Pietá, the situation changes depending on from which angle it is viewed.

Verdi may have been the master of this device, but he was not the only great composer to use it well. The ever-popular sextet from Donizetti's *Lucia di Lamermoor* is always nice to hear as a set piece, on the radio or in the recital hall. In the context of its story, it is a dramatic masterstroke. The gorgeous quintet in act III of *Die Meistersinger von Nürnberg* makes many people wish Wagner had discarded all his theories about music drama and simply written more lovely music of this type. Two pairs of lovers break up at the same time in act III of Puccini's *La bohéme*. One pair is tender and romantic, the other vulgar and spiteful. They are two sides of the same coin. It is only by experiencing them simultaneously (as we can only do in opera) that we understand the full implications of a break-up. Nor is this use of multiple voices absent from our modern era that is dominated by such trends as atonality, minimalism, and expressionism. John Corigliano's and William Hoffman's

The Ghosts of Versailles (1991) uses a quintet to great effect in act III to show us five characters who each somehow find a moment of serenity while awaiting execution.

The trio has long been a popular component of opera. It is easier to keep the action moving through a trio than through larger ensembles, and the love triangle (in its many variations) is a staple of operatic plot. Again, the impetus may have come from Mozart, who created a great trio for three basses toward the end of *Don Giovanni*. There is no shortage of dramatic action in Mozart's trio. A statue shows up at the door and drags the hero down into the flames of hell. The epilogue has the remaining characters singing a sextet directly at the audience, telling us that the bad always get punished. In a sense, the trio is the finale of the opera itself. In fact, for many years it was popular to dispense with the final sextet altogether. Throughout the nineteenth century, the trio was considered perhaps the most satisfying way to end an opera and wrap up everything. Gounod's *Faust* ends with a spectacular trio, while Verdi used it for the finales of *Ernani*, *La forza del destino*, and *Aida* (although it is hardly recognizable as a trio in this instance).

Trios, of course, can occur anywhere in an opera when people's experiences are clashing. Carmen sees her own death foretold in the cards, while her friends only see good fortunes for themselves in act III. Ping, Pang, and Pong in Puccini's *Turandot* always appear together, as their names suggest. Almost every line they have is elaborated into a miniature trio throughout the opera. Even Wagner's *Ring*, almost entirely composed of vocal solos and orchestral passages, has a vengeance trio in act II of *Götterdämmerung*.

The ultimate trio in all opera, recognizable to all opera fans as "The Trio," occurs toward the end of Richard Strauss's *Der Rosenkavalier*. The situation is a love triangle where one character nobly withdraws from the situation, allowing the two young lovers a future. The plot situation has an antecedent in Wagner's *Meistersinger*, but the music incorporates lessons from Mozart and even Verdi as well. The three characters sing very similar music. Some of it is even the exact same music. How-ever, the meaning is different for each because of its relation to the context of the rest of their music. Most of all, "The Trio" drips in wisdom. It is not an experience that can be achieved in any medium but opera.

The Chorus

The chorus represents greater society, to put it succinctly. Sometimes, this society can be a monolithic structure, though it must be admitted that some operas only use the chorus as a loud punctuation for the lead characters. In baroque opera, the chorus (which was usually small anyway) was almost always used merely to bring down the curtains at the ends of acts and occasionally to add a little pomp to public scenes. Beethoven gave the chorus an important and poignant role in *Fidelio*. Rossini, perhaps influenced by Beethoven, also sought to expand the role of the chorus in his operas *Moïsé* and *Guillaume Tell*. Generally speaking, however, the chorus did not evolve into a more complex role until the middle of the nineteenth century.

The more rudimentary early choruses could attain great heights. The celebrated chorus "Va, pensiero" from Verdi's *Nabucco* is powerful when sung by itself, but truly brilliant in the course of the opera. Most of that opera is wild, raw, and a bit out of control. The calming sounds of the unified chorus in act III imply that fragmented individuals driven to extremes can find a sense of calm and composure within a community. It was a powerful statement to make amid the fragmented fight for Italian unification, and in fact it still gets people teary-eyed today.

After *Nabucco*, Wagner, Verdi, and Meyerbeer all succeeded in finding more for the chorus to carry. They no longer needed to represent a single frame of mind; they could show sentiments spreading through a community, such as the magnificent final scene of Wagner's *Die Meistersinger von Nürnberg* or act III of Verdi's *Otello*. In *Aida*, Verdi put the opposing forces of two nations, and various factions within those populations, in the great Triumphal Scene of act II. Later composers took even greater risks and accomplished even more with choruses. Puccini mastered a situation Verdi and Wagner had been aiming for throughout their careers with the choral finale of *La fanciulla del West*. The soprano has encapsulated her belief in redemption with a brief theme (a leitmotiv, as the Wagnerians would say). Each of the members of the chorus (all male, in this case), sings the theme, one at a time, until it is transformed into a unified melody. The community is redeemed by the faith of a single woman. Gershwin incorporates musical devices of the Gullah people of South Carolina in the great choruses of *Porgy and Bess*, including forays into atonality that chillingly depict the terrors, prayers, and bravado of different members of the community as they await a hurricane. Arnold Schoenberg made the chorus the lead character, so to speak, in his twelve-tone opera *Moses und Aron*. All the various aspects of the Israelites in the Exodus can be detected in the complicated choral music. These include faith, cowardice, and rebellion, sometimes simultaneously. The movie *The Ten Commandments*, to cite a rather absurd comparison, had to take several hours to show contrasting scenes of the populace first in one phase, then the next. A chorus could represent it all at once, which is, in fact, much truer psychologically. Benjamin Britten was especially adept at nuanced choral writing. In *Albert Herring*, the hypocrisies of society are amusingly exposed in the chatterings of the chorus, while society becomes an even more stifling and oppressive specter in *Peter Grimes*. In *Billy Budd*, the sailors' choruses build and dissipate like the fogs through which they sail, yet the sailors are always recognizably human in their emotions. The dramatic import within this fable of Good and Evil is stupendous. Humanity itself is depicted as driven by unseen forces as daunting as Nature herself. Philip Glass has used the chorus to great effect, building themes incrementally to create an irresistible wall of human sound. At their best, his choral moments can encompass all the aspirations of humanity, an important concept in nonnarrative operas such as *Satyagraha*.

People may well complain about the deficiencies of twentieth century composers, but the last century has shown a steady improvement in the mastery of the chorus as an important and endlessly fascinating aspect of opera.

The Orchestra Alone

The orchestra, of course, plays throughout an opera, and its relation to what is being sung is a life's study. In and of itself, however, the orchestra without vocal accompaniment is also an important component of opera. First off, there is the overture. Traditionally, this is a set piece of orchestral music played before the curtain is raised. Before electric lighting, all theaters stayed lit during performances and audiences needed something to get them in the mood for an opera. After electricity came into use, composers experimented with the overture. Some dispensed with them altogether, while others made use of a few loud chords. Puccini was especially fond of this. But a good overture can set the tone for everything that is to follow. It provides a bridge between the "real world" people have just left and the surreal world of opera. It also gets the audience settled in their seats and perhaps even begins the process of careful listening. Lately, it has been fashionable in opera houses to stage the overture; that is, to have some sort of stage business performed while the overture is played. This blasts out any sort of benefit we might derive from the transitional nature of purely orchestral music.

Also, who says overtures aren't interesting enough in their own right? All of Mozart's mature overtures are masterpieces, and legend says that he composed the overture to *The Marriage of Figaro* during lunch on the day of the premiere, using all new material and not "stealing" any themes from the opera itself. (This legend cannot be proved and seems unlikely, but, as the Italians say, perhaps it *should* be true.) All of Rossini's overtures have great charm at the very least. Beethoven worked so hard to write the perfect overture for *Fidelio* that he ended up writing four. Two of them are popular in the concert hall (where they are called *Leonora Overtures*, after the heroine's real name) and one of them usually pops up as a sort of orchestral interlude in act II of the opera. Beethoven's problem was how to encapsulate the issues in the opera without giving away too much, and it is a problem that has never been fully solved. Wagner wrote tremendous orchestral introductions to all of his operas. All (except the relatively short prelude to the beginning of *The Ring of the Nibelung*) are symphonic masterpieces and are staples of the concert halls. Italians in general have been less interested in symphonic music than the Germans since the eighteenth century, so few Italian operas after the bel canto era have notable overtures. Verdi composed one for *Aida*, but decided against using it, and settled for a shorter prelude instead. (A prelude is technically different from an overture in that there is no break when the curtain rises. There is, however, a great blur between the two in common usage.)

Besides the overtures and preludes in opera, there are many opportunities for purely symphonic music within the course of the opera itself. Marches are a popular way to wake up those in the audience who have been dragged to the opera by spouses. Meyerbeer's *Le Prophète* has a magnificent Coronation March that even made Verdi green with envy. The Italian struck back a decade later, however, with the unforgettable march from *Aida*. Hector Berlioz's "Rákóczy March" from *La damnation de faust* is almost the only part of that opera to survive outside of the scholars' bookshelves. The jaunty march from Prokofiev's farcical fable *The Love for Three Oranges* had a highly unexpected second career. It became the theme song of television's *The FBI*, despite the fact that the terribly serious television show ran during the height of the Cold War and a loyal Soviet citizen had composed the music as a comic piece.

Dance music is also a staple of opera. At the Grand Opéra in Paris, of course, a full ballet was required of every opera given throughout the nineteenth century. Even Wagner was required to insert one into his *Tannhäuser* in order to get it produced in Paris. (Wagner complied, but only partially. He wrote the ballet for the beginning of the opera rather than the traditional middle, and an actual riot ensued.) Verdi accommodated the Grand Opéra with ballet music for productions of his works there, but much of it is pro forma, and Verdi himself was rarely enthusiastic about it. One exception to this was the extended ballet music he wrote for the Triumphal Scene of act II of *Aida*. Verdi liked what he heard in Paris so much that he instructed his Italian publisher to include the new music in all editions of the score, and this is the version we invariably hear today. The ballet music for *Otello* and *Le Trouvère (Il trovatore)*, while lovely, has been relegated to the file of curiosities, at least for the present time.

It is easy to ridicule the Parisians of yore for their insistence on stopping all operas in the middle to enjoy a ballet, but perhaps they were onto something. The long operas to which they were accustomed (and the Grand Opéras of Meyerbeer and the others were very long) needed a break. One can become inured to the human voice quite quickly. Wagner left Paris in a huff after his *Tannhäuser* debacle, but he learned some good lessons from the Parisians. Perhaps he also had Beethoven in mind who achieved a rather accidental success with his miniature symphony in the middle of *Fidelio*. Wagner wrote two extravagantly beautiful orchestral interludes for the very long opera *Götterdämmerung*, the final of the four operas that comprise *The Ring*. Even those who think they could never bear a full-length opera easily enjoy "The Rhine Journey" and "Siegfried's Funeral."

Those who wrote shorter operas also saw the advantages of orchestral interludes. The Italian composers and others of the *verismo* period used intermezzi, as they called them, to great effect. Those from Mascagni's *Cavalleria rusticana* and Leoncavallo's *I pagliacci* are justly celebrated, while the intermezzi from Franz Schmidt's *Notre Dame* and Ermanno Wolf-Ferrari's *I gioielli della Madonna* should be even more popular than they are.

Many of the Modernist composers who came to prominence

after World War I were primarily instrumental rather than vocal composers, and the orchestra assumed ever higher prominence in this period. Even those who mastered the voice and the dramatic sense of opera gave the orchestra a role that would have been unthinkable in the bel canto era. Perhaps the greatest example is Berg's *Wozzeck*, comprised of short dramatic sequences separated by musical links. One of these interludes is especially remarkable. It is one minute long and contains only two orchestral crescendi with drumbeats in between. Both crescendi are the note B orchestrated in different manners; that is, instruments join in and play the note at different times. Berg proved what Mozart's music had demonstrated; only the greatest geniuses should attempt the effects that seem simplest. The B crescendi in *Wozzeck* are startling, thrilling, and shattering.

Other modern composers have been more lyrical in their approach to the orchestra. Britten's *Peter Grimes* uses "Sea Interludes" to paint a background to the story and also to compare the characters with forces of nature. Richard Strauss's late opera *Capriccio* (1942) packs much of its emotion into a lush intermezzo that precedes the heroine's great narrative monologue. Much of the "action" of that conversational opera is deliberately trivial, while the orchestra alone can show us what "lies beneath."

Most of these examples can be, and are, enjoyed as separate pieces, either on recordings or on radio and in the concert halls. But something is lost when these are heard out of context. Many people have been able to write interesting or beautiful music. Only a very few have been able to harness all the power of the symphonic orchestra into the service of drama.

Other Elements

An operatic score has, of course, many more subdivisions and additional components than those listed above. People can (and do) study even individual scores for a lifetime without exhausting all that is to be found in them. Many find this a fault. Opera is called a "bastard" art form, and not without reason.

All kinds of music and every variety of song ("all the tricks in the book," we might say), are employed in its service. For the listener, less concerned with theories of aesthetic purity than the scholar, this is a boon rather than a problem.

Putting It All Together

There is more to opera than the purely aural. Opera, at its best, is experienced live. It is a visual art form as well as an aural one. This means that there are even more considerations: productions, dance, acting abilities, and everything else that goes along with live theater. These days, audiences tend to be much more sophisticated than our predecessors in visual terms, but perhaps a bit less in aural terms. Our ears are assaulted with much noise in the course of the day. We leave the television on even when we are not watching it. Our appliances beep and ring and squeak constantly. Few of us sing in the course of our day, and even fewer play a musical instrument. So while there is much to be learned from the visual aspects of live opera, we all can derive great unexpected pleasure from the sheer act of listening, whether in the theater or in our homes. We are gifted with much technology that can help us to experience opera as primarily music. All we need is a little ability to sit still for a bit, concentrate, and try to decipher the patterns and conventions of the composers of opera.

The rewards are greater than merely decoding a complicated art form. In an ideal experience of opera, the listener or viewer is blissfully unaware of the many components creating the moment. Like great cuisine, the greatest moments are when one forgets or ignores all the technicalities and revels in the experience itself. The reward of opera is a unique, profound, and intensely satisfying experience of the human condition.

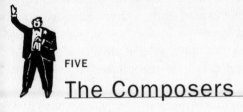

FIVE

The Composers

Opera is a collaborative effort, requiring hundreds of specialists to mount even a single production. The center of all the work is, of course, the score itself, and it is little wonder that the level of adulation afforded to successful opera composers surpasses even the demented worship given the greatest singers. In fact, opera composers have been so idolized (and disparaged), that it is easy to forget that these were human beings plying their craft. Almost all of them have had biographies written about them, and these biographies are always interesting at the least. Some, like Wagner, are as fascinating as they are disturbing. In any case, the near-deification of opera composers becomes comprehensible the more one knows about opera. Composers are often referred to as representatives of artistic developments, beyond their own accomplishments. When reading any literature about opera, one will always come across many references to other composers, and authors often assume familiarity with the canon of the officially great creators of opera.

This chapter includes brief information on the composers that one is likely to come across most often in the exploration of opera. Some, like Beethoven and Camille Saint-Saëns, are much more famous for their musical accomplishments outside of the opera world, but made significant contributions and are necessary in any discussion of the form. Others, such as Cilea and Zandonai, are almost never mentioned by anyone but the most dedicated opera fans. All have earned their place in the annals of opera history and debate of the subject.

John Adams (1947–): A popular American composer whose two operas, *Nixon in China* and *The Death of Klinghoffer* have been widely produced throughout the world. Adams was initially categorized as a Minimalist, but his success seems to derive from a nondogmatic approach to composition. His work contains much lyric romanticism and he has lately made forays into such eclectic idioms as swing music. Adams is also a great believer in collaboration, taking much time to work with excellent directors, librettists, and choreographers.

Dominick Argento (1927–): Contemporary American composer whose operas, especially *Casanova* and *The Aspern Papers*, have been well received by audiences in the theater and on television. Argento's operas are essentially traditional in both form and content, which draws some ire from the theoreticians. However, they also have excellent subtleties, are written for (rather than against) the voice, and are built with careful attention around excellent source material.

Samuel Barber (1910–1981): For a time, Barber was the "Great Hope" of the American opera scene, even though there was nothing especially American about Barber's operatic music. He followed the format of European Romantic Modernism and was not known as an innovator. His *Vanessa* (1957) is still popular, with its traditional dramatic and vocal narrative and tonal accessability. Barber had the honor of premiering his *Antony and*

Cleopatra for the opening night of the new Metropolitan Opera, a night that went down in history as one of the great fiascos of operatic history. (Production issues didn't help. Diva Leontyne Price was literally eaten on stage by the papier-mâché Sphinx.) With the benefit of hindsight, *Antony and Cleopatra* has much to commend it, but the music strikes many today as overly strident and noisy.

Ludwig van Beethoven (1770–1827): Beethoven's importance as a composer far outweighs the contributions of his single opera, *Fidelio*. It was Beethoven who broke the bounds of convention and restraint, in both the orchestra and singers' voices, that had contained the Baroque period within a framework of acceptable guidelines. This ushered in the Romantic era in opera, with all of its emotional intensity and even bombast. Beethoven's life was every bit as turbulent as his music, with his two most intense relationships being his nephew, over whom he obsessed, and the mysterious woman with whom he communicated only by letter, the "Immortal Beloved." The greatest irony of Beethoven's life was his deafness, which began around the turn of the nineteenth century and worsened as the years continued. It is said that he never actually heard his final works, including the monumental Symphony number 9. Rossini was among Beethoven's first admirers in the operatic field. Among Germans, Weber emulated Beethoven, and Wagner claimed him as his mentor. We know Wagner fudged the truth about attending a performance of *Fidelio* and being converted to the possibilities of German opera, but there is no doubt that *Fidelio*'s declamatory vocal style based on the inflections of speech had a huge effect on Wagner and all subsequent composers. It became traditional to include one of the discarded overtures to the opera in the middle of the work itself, as a sort of extended orchestral interlude, and this opened up new possibilities for composers, a device well exploited by Wagner above all.

Vicenzo Bellini (1801–1835): One of the masters of the Italian bel canto style, Bellini wrote operas that have always been admired for their lyric beauty and opportunities for vocal display. Only in the last fifty years, however, has he been appreciated as a master of dramatic theater. The Sicilian was a success first in Naples, then Milan, and finally Paris. His operas, including *La sonnambula*, *I Capuleti ed I Montecchi* (a reworking of the *Romeo and Juliet* story), and *Norma* were enormously successful and influential internationally and were among the first popular operas in the United States. Even Wagner was moved to concentrate on the operatic theater rather than the concert hall by early exposure to Bellini's works (although he lied about this in his autobiography and claimed it was a performance of Beethoven's *Fidelio* that caused his epiphany). Bellini's premature death was one of opera's great losses.

Alban Berg (1885–1935): A student of Arnold Schoenberg, the Austrian composer Berg is often (and not always accurately) categorized as a Serialist. Berg's reputation as an opera composer was assured with the sensational premiere of *Wozzeck* in Berlin in 1925, one of the most important musical events of the century. In a rare turnabout for new operas, audiences loved *Wozzeck* while the critics twisted themselves into knots trying to figure out the actual significance of the piece. While *Wozzeck* includes lessons learned from the Serialists, it is not written in twelve-tone rows. The score is eclectic, but has the feel of single united whole, perhaps its ultimate achievement. *Wozzeck* is still discussed as a new and daring opera seventy-five years after its premiere. Berg wrote songs and chamber pieces, eventually turning to two Wedekind plays for his next opera, *Lulu*. It is as graphic as *Wozzeck* and perhaps even more sordid, a tale of sex and degeneracy capped by its heroine's murder at the hands of none other than Jack the Ripper. *Lulu* is constructed on the twelve-tone model, and Berg was uniquely qualified to adapt that formal structure for the needs of the stage, but he died from an insect bite before completing the final act. His widow forbade performances of *Lulu* using Berg's notes for the ending, but it was given in two acts and was as great a sensation as

Wozzeck. After Frau Berg's death in 1977, the final act was orchestrated and Lulu began a second round of triumphs throughout the world. The reason *Lulu* and *Wozzeck* continue to amaze audiences is that, ultimately, they are great operas. Berg never allowed his theories to detract from the goal of engaging audiences within a theater, a lesson that many of his followers should have followed better. Now that the polemics surrounding Berg's music have died away, audiences are free to appreciate his musical and dramatic genius.

Hector Berlioz (1803–1869): Known in his day as a journalist and musical theorist, the French composer Berlioz's importance as a composer has been acknowledged by posterity. He was the consummate Romantic, with extravagant emotions constantly at war with his superb intellect. (He actually passed out when he saw the popular Irish actress Harriet Smithson, stalked her, and married her ten months later. The marriage, predictably, was not a success.) Berlioz pushed the limits of music, and opera, beyond the confines of his own time. His works were longer, more massive, stranger, and more tonally unfettered than anything that had been heard. Most of his contemporaries thought of him as unhinged, a reputation he seemed to savor. His most ambitious work, *Les Troyens*, a reworking of Virgil's *Aeneid*, was insanely long, difficult to sing and to fathom, and a flop at its premiere. Only in the later twentieth century did it find its way into the repertory, and then usually given in two parts.

Georges Bizet (1838–1875): The French composer Bizet was an excellent musician, a child prodigy and popular as a pianist in Paris, and whose operas were coolly received by the public in their day. *Les Pêcheurs de perles (The Pearl Fishers)* and *La jolie Fille de Perth (The Pretty Maid of Perth)* are usually popular with audiences today on the rare occasions when anybody bothers to perform them, but his fame rests primarily on the immortal *Carmen*. The initial lack of success of *Carmen* at the Opèra-Comique in Paris is said to have killed Bizet, who died shortly afterward. Furthermore, it led to some tinkering with the original, most notably its original spoken dialogue being replaced with recitative by the New Orleans native Ernest Guiraud. Even with the dreaded issue of multiple editions, however, *Carmen* remains a mainstay of the repertory, and is, according to many, the perfect opera. Abundant melody, a gift present in Bizet's earlier works, is matched by a perfect mastery of the orchestra within a framework of magnificent dramatic sweep. Nietzsche heard it and literally went insane, declaring that all of Wagner's work was a "disease" compared to this burst of Mediterranean sunlight. It has never been absent from the world's stages since that time. The growth from the beautiful *Pearl Fishers* to the sublime *Carmen* is so great that we must regard Bizet's premature death in the same category of artistic tragedy as Mozart's, Bellini's, and so many others.

Arrigo Boito (1842–1918): A great character and a bit of a mystery, the Italian composer Boito appeared on the Milan music scene at the moment of Italian independence and unification. An internationalist and a progressive (his mother was Polish and he had spent his formative years on a grand tour of the continent), Boito wrote fiery articles denouncing what he saw as Italian decadence and calling stridently for destruction of the status quo. Verdi understood Boito's diatribes as a direct insult, and avoided contact with the young radical for a while. Boito stepped up to the plate with an opera of his own, *Mefistofele*, which was a spectacular flop at its Scala premiere in 1867. He began work on a second opera, *Nerone*, and worked as a librettist for other composers, including Ponchielli, for whom he wrote the fiery *La gioconda*. Verdi and Boito were reconciled (Boito never knew how insulted Verdi was by his writings), and together they refashioned Verdi's only mature failure, *Simon Boccanegra*, into an excellent work. Their correspondence at this time is a lesson in the mechanics of creating a great opera. Boito provided the librettos for Verdi's greatest masterpieces, *Otello* and *Falstaff*. In addition to providing librettos, Boito acted as agent, muse, and often therapist for the grumpy Verdi. *Nerone* languished. Boito carried on a poetic affair with Eleanora Duse, the great actress whose fame rivaled Bernhardt's, and remained her "only true friend" even after she left him for the poet Gabriele D'Annunzio. Boito became a force in national arts policy, and died a greatly respected figure in 1918. Toscanini prepared an edition of the never-completed *Nerone*, but the work has been found unwieldy. *Mefistofele*, however, continues to delight audiences and frustrate us, making us wonder what else Boito might have created had he not been quite such a perfectionist.

Benjamin Britten (1913–1976): The most popular English composer of the twentieth century and probably the only one whose operas have achieved a great popularity on the international scale. Britten is particularly admired by musicians, but audiences have learned to appreciate his mastery of summing up a dramatic situation in quick and perfect phrases. Britten's operas, such as *Billy Budd, Death in Venice, Peter Grimes*, and *The Turn of the Screw*, are also well regarded because of their good use of excellent source literature. Many of his works were written for the particular talents of his longtime lover Sir Peter Pears, a tenor with a unique vocal presence and bordering on a counter-tenor sound. Many assumed Britten's operas would not be viable stage works without Pears's talent, but a wide variety of interpreters, including the heroic tenor Jon Vickers, have found their own methods of interpreting the music, and the operas are now considered standard repertory.

Francesco Cilea (1866–1950): An Italian composer of the *verismo* style who, like many of his colleagues, seemed to run out of steam, compositionally speaking, at a young age. His most enduring success has been the potboiler *Adriana Lecouvreur*, a work never highly regarded by critics or experts but with a title role so enticing to divas that it refuses to go away. At its best, Cilea's work is lyric and provides much opportunity for displaying the voice from the bottom to the top.

John Corigliano (1938–): A New Yorker from a gifted musical family, Corigliano has made a name for himself as a teacher and a composer of symphonies, vocal music, film scores (*Altered States* and *The Red Violin*, among others), and a single opera to date, *The Ghosts of Versailles*. Commissioned by the Met, *Ghosts* was a great success with the public at its premiere in 1991, but the long gestation period of the piece left Corigliano and librettist William Hoffman so exhausted both have claimed they would never write another opera. Fans hope this is mere operatic overstatement.

Claude Debussy (1862–1918): The French composer Debussy's innovations in harmony and structure made him one of music's most important names. He has also been admired by virtually every other composer who has heard his music—an admiration he rarely returned (since he was, in his own way, almost as much of a curmudgeon as Wagner). He worked for ten years on an opera, *Péllas et Mélisande*, a great and surprising success at its premiere in 1902. It was the only opera he ever completed. For many years, audiences have found *Pélleas* challenging in its apparent formlessness and reliance on orchestral color, but the brilliant music and the appeal of the lead roles for big-name stars have assured its presence and popularity over time.

Gaetano Donizetti (1797–1848): One of the greats of the bel canto style, the Italian composer Donizetti was something of a factory, who could churn out operas at great speed. In fact, he had written thirty operas before he had an international success with *Anna Bolena* in 1830. Donizetti enjoyed some success throughout Italy and especially in Paris in the 1840s, with comic operas of great melodic buoyancy (*L'elisir d'amore, La Fille du regiment, Don Pasquale*), tragic operas with magnificent diva roles (*Lucrezia Borgia, Roberto Devereaux*), and even a Parisian Grand Opéra (*La Favorite*). Unfortunately, he became insane as a result of syphilis and died before he could enjoy and truly exploit his fame. For years, Donizetti was held in low esteem

(Wagner set the tone when he called his music "trash"), and only his masterpiece *Lucia di Lamermoor* was heard with any regularity. Donizetti, however, had written for several specific virtuoso singers of his day, and his reputation was rehabilitated when several great singers of the 1950s and 1960s (including Callas, Sills, Sutherland, and Caballé, among others), rediscovered the dramatic intensity lurking behind the pretty showpieces.

Antonín Dvořák (1841–1904): Most famous as a composer of symphonies, songs, and religious music, Dvořák (DVOR-zhak) is also idolized in his native Bohemia (Czech Republic) as an opera composer and as a founder of a national music style. Dvořák was popular as a composer and conductor in London and especially in New York, where he lived for three years and composed some of his best music (including the famous *New World Symphony*, incorporating Native American themes). Interestingly, he claimed that the African-American music he heard in the States made him unbearably homesick, and he returned to his native country to great acclaim and became director of the Prague Conservatory. His opera *Rusalka*, based on a local myth and including a famous "Hymn to the Moon," has achieved some popularity in the United States.

Carlisle Floyd (1926–): American composer whose operas *Susannah* (1955) and *Of Mice and Men* (1970) have held a steady and growing popularity with the public. Floyd uses a lyric rather than an academic vocabulary, and relies upon folk motifs and everyday sounds (such as sirens), making his work eminently approachable yet always creative. His operatic work always includes social commentary, but in a natural and dramatic context rather than the didactic ham-fistedness that has marred much recent opera. Floyd has been praised for his vision in consciously attempting to create a national American idiom for opera, and his work compared to Britten's accomplishment for English opera.

George Gershwin (1898–1937): One of the great lights of American musical history and whose early death was a national artistic disaster. Gershwin defied categorization, and from early in his career sought to blur the distinctions between popular, classical, and jazz music. In 1922, he composed a fascinating, one-act opera, *Blue Monday*, as a number in Broadway's *George White's Scandals*, but audiences were, frankly, perplexed and it was removed after a single performance. After his phenomenally successful *Rhapsody in Blue* took jazz to the concert hall, Gershwin began to ponder composing a full-length opera. Gershwin discussed a commission for the Metropolitan with financial backer Otto Kahn, but the project fell through. Instead, Gershwin worked with his lyricist brother Ira and novelist DuBose Heyward on the latter's novel *Porgy*, set in a tight-knit black community in Charleston, South Carolina. *Porgy and Bess* was a sensation when it opened in Boston in 1935, but Gershwin was nervous about the work's length (almost four hours) and cut much of the atmospheric music when he moved it to Broadway. It is a paradoxical truism in opera that cutting a work generally makes it seem longer, and in its cut form *Porgy* was seen mostly as a showcase for great songs rather than a masterful opera. The work as a whole is devilishly difficult to perform, requiring great vocal agility for its fifteen solo roles, complicated choruses written in idiomatic counter rhythms, Broadway charisma, sudden changes of mood in the orchestra, and even a virtuoso, solo, jazz pianist. Several important revivals in the United States and Europe in the 1970s and 1980s, however, have secured *Porgy and Bess's* position as a great opera, and possibly the ultimate American opera.

Umberto Giordano (1867–1948): One of the composers of the verismo school of Italian opera, Giordano's most enduring successes were *Andrea Chénier* (1896) and, to a lesser extent, *Fedora* (1898). Both built around brief melodic lines of intense passion, a style not well suited to today's singers. These operas have become associated with legendary performances by great tenors and divas of the twentieth century, one of the reasons why a selection from *Chénier* was chosen for a memorable and transcendental scene in the movie *Philadelphia*.

Philip Glass (1937–): The American composer Glass's large-scale operas have been popular with audiences, but leave many expert musicians wringing their hands in dismay. The issue at stake is Glass's famous sound, using rhythm over melody (or even atonality) to create his lyric pictures. Critics often fail to notice Glass's ability to write for the human voice, an ability notably absent in many would-be opera composers. His first opera was the enormous *Einstein on the Beach* (1976), initially more of a hit with the avant-garde set than with operagoers or musicologists. Since then, he has written *Satyagraha* (1980) and *Akhenaten* (1984), both lyric works built along nonnarrative librettos, and the humungous multi-media event *The CIVIL WarS* (1984). In 1992, Glass, a one-time taxi driver in New York, conformed his ambitions to the exigencies of the Metropolitan Opera, for whom he wrote *The Voyage*. Glass's durability is forcing some reconsideration of his work, which had previously been so pegged within a certain category that it has been satirized on network television.

Christoph Willibald von Gluck (1714–1787): The German composer Gluck's role as "reformer" of opera, a role in which he was fetishized by Wagner and others, has distracted from public appreciation of his excellent operas. On the first level, his operas, such as *Orfeo ed Eurydice* (1762) and *Iphigénie en Aulide* (1774) are astounding in their sheer grace and beauty. Upon closer or repeated listening, however, their dramatic intelligence becomes apparent. Gluck became involved in a notorious "rivalry" with Italian composer Niccolò Piccinni in Paris in the 1770s. While the rivalry was largely what we could call a media ploy, Gluck enjoyed the increased attention given his works as a result. He retired to Vienna and lived the good life, bragging of his abilities and spending beyond his means. A doctor told him to curtail his vices immediately or risk death. Gluck promptly poured himself a brandy, drank it, and died.

Charles Gounod (1818–1893): The French composer Gounod's operatic reputation rests firmly on two works, *Roméo et Juliette,* and, even more, *Faust.* These two operas were given frequently in every opera house until the First World War. Singers appreciated the expansive vocal lines that showed off their voices and refined techniques, while audiences responded to the beautiful melodies of arias, choruses, and ensembles, all deftly interspersed and crafted into a satisfying whole. Critics, however, grew bored quickly, and faulted Gounod's operas as sentimental and insufficiently integrated theater works (that is, they did not conform to Wagner's notions of music theater). The fact that the public demanded these works only widened the rift between experts and audiences. Yet the beauty of these operas prevailed. Sir Thomas Beecham, the crusty London conductor, caused a mini-scandal when he proclaimed in the 1920s that he would trade all of Wagner's work for the simple run of notes up the C major scale that introduces the big theme in the overture to *Faust.* Eventually, the experts realized that, while Sir Thomas may have just been exaggerating to make a point, there was much to celebrate in Gounod's scores. While they may not be as ubiquitous as they once were, *Faust,* in particular, is still central to any opera company's arsenal.

Georg Friedrich Handel (1685–1759): Although the German composer Handel's music, including such hits as *The Water Music Suite* and the ubiquitous oratorio *Messiah,* has always been popular with audiences, his operatic fortunes have wavered. This is especially ironic since he considered himself primarily an opera composer and certainly expended his greatest energies within that form. He had successes in Italy but hit the heights of fame and fortune running an opera company in London. During this time, he would travel frequently to Italy, shopping, so to speak, for librettos and singers and keeping abreast of musical developments. The "Italian" operas he produced in London, including *Rinaldo, Giulio Cesare*, and *Ariodante*, caused unprecedented sensations in that city, as well as a good deal of resentment at the "artificial" art form. Eventually, the company closed down and Handel turned to other forms of composing. His operas languished for many years, but general revival began in Germany in the 1920s and has continued to the present day. It is often difficult to find the exact, right formula for singing a Handel opera. For one thing, we lack the basis of all of them, the castrato. Furthermore, there are many repetitions in a typical Handel aria. We know that the repeated passages must be sung in a different manner, to avoid tedium, but unless a singer has great musical taste it is very easy for him or her to move from ornamentation into hollow, vocal display. As if this weren't challenging enough, the music as written is incredibly demanding since the castrati and their diva rivals were without doubt the most agile singers ever known. Still, a Handel opera is a great vehicle for singers who have intelligence as well as natural ability, and that's when the psychological perception and inherent drama of the works comes alive in a way that would have seemed impossible a century ago.

Leoš Janáček (1854–1928): It is hard to believe now, but for many years Janáček was unknown outside of his native Bohemia (the Czech Republic), where he has always been idolized. Janáček lived a fairly quiet life as a teacher and composer of songs and religious music, the whole time trying to get his opera *Jenůfa* produced. It was a sensation when it finally was given in Prague in 1916. The fifty-eight-year-old composer embarked on the most productive phase of his career, providing a great role model for late-bloomers everywhere. His satirical opera *The Excursions of Mr. Broucek* (1920) makes free use of time and space travel, and might well be regarded as an operatic contribution to the genre of science fiction, which was budding in Eastern Europe at that time. His style was modern without being dry, and his operas include much of the emotional rawness and intensity of the *verismo* school without its excesses of sentimentality. *Katya Kabanová, The Makropoulos Affair,* and *The Cunning Little Vixen* have joined *Jenůfa* as staples of opera companies everywhere, invariably pleasing what audiences have been convinced to attend.

Erich Korngold (1897–1957): A child prodigy of great promise whose first full-length opera, *Die tote Stadt (The Dead City)* was a huge success at its premiere in 1920. *Die tote Stadt* combined the best elements of several genres of contemporary opera within a refreshing and dramatic harmonic language. The Austrian composer's subsequent operas left everyone puzzled, and he never achieved the same success again. Moving to Hollywood in 1935, Korngold wrote film scores (including *Captain Blood* and the marvelous *Private Lives of Elizabeth and Essex*) which he infused with all the orchestral passion of the Viennese environment that had shaped his work. *Die tote Stadt* languished until several important productions in the 1970s (especially one by the New York City Opera) brought it back to the public.

Ruggiero Leoncavallo (1857–1919): In sum, the Italian composer Leoncavallo must be regarded as another "one-hit wonder" of the *verismo* period. His short, intense opera *I pagliacci (The Clowns)* has been enormously popular since its premiere. It has been welded to its fellow versimo masterpiece, Mascagni's *Cavalleria rusticana,* by most opera companies, and together *Cav* and *Pag* have become staples of the operatic circuit. They work well together, both dealing with the overflowing emotions of everyday people who have been driven to extreme acts by life's realities. *Pagliacci,* in particular, with its familiar aria *"Vesti la giubba,"* has come to stand for all Italian opera in the public mind, as misleading as this may be. Like Mascagni, Leoncavallo never repeated this early success. He wrote a *Bohème* the year after Puccini's, but Puccini won the *Bohème* battle and Leoncavallo's has been relegated to the curiosity file. Leoncavallo turned to operetta, but his gifts of depicting passionate outburst were ill-suited for the form, and he turned to teaching.

Pietro Mascagni (1863–1945): One of the great enigmas of operatic history, the Italian composer Mascagni burst upon the scene with the definitive *verismo* opera, *Cavalleria rusticana,* in 1889. That one-act thunderbolt took Italy by storm with its raw, emotional bluntness and its direct portrayal of simple, everyday people. Most assumed Mascagni, rather than Puccini, would assume Verdi's mantle as the king of Italian opera. People waited in vain, however, for Mascagni to repeat his triumph. Mascagni's later operas never fulfilled the hope, although *L'amico Fritz* (1891) and *Iris* (1898) have sometimes been popular in Italy and occasionally beyond. Mascagni had studied with Ponchielli, and an aging diva in Italy, who had worked with Mascagni during the heady, early days, once blithely stated in an interview that "Everybody knew Ponchielli had written *Cavalleria.*" She promptly died before being interrogated further, leaving posterity with one possible explanation for the Mascagni puzzle. Mascagni became somewhat embittered about his lack of subsequent success, especially in comparison with the international fame of Puccini, with whom he attended the Conservatory of Milan. In an attempt at official recognition, he severely compromised himself by his association with Mussolini's government, where he is said to have spent more time promoting himself than developing Italian music. *Cavalleria,* however, remains firmly in the most basic of operatic repertories.

Jules Massenet (1842–1912): The greatest exponent of the French Romantic style, Massenet wrote beautiful, refined works whose delicacy require superb interpretation. Like many French musicians of his generation, he showed great musical promise even as a child. He was given the prestigious Prix de Rome and lived for three years at the Villa Medici, absorbing Italian dramatic notions. This experience seems to have given Massenet the ability to challenge prevailing French notions of operatic production upon his return, yet his art is quintessentially French. His masterpiece, *Manon,* has remained a favorite of divas since its premiere, while *Werther* and *Don Quischotte* disappear periodically, only to reemerge when great artists translate their vitality through performance. Massenet learned the lessons of the leit motiv from Wagner, but wisely used them only within his own shamelessly lovely musical vocabulary.

Gian Carlo Menotti (1911–): Menotti has been a crusader throughout his long career, fighting to make opera as much a part of the American popular landscape as the Broadway musical. Critics have faulted his music as dumbed-down and insufficiently daring (he has long been known as a sort of Puccini *manqué*), but Menotti has held to his vision and written some popular operas along the way. His *Amahl and the Night Visitors* (1951) was written for the then new medium of television, and is actually the single most performed opera in America. Others include *The Medium* (1945), *The Consul* (1947), and *The Saint of Bleecker Street* (1954). The Italian-born composer has long championed American music, and his Spoleto Festival in Charleston has been an important feature of the American opera scene since the 1950s. While opinion of Menotti's operas is at a rather low point just now, their accessibility will guarantee their duration for some time, and Menotti will probably go through a few more critical gyrations in the coming years.

Olivier Messiaen (1908–): The great French organist, composer, and Catholic mystic created music in a wide variety of genres and styles, but only one, single, massive opera, *Saint François d'Assis* (1983). Long attracted to the transcendental themes in the life of St. Francis, Messiaen had even studied birdsong. While birdsong of course plays a role in *Saint François*, recent productions of the work (which can run up to six hours in performance) have shown the excellent dramatic range of the work.

Giacomo Meyerbeer (1791–1864): Meyerbeer was born Jacob Beer in Berlin, but as a child prodigy became enamored of Italian music techniques. His greatest success came in Paris after 1830, where he hit upon a formula that defined the style of the Paris Opéra throughout the nineteenth century: great historical spectacles with rousing choruses, marches, and a full ballet, interspersed with bravura vocal solos tailored to the biggest stars. One great success, *Le Prophéte*, even included a ballet on roller skates, causing quite a *furore* (and starting a new athletic fad) in 1836. The public adored his works, and Meyerbeer was, in a sense, the George Lucas of his day. Although there is every indication that Meyerbeer helped the young Wagner in both Berlin and Paris, Wagner, who spewed hatred at everyone, decided Meyerbeer was his Great Enemy. He attacked Meyerbeer wherever he could, most famously in his notorious pamphlet "Judaism in Music." Meyerbeer's role as a symbol of the French musical establishment of his day has tended to obscure judicious consideration of his music, which was more than pablum for the Parisian public. His great arias, in particular, are infused with enough talent—some would say genius—to keep them popular with singers today. The operas as a whole, however, tend to be unwieldy to perform, and only remained popular (interestingly enough) in Italy down to recent times. Their reputation as showcases for great singing make these operas a special favorite among devotees of the great singers and recordings of the twentieth century. Other composers, however, were not immune to what Meyerbeer could achieve at his best. Verdi was haunted by the magnificence of the Coronation Scene in *Le Prophète* and consciously worked to emulate it in the Triumphal Scene of his own *Aida*. Even Wagner can be seen imitating Meyerbeer in some of his earlier works. An undeniably important chapter in the story of opera that cannot be easily dismissed.

Claudio Monteverdi (1567–1643): Opera might well have become a mere footnote in Italian cultural history were it not for this great composer, who was among the first to recognize the potential of the then-new genre. A composer of motets, songs, and religious music, Monteverdi composed the opera *Orfeo* for the court of Mantua in 1608. It is the earliest opera still heard today, and its music, while recognizably antique, does not sound dated in the least. Monteverdi moved to Venice, where the absence of an aristocratic court forced him to write for what was then a new institution, the public theater. If a work bored the public, they would simply stay away (unlike at courts, where attendance at functions was anything but optional). Monteverdi therefore had to find a way to engage the audience in a new way, and he did so by discovering the key to opera's appeal: dramatic tension. With great nuance and subtlety, Monteverdi began the long process of discovering opera's ability to unpack the human psyche within a unique dramatic language. Although he composed over forty operas for Venice, only two survive, *Il ritorno d'Ulisse in patria* and *L'incoronazione di Poppea*.

Douglas Moore (1893–1969): An American composer who relied heavily on folk music in his compositions, of which *The Ballad of Baby Doe* (1956) is his most popular. Moore studied at Yale and with the legendary teacher Nadia Boulanger in Paris, returning to New York to teach composition at Columbia University for many years.

Wolfgang Amadeus Mozart (1757–1791): Mozart's name, like Einstein's, has become a popular byword for an almost otherwordly level of genius. His musical feats as a child prodigy alone would have guaranteed his legend. However, the Austrian Mozart has never been relegated to a place of incomprehensibility. Perhaps his greatest genius was his ability to make the most difficult music appear effortlessly written and spontaneous. He excelled in every genre of music he attempted (which was virtually all forms of music known in his time and place). Mozart began composing operas at the age of ten, works that already demonstrated musical maturity and sophistication. His childhood must have been both glamorous and dreadful as his composer-father Leopold marketed the boy around the many courts of

Europe in search of patronage. As he grew into adulthood, Mozart added his keen insights into human nature to his operatic compositions, and his three operas composed to the brilliant librettos of Lorenzo da Ponte (*Le nozze di Figaro, Don Giovanni,* and *Così fan tutte*) remain paragons of what the genre can achieve. Legends naturally accrued around such a man, exaggerated in future generations. He did not starve to death, as some would have it. He did not have any great rivalry with the imperial court composer Salieri, whose rumored jealousy has provided dramatic material for playwrights from Pushkin in the early nineteenth century to Peter Schaeffer (*Amadeus*). Neither did the Emperor Joseph II actually say that Mozart's opera *The Abduction from the Seraglio* had "too many notes," nor did the Queen of Naples ever call *La clemenza di Tito* "*porcheria tedescha*" ("German garbage"). Still, these legends have some basis in fact. Mozart was famously incapable of the social and professional niceties that would have ingratiated him more with colleagues and patrons and that could have provided him with a more comfortable life. His operas puzzled many of his contemporaries, and (unlike Gluck, Wagner, or Stravinsky) he spent no time attempting to explain them. His personality quirks (also including a scatalogical obsession) were perhaps hallmarks of his genius, or possibly they were by-products of his irregular childhood. Within a few years after his death, his popularity soared among the public and his legend, carefully nurtured by his widow Costanze, grew accordingly. The notion that some operas require several viewings before revealing their true beauties, a notion that is the core of today's repertory system, owes more than a little to Mozart's posthumous popularity.

Modest Mussorgsky (1839–1881): Creator of two Russian national epic operas, *Boris Godunov* (1868–1873) and *Khovanschina* (1873). Although *Boris* has been popular throughout the world for a long time, Mussorgsky kept revising it, and it was later "improved" in orchestration by Rimsky-Korsakoff. Every time *Boris* is produced, therefore, it is in a new (and self-proclaimed "authentic") edition. The composer, who was a sloppy alcoholic sort right out of the Russian literature of his time, likewise never completed *Khovanschina*, his other operatic endeavor. In whichever guise they appear, however, Mussorgsky's operas cannot fail to impress audiences with their grandeur and passion. The vocal solo writing, also, is impressive. The title role of *Boris* is considered the career goal of every bass in the opera world.

Jacques Offenbach (1819–1880): The toast of Second Empire Paris, Offenbach was born in Germany, the son of a cantor, and had an endless gift of melody. His operettas were the hot ticket of Paris in the 1860s, and his fame spread around the world. People loved to whistle and hum his tunes as soon as they heard them, as people still do (i.e., the famous "Can-Can," from *Orphée aux Enfers*). *La Grande Duchesse de Gérolstein* was the hit of the Exhibition of 1867, and Bismarck was seen to laugh heartily at the portrayal of the squabbling German princelings. About the only person who didn't appreciate Offenbach was Wagner, who railed against such "Jewish triviality." Offenbach aspired to greater heights, though, composing his opera *Les Contes d'Hoffmann* (*The Tales of Hoffmann*) but dying shortly before it went into rehearsals. Since there is no definitive edition of this opera, it is constantly being rearranged and tortured into "authentic" editions. Still, *Hoffmann* cannot fail to impress in whichever edition it appears. The lyricism of the vocal lines, the clever use of the orchestra, and the beauty of the music make it one of the staples of every opera house. In a good performance, *Hoffmann* holds its own in comparison with anybody's works.

Amilcare Ponchielli (1834–1886): A teacher and composer, Ponchielli is remembered today as the composer of the great all-time potboiler of Italian opera, *La gioconda*. It is now fashionable to dismiss this opera as the nadir of opera, with its constant stream of overflowing passion, but opera fans continue to cherish it as a guilty pleasure. Ponchielli also wrote several other operas that achieved varying degrees of success in his lifetime, but he was primarily cherished as an able administrator of the conservatory and a teacher of such composers as Puccini, Mascagni, and Cilea.

Francis Poulenc (1899–1963): One of the century's most popular composers of songs, the French composer Poulenc also left us three operas of enduring power and appeal, *Les Mamelles de Tirésias* (1944), *Dialogues of the Carmelites* (1956), and *La Voix humaine* (1958). Poulenc's work is cherished for its vocal primacy and awareness of various musical genres without descending into dogmaticism. *La Voix humaine* is an opera of about a half-hour's length with a single part for a woman who is breaking up with her lover on the telephone, and therefore is a great vehicle for divas who can act. Poulenc's career crossed several artistic trends. In his youth, he was identified with a group of iconoclastic composers known as Les Six, who idolized Stravinsky, but also sought to keep French music from didactic formalism. (Poulenc was very vocal about his admiration for music-hall star Maurice Chevalier, for example.) In the 1930s, Poulenc rediscovered the spiritual dimensions of his Catholic faith, and began composing religious music remarkable for its unmistakeable humanity. (He once described himself as "half monk, half guttersnipe.") The ability to encompass both the human and the ethereal became one of the main reasons for the popularity of his operas, culminating in *Dialogues of the Carmelites*, 1958.

Sergei Prokofiev (1891–1953): A giant of twentieth century music and a great puzzle of an opera composer. Prokofiev was considered to be wild and avant-garde by the musical establishment of his youth in Russia, but he soon proved he could write in any style he chose. *The Gambler*, probably his most digestible opera, was premiered in 1917 and revised ten years later. *The Fiery Angel*, an exciting opera that fully validates Prokofiev's early reputation as a dissonant shocker, was also written and revised at this time. Leaving Russia after the Revolution, Prokofiev wrote *The Love for Three Oranges*, based on an Italian fairy tale, for the Chicago Opera in 1921. (The famous march from this opera was used as the basis for the theme song for American television's *The F.B.I.*, a remarkably inappropriate choice in view of subsequent political developments.) Prokofiev made the strange decision to return to Russia in 1933, just as Stalin was imposing his ideas on his "people's artists." Prokofiev wrote the requisite patriotic works and film scores. His scores for *Alexander Nevsky* and *Ivan the Terrible* are among the best ever written for film, bringing that art form and opera to their closest contacts. Prokofiev returned to the opera house for *Betrothal in a Monastery* (1941) and a setting of *War and Peace* (1942, revised continually until his death). Many outside of Russia criticized Prokofiev for his willingness to accommodate Stalin's dictates, and his exact political leanings remain difficult to fathom. He freely confessed that he was not a hero, however, and accepted his occasional wrist-slaps from the Kremlin with a philosophical attitude.

Prokofiev's place as an opera composer is redefined almost yearly. His works are dismissed until a new production shows their many facets. *The Gambler* receives a certain amount of attention outside of Russia, but *The Fiery Angel* has impressed today's less easily shocked audiences in performances throughout the 1990s. *Betrothal* is popular in Europe, but has yet to conquer America. *War and Peace*, predictably, remains unwieldy. It is written for over twenty vocal solo parts, in addition to choruses, ballets, and, yes, battle scenes. (Napoleon, a bass baritone, expounds his military strategy at some length.) It has been difficult for America to appreciate. *Oranges* becomes popular again only when great performers and clever productions bring it alive.

Giacomo Puccini (1858–1924): One of the five pillars upon whom all opera houses are built, the Italian composer Puccini has remained popular since his time to our own. He had a tremendous ability to encapsulate great passions in brief, instantly recognizable phrases, an ability that was bolstered by the advent of the recording industry with its short cylinders and 78s. Puccini's short, powerful arias formed the bulk of the recording industry's first hits, but growing familiarity with the whole of his operas (particularly through radio and television, where their accessibility has ensured their popularity) has increased appreciation for the composer's abilities. While audiences were enraptured by Puccini's romanticism, critics and music experts of his time found him sentimental and insufficiently modern. This point of view has eased in recent years, and Puccini's craftsmanship and dramatic aptitude are now universally admired. In many ways, Puccini represents the culmination and perhaps the finale of the Italian lyric tradition since few composers since have emulated his style and those who have tried have not done so with his ability. In his lifetime, he was the consummate "artist-personality," handling media and fans with great aplomb. He had torrid affairs and dressed superbly, usually in a rakish fedora and an ever-present cigarette holder (which contributed to his early demise).

Nicolai Rimsky-Korsakov (1844–1908): The Russian composer Rimsky-Korsakov was born into a rural family with a long tradition of naval service. At the age of twelve, he was sent as a cadet to the Imperial Naval Academy in St. Petersburg, but once in the capital found himself attending concerts and operas as often as possible. He persevered in both musical and naval studies, however, and wrote much of his first symphony while on a two-year, round-the-world tour of duty aboard the clipper ship *Almaz*. At the age of twenty-seven, he was able to leave the navy altogether and assume a teaching position at the St. Petersburg Conservatory. He held that position, as well as several other official music posts, until his death in 1908.

Essentially a conservative composer with a marvelous command of the orchestra, Rimsky-Korsakov wrote about a dozen operas that are staples of the Russian repertory. Their popularity outside Russia, however, has always been precarious. They have been presented with more frequency in the last decade in some American cities, but whether they will take root remains to be seen. Nationalist epics such as *Sadko* and *The Tsar's Bride* brim with all the pageantry of old Russia, while his folk-based fables such as *The Snow Maiden* and *The Golden Cockerel* (usually known under its French title, *Le Coq d'or*), provide much exotic beauty. Beverly Sills made the difficult role of the Queen of Shemakah in *Coq d'or* one of her signature roles. Rimsky-Korsakov is also known as an orchestrator of other composer's works, most notably Mussorgsky's *Boris Godunov* and Borodin's *Prince Igor* (which includes the familiar Polovetzian Dances).

Gioacchino Rossini (1792–1868): One of the greats of opera, always beloved but also increasingly respected in the last two generations. The Italian composer Rossini came of age in an Italy much disrupted by the Napoleonic interlude. The conservatories were shriveled, aristocratic and ecclesiastic patrons bankrupt, and all traditions challenged. Rossini offered operas of great buoyancy, comedies that seemed to contain laughter in the music, and dramas of extravagant vocal dynamism. He was aided by his acquaintance with the remarkable García family, singers who understood the spirit of the music and who brought it alive to audiences around Europe and even North America, where they sang Rossini's *Barber of Seville* on the first overseas opera tour. *The Barber* had been a notorious flop when it premiered in Rome in 1816, but it shortly found its audience, and has reigned as the definitive comic opera ever since. Too much, perhaps, for the good of its creator's reputation, since there is much more to Rossini than the charm of *Barber*. The balance of Rossini's work benefited from the general bel canto revival of the 1950s and 1960s, and productions of his long-lost drama *Semiramide* in 1979 were called the "performances of the century" by one critic. After several successes in Italy, Rossini moved to Paris, where he did much to codify the genre of Grand Opèra, which would reign in that city throughout the nineteenth century. His opera *Guillaume Tell* (1829) was on a grand scale, five acts, with bravura arias, rousing choruses, orchestral interludes, and of course the most ripsnorting overture of all time. It was admired but found unmanageable. Once in later years, when an excited fan told Rossini that there would be a performance of *Guillaume Tell*'s act II, Rossini wryly asked, "What, *all* of it?" Meyerbeer learned to take the Grand Opèra format as defined by Rossini and make it not only manageable but de rigueur for all works given at the Paris Opèra. Rossini did not seek to try again. He never wrote another opera throughout his long life, much to the consternation of his contemporaries and posterity. Explanations for this retirement range from a general laziness on Rossini's part to an inner knowledge that he was incapable of keeping up with the changing times. Whatever the real reason, we know Rossini retired to an excellent life outside of Paris, where he wrote some scurrilous songs ("The Sins of My Old Age"), two marvelous religious pieces, grew fat, and got *tournedos* and other tasty dishes named after him. He also charmed everybody he met, including, of all people, Wagner.

Camille Saint-Saëns (1835–1921): This great French musician composed many operas, but today only *Samson et Dalilah* is performed with regularity. The heroic tenor role and the sensuous mezzo role are prized by star singers, while audiences appreciate the great melodiousness and occasional great fun of the score. Saint-Saëns was a notable musical prodigy even as a child, and in adulthood was prized as an organist, composer of symphonies, and teacher. He was noted for being able to imitate star sopranos with scathing impressions of their vocal colors, foibles, and, on special occasions, their outfits.

Arnold Schoenberg (1874–1951): One of the most important composers of the twentieth century with a huge effect on opera, even though he only wrote one, *Moses und Aron*, and it was never completed. The Austrian Schoenberg had moved into atonality by 1909, and in 1911 premiered a large-scale choral cantata, *Gürrelieder*, in this style. (*Gürrelieder* has been staged as a sort of opera, but not successfully). In 1921, he presented his new format for music, called Serialism, based on series of all twelve notes in an octave used once, and only once, per series. Schoenberg's student Alban Berg was greatly impressed, and incorporated this method in his opera *Lulu* even before Schoenberg wrote *Moses un Aron*. Serialism became the subject of heated debate throughout the balance of the century. *Moses und Aron* is a difficult work to produce, but has favor with mainstream audiences, otherwise uninterested in musicological polemics, because of its drama and musicality. Like so many other great artists, Schoenberg left his homeland with the advent of the Third Reich. He settled in Los Angeles and taught for several years at UCLA. (For a while, he and Stravinsky were neighbors, but they avoided each other.) His son, Ronald, became a judge and, in fact, sentenced OJ Simpson to counseling sessions in 1989 for spousal abuse.

Dmitri Shostakovich (1906–1975): One of the twentieth century's most important composers, the Russian composer Shostakovich was prevented by circumstances in his native Russia from becoming one of the great operatic composers as well. After writing three patriotic symphonies in the 1920s, Shostakovich wrote a grotesque but deft satirical opera, *The Nose*. Encouraged by positive feedback from musicians, he wrote *Lady Macbeth of the Mtsensk District*. The new work was also satirical and a bit grotesque, but informed with a powerful sense of conviction and a shattering dramatic sweep, winning a measure of international fame for the composer. Not everyone was pleased. A review called "Muddle Instead of Music," widely assumed to have been written by Stalin himself, appeared on the front page of *Pravda*. The opera, and its composer, were excoriated as infantile, counterrevolutionary, demented, and evil. Shostakovich was effectively silenced as an opera composer. He turned to composing excellent film scores and the best symphonies of the century. After Stalin's death in 1953, Shostakovich revamped the opera as *Katerina Ismailovna*, as which it occasionally still appears. *Lady Macbeth of the Mtsensk District* in its original form, however, has been acknowledged by audiences and critics alike as a powerful and impressive work. With its brash music and unflinching story line, it is even still a bit shocking, although few nowadays have a Stalinesque experience of the vapors when they hear it. Shostakovich was deeply embittered by his experiences with the Soviet government. His autobiography, *Testimony*, is a powerful, depressing, and important work.

Richard Strauss (1864–1949): One of the most important opera composers of all time, and one whose career stretched over a time of great change in art and in the world. Strauss, though no relation to the waltz family, grew up in a musical family of his own. Strauss was German, and his father was first horn player in the Munich orchestra and worked (and argued) frequently with Wagner. Richard wrote songs and vast "tone-poems" (symphonic works in a single movement concerning a dramatic subject such as Don Juan or Til Eulenspiegel) before he moved into creating operas. After two relative failures, Strauss hit the jackpot with *Salome*, a scandalous and powerful work with all the intensity of a Wagner opera packed into a mere hour and twenty minutes. This was followed by *Elektra*, where Strauss pushed the bounds of the operatic to the very limits (but not beyond) of tonality itself. People wondered what direction Strauss would take after *Elektra*. The obvious next step seemed to be into sheer cacaphony and complete disregard for Western notions of tonality. Strauss surprised the public by collaborating with Austrian poet Hugo von Hofmannsthal on a baroque opera of grace and great charm that is in many ways an homage to Mozart's *Marriage of Figaro*, *Der Rosenkavalier*. It was a smash at its premiere in 1911, and has never wavered in public esteem. Yet the grace and beauty of *Der Rosenkavalier* are deceptive. Many musicians say it is the single most difficult score in all standard opera, and Strauss himself avoided conducting it. "It's very difficult," he complained. "Especially that third act." The balance of Strauss's long career saw the completion of ten additional operas, some popular, (*Ariadne auf Naxos, Die Frau ohne Schatten*), others still clawing their way into the public heart (*Intermezzo, Dafne, Capriccio*), but none as widely adored as *Rosenkavalier*.

Strauss's operas are especially admired for his champion orchestral mastery and for his particular devotion to the female voice, an area in which he may have been aided by his soprano wife, Pauline. They are so well balanced between the Romanticism of the nineteenth century and the Modernism of the twentieth that they seem timeless. Strauss himself was a jovial man whom everybody seemed to like, unpretentious in the extreme and loving nothing more than a good game of cards with friends or strangers. It is therefore truly sad that Strauss accommodated himself to the Third Reich in 1933, conferring great legitimacy on the Nazi regime's artistic agenda. Strauss was no Nazi, and he felt that remaining in Germany was the best way he could help Jewish musicians and collaborators (such as his librettist Stefan Zweig) as well as protect his family, which included some Jews by marriage. Yet his collusion remains a documented fact. When Toscanini quit the Bayreuth Festival in 1933, Strauss stepped in and conducted. Many have never forgiven him, and it remains almost (but not quite) as difficult to perform Strauss's music in present-day Israel as it is to perform Wagner's. Yet Strauss's operas are popular elsewhere, with a steady increase in the number of productions of the lesser-known works. The Santa Fe Opera, in particular, has built an international reputation with its championing of these works.

Igor Stravinsky (1885–1971): One of the twentieth century's greatest composers, his sudden and total switches of style have left musicologists who try to categorize him in a state of permanent confusion. Sometimes avant-garde and dissonant, at the next turn deeply spiritual, suddenly redefining neoclassicism, and finally proclaiming himself as a Serialist, the Russian Stravinsky enriched the century with a huge range of music. His operatic output is small, but demonstrates his versatility. The early, one-act "Chinese" opera *The Nightingale* (1909) is both brash and lyrical. He wrote a very self-consciously Russian work in *Mavra* (1922), and shortly after produced *Oedipus Rex* (1927, with a libretto in Latin). His most notable operatic work, however, came after World War II and was in a completely different style. *The Rake's Progress* was premiered in Venice, significantly, and New York in 1951. Based on Hogarth's famous engravings of life in eighteenth century London and with a libretto by W. H. Auden and Chester Kallman, *Rake's* is composed in a masterly style that is both classical and very modern. Audiences at the time, accustomed to new operas that were either too brainy or too derivative to enjoy, were both stunned and delighted. One famous critic, Alberto Moravia, saw in *Rake's* a plea for the continuation of European civilization after the horror of World War II. Nowadays, *Rake's Progress* is an accepted fact of operatic life, often seen throughout America in an especially evocative production designed by the artist David Hockney.

Stravinsky lived in many places in Europe and the United States. Los Angeles was one of his favorite haunts, and he and Walt Disney met on several occasions to discuss a joint project. The project never materialized, but Stravinsky was grateful for the royalties Disney paid him for the use of his ballet music *The Rite of Spring* in the film *Fantasia*. Stravinsky was eccentric and often quite gruff; he loved being photographed in the nude. In 1928, George Gershwin asked Stravinsky to give him music lessons. "How much money do you make, Mr. Gershwin?" Gershwin admitted his income was over a hundred thousand dollars a year. "Then I should take lessons from you!" was the reply.

Peter Ilyich Tchaikovsky (1840–1893): Most people think of Tchaikovsky as a composer of symphonies and ballet scores, but he also wrote ten operas. Only two are well known outside of his native Russia, *Eugene Onegin* and *The Queen of Spades*. This is a shame, since they are all at the least interesting and blessed with Tchaikovsky's gift for nailing an emotional situation with unforgettably beautiful music. *Onegin* in particular is easy to appreciate, combining acute psychological insight of characters with a panorama of an entire society. Tchaikovsky traveled throughout much of his career, especially to favorite haunts in Italy, and to the United States, where he conducted the inaugural concert of New York's Carnegie Hall in 1892. For years, Tchaikovsky was considered emblematic of the tortured homosexual artist who poured out his sorrows into his music. Recent scholarship that has shown Tchaikovsky as reasonably well-adjusted and sexually active has, in fact, met with great hostility from the musical establishment. Nor is there any reason to seek depressing messages from his music. Russians have long excelled at depicting melancholy, and Tchaikovsky was quintessentially Russian.

Virgil Thomson (1896–1989): A brilliant critic and indispensable feature of the American music scene for nearly six decades, Thomson's own compositions for the stage have only recently begun to be appreciated by mainstream audiences. *Four Saints in Three Acts* (1928) and *The Mother of Us All* (1947), both set to librettos by Gertrude Stein, were admired when they first appeared, but thought of mainly as exercises in cleverness. Repeated exposure has revealed them to be dramatically compelling as well. *The Mother of Us All*, in particular, has moved audiences in recent years. It is impossible to characterize the nature of Thomson's music style in a brief summary. He wrote disjointed snippets to accompany Stein's words, and quoted vernacular styles, but could also allow his scores to soar over long and passionate vocal lines when necessary. Perhaps because of this adaptability, it might be most accurate to describe Thomson as quintessentially American.

Giuseppe Verdi (1813–1901): The acknowledged supreme exponent of Italian opera, and, along with Wagner and Mozart, of

opera itself. Giuseppe Verdi lived long and never stopped growing as an artist. Born to a family of humble, country taverners,
Verdi became the village organist at the age of nine and studied
with local musicians, but he was refused entry to the Milan
Conservatory. Perhaps this was for the better since it forced
Verdi directly into the theater, and he remained an opera composer almost exclusively for the balance of his long career. Success came with his third opera, *Nabucco*, a sensation that still
holds performance records at Milan's La Scala. He churned out
more than a dozen operas over the next eight years, some failures, but most international successes. Verdi's works were cherished for their sheer vitality and raw power. He also became
associated, through his temperament as well as his allegiances,
with the growing Italian unification movement, the *risorgi-
mento*, and has ever since been regarded almost as a "founding
father" by patriotic Italians. Around 1850, he began to imbue
his operas with a new and profound level of dramatic acumen
and psychological insight (*Rigoletto*) in addition to musical intensity (*Il trovatore*) and even foreshadowed the subsequent
Modernist interest in everyday people and real-life situations
(*La traviata*). Like Mozart, Verdi preferred to rely upon his own
talents rather than novel effects to create his impressions. Unlike Wagner, he was entirely uninterested in theories of art or
aesthetic didactics, insisting that the mark of a good opera was
a full theater. His final masterpieces, *Otello* and *Falstaff*, completely surprised critics, who had dismissed him as old-
fashioned, with their freshness and innovations, yet even these
works can be easily classified within the traditions and context
of Italian opera. Verdi preferred to make the old techniques
new rather than find new ones altogether. His death in Milan
in 1901 occasioned a huge outpouring of mourning and three
days' business closure throughout Italy. Since his death, Verdi's
art has never been absent from the world's stages, but has en-
dured some swings of taste. A few of his operas, notably *Traviata* and *Aida*, have always been on the boards, but many of
his early works languished outside of Italy. Since World War

II, there has been a steady increase in the performance of all of Verdi's works, and within the last generation or so the world might well be said to have experienced a second round of Verdimania. About a quarter of operas performed by American companies are Verdi's, and the entire corpus of his output is represented.

Carl Maria von Weber (1786–1826): The German Weber had all the ingredients to become a great opera composer. He was a virtuoso pianist, a theater impressario, and, not least, was the cousin of Mozart's wife Constanze. He is credited with being among the first conductors in the modern sense, and certainly his exploitation of the full potentials of the orchestra had an effect on subsequent composers. His most enduring success has been *Der Freischütz*, an opera whose magical setting and otherworldly feel greatly influenced the German Romantic movement.

Richard Wagner (1813–1883): A colossus of music, a master reinventor of lyric theater, and probably the most controversial figure in all of art, there can be no discussion of opera without Wagner. He was a megalomaniac who sought to explain himself in twenty-two volumes of often insane prose, and the man could not sneeze without making those sneezes the format of a new world order. Wagner achieved success with the six-hour long opera *Rienzi*, and with the shorter *Fliegende Holländer* (*The Flying Dutchman*), his earliest opera to remain in the repertory. Wagner grew further from the standard operatic compositions of his day with the subsequent *Tannhäuser* and *Lohengrin*. By the time of the revolutions of 1848, which forced Wagner into a thirteen-year exile from his native Germany, he had come to believe that nothing more could be accomplished with operatic forms or the arts establishment as it existed. He conceived of a new sort of work, a "Total Work of Art," that would be the synthesis of the best poetry, music, and stage presentation, and looked to Norse and Greek mythology for models. He could not even bear the term *opera* for his works after this point, and referred to them only as "music dramas." The project obsessed him for twenty-eight years until he finally produced *The Ring of the Nibelung* at a specially constructed festival theater at Bayreuth, Germany, in 1876. In the meantime, after a disastrous spell in Paris, he had become the idol of the young and eventually insane King Ludwig II of Bavaria, who invited him to Munich and who paid off all of Wagner's debts. Wagner immediately got himself exiled from Munich through absurd intrigues with government ministers, but still remained on good terms with the king, and the utterly revolutionary *Tristan und Isolde* and the popular *Die Meistersinger von Nürnberg* were premiered in the capital city. After the first Bayreuth festival of 1876, Wagner began his final work, a pseudo-religious "festival-consecration play," *Parsifal*. All who traveled to Bayreuth for this work (the only place one could hear it until the Metropolitan Opera stole a copy of the score and produced it in New York in 1903) were impressed, most favorably, and some said the composer would surely die soon. There was little one could say after *Parsifal*. Indeed, Wagner died in Venice six months after the premiere of *Parsifal*.

Kurt Weill (1900–1950): It is difficult to discuss the German composer Weill without falling into the exact sort of reductive categorization that Weill himself fought so hard against. The eclectic composer maintained that he could not discern any difference between "light" and "serious" music, only between good and bad music. Weill's willingness to blur lines of distinction extended beyond styles of music into structures as well. Some would say he only wrote one full-length opera, *The Rise and Fall of the City of Mahagonny*, but his many other stage compositions include at least gestures toward opera. Even when his songs are self-consciously nonoperatic, Weill seems to be making a statement about opera itself. Born the son of a cantor in 1900, Weill studied music and theory in Berlin, but found formal training stifling. He wrote cantatas, songs, cabaret music, and whatever else caught his imagination, seemingly at random, all of which became increasingly imbued with his sense of social justice. In 1927, his *Dreigrosschenoper*, an updated gloss on John Gay's *Beggars' Opera*, with collaborator Bertolt Brecht, was an international sensation and a bit of a scandal. After fleeing the Nazis in 1933 and arriving in the United States two years later, Weill dedicated his talents primarily to Broadway, where he collaborated with such authors as Ira Gershwin, Maxwell Anderson, Elmer Rice, and Alan Jay Lerner. In recent years, Weill's music has gown popular with a huge range of singers, from opera stars to the most alternative performers, perhaps fulfilling at last his goal of creating art without social boundaries.

Hugo Weisgall (1912–1997): Weisgall was born in Moravia (now the eastern Czech Republic) but moved to the United States as a child and became what many considered one of America's most important composers. His work is especially prized for transforming source material of extraordinary quality into a viable and moving operatic idiom beyond the mere "word-painting," typical of much new opera. His most performed work, *Six Characters in Search of an Author* (1959), based on Luigi Pirandello's influential and challenging drama, is praised by fans for unpacking and perhaps even surpassing the emotional intent of the play. *Esther* (1993), based on the biblical story, was likewise warmly received by New York City Opera audiences and continues a slow but steady growth in popularity because of its approachable yet sophisticated score.

Riccardo Zandonai (1883–1944): The Italian composer Zandonai's greatest success was his opera *Francesca da Rimini*, of 1912, with a libretto by Ganriele D'Annunzio, based on an episode in Dante's *Inferno*. Set aside for several decades, *Francesca* was revived in Italy in the postwar period and eventually found an audience in the United States because of its lush score and plummy, romantic lead roles.

SIX

The Performers

Ultimately, opera depends on the performers who bring it alive. Opera fans love to discuss singers, to a maddening degree sometimes. In fact, opera fans will discuss singers they have never heard, even on recording. The various attributes of a Farinelli (d. 1782) or a Malibran (d. 1828) are discussed as if they were on television the previous night. Of course, some of this is name-dropping, but there is more to it as well. Opera singers come to represent certain aspects (and certain antics) of the art that are difficult to describe, and become in this way bigger than life. It is therefore perfectly natural to refer to singers one could never have heard in the course of a conversation. Conductors, too, have reputations that outlive them, remembered for the art they created and helped others to create.

Below is an alphabetical survey of many of the singers—and the conductors—whose names are bandied about by opera fans as if they are old friends, and, in a sense, they are. The list is far from complete. It is meant to give a glimpse into the marvelous diversity of people who, at base, are the essence of this art form.

Claudio Abbado (1933–): For years the reigning genius at Milan's La Scala, famous for rich renditions of the standard repertory as well as successful forays into newer works, Abbado made the rare leap from opera to symphonic conductor, and has been chief conductor of the august Berlin Philharmonic for the past decade. His recordings from the 1970s are generally marvelous.

Marian Anderson (1897–1993): A contralto whose place in operatic history is assured more by what she did not sing than by what she sang. As an African-American woman in a time of segregation, Anderson was repeatedly denied entry into conservatories and instead studied privately. Since she could not work with opera companies, she became a noted concert artist, singing songs and arias primarily in Europe. Even booking concerts in the United States was difficult for Anderson, as she discovered in 1939 when the Daughters of the American Revolution refused to allow her the use of their Constitution Hall in Washington, D.C. First Lady Eleanor Roosevelt resigned from the D.A.R. in protest, and Anderson moved her concert to the Lincoln Memorial, where she sang before a rapturous audience of 75,000 people. Shortly afterward, she sang for King George V and Queen Elizabeth on their tour of the United States. Anderson's long-delayed debut at the Metropolitan occurred in 1955 in Verdi's *Un ballo in maschera*, but by that point Anderson was in no position to begin an operatic career. However, the indefatigable woman continued to give concerts for many years, and sang at President Kennedy's inauguration in 1961. Anderson will be remembered not only for her uniquely rich voice, but for her exceptional spirit, which has made her an American icon.

Cecilia Bartoli (1966–): One of the most interesting and controversial singers working today, Bartoli is a mezzo-soprano with an extraordinary command of coloratura technique. As such, she has become noted for her blazing portrayals of Rossini's heroines, as well as Baroque roles and a few forays into the French Romantic repertory. The voice is small (to a fault, according to some), but focused, and the breath control is astounding. Bartoli also projects all the personality of her native Rome, which delights some and annoys others.

Kathleen Battle (1948–): Although Battle's voice was not large, it was clear, flexible, and always perfectly focused. She was sometimes criticized for making difficult music (such as Zerbinetta's grueling aria in Strauss's *Ariadne auf Naxos*) sound *too* easy. Widely rumored to be partial to diva antics of a bygone era, La Battle's performances were always a great source of gossip for fans and detractors alike.

Carlo Bergonzi (1924–): This beloved tenor from the Parma province has the music of Verdi in his very blood, although he has also excelled in other roles by Italian and French composers. His phrasing and vocal production, which often sound weird to Americans, are always fascinating and often transcendental, although it must be admitted that some of his choices are a bit quirky.

Jussi Bjoerling (1911–1960): A Norwegian tenor very popular through the 1950s, Bjoerling was known for an instantly recognizable ringing tone that sometimes can be accused of brassiness.

Grace Bumbry (1937–): First a mezzo, then a soprano, with occasional trips between the two, this star from St. Louis was thrilling in a wide variety of roles, especially Carmen, Salome, and, later in her career, Bess. Bumbry was also the first black singer to perform at the Wagner Festival in Bayreuth, where her portrayal of Venus in *Tannhäuser* is still recalled as one of the great moments in that theater's history.

Montserrat Caballé (1933–): This famous Catalan soprano has an undeniably gorgeous voice, vocal precision, and the ability to spin out a note or a line over several continents. Her renditions of Rossini's *Semiramide* in Orange, France, and San Francisco, with Marilyn Horne, were called the "performances of the century" even by some of the most unflappable critics. She was also famous for forgetting the words in midperformances and tra-la-la-ing her way through. Few cared. One side note: Caballé collaborated with the late Freddie Mercury (of the rock group *Queen*) on *Barcelona*, one of the strangest albums ever released and a must for students of the unusual (if you can find it).

Maria Callas (1923–1977): Probably the major operatic phenomenon of the twentieth century, La Callas commanded a fanatical following that shows no signs of waning years after her untimely (and somewhat mysterious) death. The New York–born soprano moved to Athens with her mother just in time to be caught in World War II and the subsequent civil unrest in Greece, and her life barely became calmer in peacetime. The publicity that she cultivated became unbearable after a series of personal setbacks, particularly a thoroughly rotten relationship with Aristotle Onassis, (who, it appears, never bothered to inform her of his plan to marry Jacqueline Kennedy). Her voice was rarely beautiful in the classic sense, but it was always intense and simply cannot be ignored when heard, earning her the title La Divina. Callas sang an insanely diverse repertory, from Wagner to Verdi to Puccini to the bel canto repertoire, which she imbued with such energy that she is usually credited with the revival of this all-but-lost art form. Her image as an emblem of the tragic diva has confused judicious discussion of her artistry, but her recordings still outsell other sopranos' and her performances on videotape continue to electrify audiences.

José Carreras (1946–): Although he is unfortunately now known as the "Third Tenor," this great Catalan would be better honored by audiences for his years of beautiful singing on the operatic stage. During those days, before his near-fatal bout with leukemia when he was only forty-one, Carreras took many chances in his singing choices. Some were more successful than others, but this gambling tendency was a great boon to opera lovers. He made a specialty out of recording then-obscure Verdi operas, many of which are being performed throughout America today and whose current popularity owes much to Carreras. He has been celebrated for the timbre of his voice, which, for some reason, all critics agree can be summarized as "silvery."

Enrico Caruso (1873–1921): This Neapolitan is so legendary, often credited with launching the nascent recording industry, that people sometimes forget just how good a singer he actually was. His voice was clarion and is still instantly recognizable, and he recorded many hits of the Italian and French repertory (generally in Italian), as well as many popular Italian songs. Born in poverty in Naples (he claimed that he and his several brothers shared a single shirt and could only leave the house one at a time), he became fabulously wealthy and was adored by both high society and the poor alike. He was celebrated for his portrayals of the great romantic heroes, such as Don José in *Carmen*, Des Grieux in Puccini's *Manon Lescaut*, Raoul in Meyerbeer's *Les Huguenots*, the Duke in *Rigoletto*, Radames in *Aida*, and Alvaro in *La forza del destino*. He created the tenor roles in Cilea's *Adriana Lecouvreur* and Giordano's *Fedora*, as well as the spectacular world premiere of *La fanciulla del West* at the Metropolitan in 1911. The legendary tango singer Carlos Gardel claimed that Caruso knew a method of simultaneously inhaling and exhaling, thereby creating a thrilling legato line, and that Caruso taught Gardel this secret on a visit to Buenos Aires' Teatro Colón. Although he traveled extensively, Caruso was primarily associated with the Metropolitan Opera of New York, where he sang over six hundred times. He eventually became a popular character in the city's social life. He took ill after a performance at the Brooklyn Academy of Music in 1920, when he coughed up blood. Diagnosed with throat cancer (he smoked two dozen cigarettes and eleven cigars daily), he returned to his native Naples to die (although he had avoided singing in that city ever since his lukewarm debut at the Teatro San Carlo). His life, in somewhat altered form, was the subject of a popular 1951 film, *The Great Caruso*, starring Mario Lanza.

Feodor Chaliapin (1873–1938): A great Russian bass who exuded sex and great musicianship, Chaliapin is still remembered for his triumphs in the two title roles of Mussorgsky's *Boris Godunov* and Boito's *Mefistofele*.

Franco Corelli (1921–): This tenor from Ancona, Italy, a great star from the '50s through the '70s, is criticized for his lack of experimentation, his uneven performances, and his partiality for some of the cheesier effects of the tenorial arsenal. Maybe, but the fact remains that he could deliver the thrills in the grand manner. There was a total confidence, sometimes unwarranted, in his delivery, and one can sit back and enjoy his macho heroics without worrying if he'll survive. Corelli was also devilishly handsome, knew it, and somehow communicates this knowledge in his voice. This doesn't always make for high art, but it usually makes for great opera for the Italian and French repertories in which he excelled.

Régine Crespin (1927–): A great French diva with an insanely diverse repertory, from Wagner (for which she was particularly noted) to Berlioz to Offenbach to a still controversial Carmen, in which she combined the best Gallic extremes of sensuality and earthiness.

Mario del Monaco (1915–1982): These days, it is fashionable to speak condescendingly of this great Florentine, focusing on his supposed bombast. Yet if another del Monaco showed up, people would jostle to lay palms on his path. Superbly heroic, he was unique in that his voice was solid from top to bottom, and he also sang the roles (particularly Otello, his signature role) exactly as marked in the score, a feat for which he is rarely credited.

Plácido Domingo (1941–): As much a phenomenon as Callas and Caruso before him, Domingo is rightly idolized for his consummate musicianship, his ability to learn diverse new roles in six languages, and his rigorous self-discipline. He continues to impress audiences by his determination to rethink and restudy roles he has sung hundreds of times (spurred on, he insists, by his most severe critic, his wife, Marta). Domingo has managed to command the respect of even those critics and musicians who fault him for his forays into popular culture and his media ubiquity. Domingo is known for his boundless energy, which has taken him to countless television appearances, conducting, performing piano recitals, and even directing two (at last count) growing opera companies, Washington, D.C. and Los Angeles. With a natural stage presence (his parents were performers in the zarzuela, the traditional Spanish form of operetta) and dark good looks that translate well from the stage, Domingo could easily have been a famous actor if he had chosen never to sing. Indeed, Olivier once commented that Domingo's interpretation of the role of Othello was better than Olivier's own, adding, "*and* the bastard can sing!" A living legend who has done much to further the cause of music in our times. Conductor James Levine recently called Domingo a "one-man Golden Age of opera."

Farinelli (1705–1782): Real name, Carlo Broschi. The legendary "greatest singer of all time," although we must of course take his contemporaries' word for this. We can tell by the music written for this castrato, however, that he must have had extraordinary abilities. He seems to have been able to sing without breathing for up to a full minute, and while medical authorities claim this is a biological impossibility, there are enough contemporary accounts of this ability to give it some credit. In 1737, the king of Spain offered him a fortune to remain at his court, which he did, singing the same four songs to the king every night for twenty-five years and being credited with restoring the melancholy king's sanity.

Geraldine Farrar (1882–1967): A mainstay of the Met during its early twentieth-century heyday, Farrar was beautiful and charismatic, making several films. Especially popular in the role of Madamé Butterfly, (which she played over five hundred times), she was idolized by her fans, the "Gerryflappers."

Kirsten Flagstad (1895–1962): The reigning Wagnerian diva of the 1930s, this Norwegian wowed audiences until the war cut a swath through the apex of her career. By choosing to remain in Norway through the occupation, she created enemies in America and her return to the Met in 1951 was widely protested. She retired from the stage in 1953.

Mirella Freni (1935–): One of the most reliable singers of the last thirty-five years, this charming native of Modena, Italy, has won audiences by her honest hard work, her clear voice, and her natural lyricism. When speaking of herself, she is refreshingly down to earth, saying that her saving grace is that she is *pigrone* (lazy), and hates to learn new roles, thereby sparing her voice much wear and tear. Perhaps, yet over time Freni has managed to conquer an impressive number of roles in the Italian and French repertories. Long involved with Bulgarian bass Nicolai Ghiaurov, the two appeared frequently together. In the later part of her career, Freni added the Russian role of Tatiana in Tchaikovsky's *Eugene Onegin* to her catalog—one of the very few operas in which the bass gets the girl. Freni will be forever known as the "last of the great Italian divas," and indeed she seems to encapsulate a particular approach to singing that does not grow on trees today.

Wilhelm Furtwängler (1886–1954): One of the first of the conductor superstars, Furtwängler rose to fame for his readings of Beethoven, Wagner, Tchaikovsky, and the Romantic classics. His conducting of Wagner's *Ring* at Milan's La Scala in the 1920s, of which there are partial recordings, is still revered by opera fans. Furtwängler became the conductor of the august Berlin Philharmonic in 1922, and retained the post for most of the rest of his life. His relations with the Nazi Party remain controversial and only partly understood. We know he fought with the Party leaders (especially with Goebbels, whom he detested) and was able to show that he protected many Jewish musicians and others to a certain extent, but the fact remains that he did find a way to work with the Third Reich. The accusations of collusion never left him. Whatever his political sins, his name as a musician remains revered for the quality he elicited out of singers and especially orchestras. His conducting is monumental (detractors say he was sometimes plodding), but also capable of a certain transcendental quality that was particularly effective in Wagner.

Manuel García (1775–1832): A great tenor and teacher from the quintessentially operatic city of Seville, and the father of opera's most remarkable clan, Manuel García, Jr., Maria Malibran, and Pauline Viardot-García. García, Sr. helped organize the first high-quality opera tour to the New World, bringing Mozart's *Don Giovanni* and Rossini's *Barber of Seville* (in whose premiere he had appeared in Rome in 1916).

Mary Garden (1874–1967): A true American original, Garden was a stunningly beautiful woman who sang in the lyric coluratura range—except when she felt like singing mezzo, or anything else. She reached her peak directly after World War I, singing French and (then) new roles especially in Chicago, a city she helped put on the international opera map. She even directed the company for a few years there.

Tito Gobbi (1913–1984): This Italian baritone's wide repertory of over one hundred roles included such diverse characters as

Berg's *Wozzeck*, various bel canto villains, and virtually every role Verdi wrote for baritone. Some find fault with his vocal tone, and he became mannered and breathy in later years, but his dramatic intensity (especially in famous performances of Scarpia in Puccini's *Tosca* with Callas) is still talked about, and his rendition of Rigoletto's "Pari siamo" is a revelation.

Marilyn Horne (1934–): As unpretentious as her Pennsylvania roots (she is universally known as "Jackie" and was often seen on talk shows and even *The Odd Couple*), Horne is, however, all business on stage. Beginning her career dubbing Dorothy Dandridge in the strange film *Carmen Jones*, then taking a soprano turn in the American premiere of Berg's *Wozzeck*, Horne settled into a mezzo repertory for three decades. Her specialties were the florid coloratura Rossini roles originally written for Malibran, whose spirit she (jokingly?) claimed to channel. Legend has it that, when a young soprano complained that the Met was too large, Horne responded, "No, honey, your voice is too small."

Herbert von Karajan (1908–1990): A conductor whose reputation, influence, and legacy can only be compared with Toscanini's. Born in Salzburg, Austria (in fact, a few feet away from Mozart's birthplace), Karajan was also known as an absolute dictator, a reputation not mitigated by his questionable associations with the Nazi Party. At one point or another, and often simultaneously, he commanded La Scala, the Vienna Philharmonic and State Opera, the Orchestre de Paris, the Berlin Philharmonic, the Salzburg Festival, the Salzburg Easter Festival (a sort of personal showcase), and the Deutsche Oper (Berlin), among other companies. He suffered the reputation of being a voice killer, yet he also elicited many singers' greatest performances, including Callas, Price, Simionato, Ramey, and many others. Although criticized for his reactionary tastes in repertory, he was also keenly interested in the latest technology, evidenced in zillions of recordings. Some purists complain about the personal stamp he put on orchestral scores, but opera lovers can only appreciate some of the marvelous effects he created, especially in Wagner's operas. A titan who will not soon be forgotten.

James Levine (1943–): Once the wunderkind from Cincinnati, for many years the chief conductor of the Met, Levine has honed the Met orchestra into one of the finest of any sort in the world. He has had particular success with Wagner. His name, incidentally, rhymes with wine.

Jenny Lind (1820–1887): The famed "Swedish Nightingale" of legend, Lind was an unassuming girl gifted with an extraordinary voice, capable of the most elegant coloratura and floating high notes. After touring, and conquering, the European capitals, she was brought to America in the 1850s by none other than P. T. Barnum amidst a publicity blitz that would put our pop phenoms to shame. A town named in her honor in California's Gold Country still exists today. Lind, however, found the publicity uncongenial, and she retired to a quieter life in London. She busied herself with running the Bach Choir and various charitable works. She was admired by her public as the definitive Victorian lady, and her concerts always ended with her signature song, "Home, Sweet Home."

Gustav Mahler (1860–1911): One of the titans of romantic composition, Mahler is adored for his magnificent symphonies and powerful songs, but never managed to produce a successful opera of his own. His operatic fame rests on his reputation as a conductor, first in Hamburg, and (after his conversion from Judaism to Catholicism in 1897) at the Vienna Court Opera, and eventually for two seasons at the Metropolitan. He was known for intense, emotional and personal readings of scores, especially of Wagner's work. In this, he was perhaps the polar opposite of Arturo Toscanini (who shared the Met podium with him for two seasons), who was famous for treating the written score as sacrosanct.

Maria Malibran (1808–1836): A diva legend of fiery temper, intense passion, and a tragic end. The daughter of Manuel García, Sr., Malibran traveled Europe and the New World with her family, especially conquering audiences in many dramatic mezzo coluratura roles written for her by Rossini. She fell off a horse in England when she was only twenty-eight, and later gave an ill-advised recital, a combination of events from which she died. The secondary opera house in Venice bears her name today.

Dame Nellie Melba (1861–1931): She of the eponymous peaches (when she was bingeing) and toast (when dieting), this lyric soprano from Melbourne, Australia, created her stage name as an Italianesque tribute to her hometown. She was popular in London, Paris, San Francisco, and New York society, much fussed over in the press, but her recordings from that industry's infancy reveal her to have been a brilliant soprano with a great gift for ornamentation.

Lauritz Melchior (1890–1973): Danish tenor, the reigning interpreter of Wagner from the 1930s through the 1950s.

Robert Merrill (1917–): This American baritone became such an American icon that his recording of "Take Me Out to the Ballgame" is still played during the seventh inning stretch at Yankee Stadium. Merrill is more celebrated for the sheer beauty of his voice than for any great rethinking of the Verdi and Puccini canon in which he specialized.

Zinka Milanov (1906–1989): Known for a magnificent pianissimo and a "white" Balkan whoop, most loved her, but she drove some people crazy. No one claimed Milanov (who never understood why she was advised to drop her maiden name, Kunc) had an authentic Italian production, but she gave honest performances every time. Her clear (to put it mildly) tones come off well on recordings, and the listener is likewise freed from the experience of lurch-and-stagger stage manner.

Sherill Milnes (1935–): This great baritone from suburban Chicago (and not a farm, as some would have it) began his career singing the Marlboro theme song on TV commercials, and within a few years was everywhere on stages and recordings. So much exposure led to a bit of carping about his less pleasant habits, including mannerisms, weird phrasings, and an occasional funny vibrato in the manner of the Cowardly Lion, but he had major vocal presence and was usually more than convincing. He also could blend his voice beautifully with tenors, an apparently dying art form among baritones.

Riccardo Muti (1941–): The current music director of La Scala and for many years the conductor of the Philadelphia Orchestra, Muti originally made his reputation by obsessively "correct" readings of the traditional warhorses of Italian opera. While many became annoyed at his pedantry, he was also credited with clearing away many encrustations of "traditions" around these pieces, and has forced many people to rethink what they thought they knew about them.

Birgit Nilsson (1937–): A great Swedish soprano whom everybody adores, Nilsson is celebrated for her huge voice and her winning, homey personality. She conquered the most daunting roles in the dramatic repertory, especially Wagner's and Richard Strauss's heroines and Puccini's Turandot. At present, she lives on a farm in northern Sweden with her two pet cows, Tristan and Isolde.

Jessye Norman (1945–): This Georgia-born artist with luscious tones in both the soprano and mezzo ranges is known for her interpretations of lieder (art songs) as well as a small but diverse operatic repertory, including Sieglinde in Wagner's *Walküre*, Cassandra in Berlioz's *Troyens*, and Madame Ledoin in Poulenc's *Dialogues of the Carmelites*. Gifted with great personal charm, Ms. Norman is particularly popular in Paris, where she sang the *Marseillaise* for the Bastille bicentennial celebrations, wrapped in an ample *tricolour*.

Elena Obrastzova (1937–): An intense, Russian mezzo who could occasionally rock the rafters in her renditions of Italian roles, especially in her peak years in the 1970s.

Adelina Patti (1843–1919): Patti is still discussed among opera people as the quintessential diva. An Italian born in Spain, she came to New York with her family in the 1850s, becoming a child star and developing a taste for high fees and caprices in the process. She sang for over thirty seasons at London's Covent Garden, commanding the highest fees of her day yet still (they say) running to the box office to count receipts during intermissions. Some recordings of her voice were made at her castle in Wales in 1904, after her retirement.

Luciano Pavarotti (1935–): This Italian tenor's truly great natural instrument, feel for phrasing, seemingly effortless high notes, and likeable persona have made him a household name at least since the early '70s. The voice itself has an undeniable shimmering beauty and an instantly recognizable quality. He is a supreme interpreter of the lyric repertory in roles like Edgardo in Donizetti's *Lucia di Lamermoor* (in which he made a spectacular American debut with Joan Sutherland in Miami in 1961), Alfredo in Verdi's *La traviata*, and Rodolfo in Puccini's *La bohème*. Conversely, critics call him musically lazy and complain about his lack of dramatic commitment, limited repertory, frequent cancellations, and wandering attention span during performances. Some of the supposedly heavier roles in the repertory, such as the lead roles of Verdi's *Otello* and *Don Carlo*, have eluded him, although experts say the problem may be more one of temperament than musical ability. His recordings from the '70s are occasionally awesome. Pavarotti is also justly celebrated for bringing the sheer beauty of operatic singing well beyond the confines of the traditional opera audience.

Ezio Pinza (1892–1957): A great Italian bass, extremely popular at the Met from the 1930s through the 1950s. Pinza was gifted with a natural refinement in his personality that extended to his most famous portrayals, especially Mozart's Don Giovanni, yet he was also a celebrated Boris Godunov. Perhaps unfortunately, he became an American household name when he took a small but important role in Rogers' and Hammerstein's *South Pacific*, where he sang only two songs every evening of the run, "This Nearly Was Mine" and of course "Some Enchanted Evening."

Pol Plançon (1851–1914): We are fortunate that Plançon's career just barely extended into the era of recordings. If he had died only a few years earlier than he did, we might be left to think that the music critics of the turn of the last century were exaggerating the greatness of some of their favorites. We would also have to wonder if there ever was any such thing as the vaunted "French Style," now as dead as the dinosaur. Plançon, a bass, had a great range, a tone as rich as a mezzo's, the power of a tenor, and yet had a trill like a lyric soprano's even in the lowest ranges—a feat almost biologically impossible. Listening to recordings of early singers can often be a chore for the average person, but listening to Plançon is a treat no one should miss.

Lily Pons (1898–1976): A tiny, perky French lyric coluratura who was a great crowd-pleaser in the 1930s, Pons carried her charm to the movies, where she appeared in several of Hollywood's campier outings.

Rosa Ponselle (1897–1981): A true American classic, Ponselle began her career as half of a vaudeville act with her sister Carmella around their native Connecticut. She studied briefly in New York before being discovered by Caruso, and made her triumphant Met debut at the ripe age of twenty-one in Verdi's difficult *Forza del destino*. Ponselle was a small woman with a huge voice, rich in tone and emotion. Many of her performances are legendary, especially as Violetta in Verdi's *Traviata*, and her recordings hold up well today, even if some of the weepy, sobby presentation is out of vogue just now. Although always adored by the public, Ponselle suffered from terrible stage fright and regularly vomited in the wings before making her entrance. She retired from the stage at the height of her popularity in 1937, teaching, coaching, and enjoying the quiet life in her appropriately named house, the Villa Pace, outside Baltimore.

Leontyne Price (1927–): A regal presence on the world's most important stages for three decades, this Mississippi-born soprano had a wide repertory, but is most cherished for her interpretations of Verdi heroines. A true American icon, (her brother was the nation's first African-American four-star general), Ms. Price was celebrated for her emotionally searing portrayals. The ovation after her rendition of Aida's "O patria mia" at her farewell performance in 1985 was one of the longest in the Met's history.

Samuel Ramey (1942–): The great bass from Kansas has tremendous versatility, a powerful yet agile voice, and a charismatic stage presence he is fond of augmenting with as much nudity as the given role will allow. On recordings, he is especially noted for his portrayals of Verdi's Attila, (one of the few lead roles Verdi composed for bass), and Mussorgsky's Boris Godunov.

Leonie Rysanek (1926–1998): The late, great diva from Vienna wowed audiences in a variety of roles with her dramatic intensity, her commanding sound, and even an occasional shriek when warranted. She enjoyed portraying some of the more demented Italian parts, such as Verdi's Lady Macbeth (in which she made her Met debut the hardest way possible—as a substitute for Callas) and Puccini's Turandot. It was, however, in the German roles of Wagner and Richard Strauss where she hit her greatest heights. In 1960, she and bass-baritone George London broke all records for longest ovations at the Met when they sang the leads of Wagner's *The Flying Dutchman*. Accounts vary as to the exact length, but it is generally agreed to have lasted over a half an hour (and Met audiences are not famous for long ovations). The record, whatever it was, held until broken by Rysanek herself at her farewell performance in January 1998, in Tchaikovsky's *Queen of Spades*. It was almost a full hour of pandemonium, made more poignant in retrospect by the knowledge, unknown at the time, that Rysanek was suffering terminal cancer. She passed away within months, and an era passed with her.

Renata Scotto (1933–): This soprano from Savona gave some immortal performances, and some horrid ones, but she never gave a boring performance in her life. Her musical intellect is tremendous, and one could feel her anger on nights when the voice would not do what she knew it should have (very like Callas in this respect). She is particularly prized for her portrayals of Verdi's Lady Macbeth, Puccini's Butterfly, and Mozart's Susanna in *Le nozze di Figaro*. She is also famous for a level of self-dramatization that is increasingly rare in this era of factory-produced celebrities. Her autobiography, *More Than a Diva*, is a genuine riot. Watch her never refer to Pavarotti by name, but only as a "certain fat tenor." Love her or hate her, (and there are plenty in both camps), there's no denying that they just don't make them like her any more, and the opera world is not noticeably better for it.

Elisabeth Schwarzkopf (1915–): This beautiful, German soprano, refined almost to the point of neurosis, was prized for her Strauss and Mozart heroines. Her Marschallin in Richard Strauss's *Rosenkavalier* remains the standard against which all others are judged.

Tullio Serafin (1878–1968): An Italian conductor who managed to appear virtually everywhere in the course of his long career. He was known as a singer's conductor, and his long experience in the theater gave him the reputation of being able to handle the most temperamental of singers.

Beverly Sills (1929–): A New York icon, the Brooklyn-born Sills has been a feature of the American opera scene for four decades. Sills delayed her debuts at the Metropolitan and La Scala until the very end of her career, preferring to work at the more intimate New York City Opera where she felt she had greater creative control over her appearances. Along with legendary portrayals with bass Norman Treigle, Sills made the French romantic and Italian bel canto roles her specialty, reviving many "lost" works for a new public. Yet her direct manner translated to her stage presence, and she was never considered obscure or arcane in her choices. She reached audiences even in operas that would have played to empty houses without her.

Giulietta Simionato (1910–): An Italian mezzo known for her lusty interpretations and dramatic rawness, along with a good deal of musical heft and musicianship. Simionato appeared in many legendary performances with Callas and her frequent collaborator, baritone Ettore Bastianini (with whom she even recorded "Anything You Can Do I Can Do Better" under the baton of Herbert von Karajan, believe it or not).

Risë Stevens (1913–): A New York–born mezzo prized for her Carmen and Saint-Saëns's Daliliah, Stevens happened to look especially good in pants, and was positively idolized for her *travesti* roles such as Cherubino in Mozart's *Nozze di Figaro* and Oktavian in Richard Strauss's *Rosenkavalier*.

Teresa Stratas (1938–): An intense Canadian soprano, Stratas is particularly noted for her portrayals of opera's most insane heroines, including Berg's Lulu, Richard Strauss's Salome, and Puccini's Suor Angelica. However, Stratas carried the same energy into other roles as well, including Mimi in Puccini's *bohème* and several works by Kurt Weill. The voice did not always cooperate with Stratas, but the drama was always in place and could be shattering.

Dame Joan Sutherland (1926–): Although this statuesque Australian was graced with a huge Niagara of a voice, she generally remained (with the coaching and advice of husband-conductor Sir Richard Bonynge) in the bel canto and Handel repertoire that had traditionally been assigned to lighter voices. The decision frustrated some but the results are extraordinary, and her portrayals of Lucia di Lamermoor and Norma are permanently etched into operatic lore.

Renata Tebaldi (1922–): Opera people always say the same thing about Tebaldi: "No top, no bottom, but a middle to die for!" Because she was heralded as the anti-Callas in the '50s and '60s, people now tend to forget how exciting Tebaldi's performances could be in terms of phrasing and, yes, sheer beauty of tone. She was regal in Verdi, Puccini, and many French roles. While the mention of her name may not get people foaming at the mouth like her famous "rival," you will never regret owning one of her recordings.

Dame Kiri te Kanawa (1944–): The beautiful New Zealander has sung in a wide variety of French and Italian roles, but has made her greatest mark in the lead roles of Richard Strauss's *Rosenkavalier*, *Arabella*, and *Capriccio*, for which she feels and projects a special affinity. Te Kanawa was seen and heard by about half the world when she sang (Handel) at the wedding of Prince Charles and Lady Diana.

Lawrence Tibbett (1896–1960): This baritone from Bakersfield, California, with a bright, almost sharp sound wowed Met audiences for a generation beginning in the 1930s, specializing in Italian and American roles. Listening to his recordings, you can tell he must have been exciting in the house, though the recorded experience doesn't always translate very well.

Arturo Toscanini (1867–1957): The colossus of conductors and a particular legend in America, the Toscanini story continues to be a lively debate years after his death. A dictatorial presence (especially interesting considering his famous anti-Fascist stance) who insulted musicians and threw batons for emphasis, he is universally admired among musicians, even those who felt the wrath of his tantrums. He was chief conductor at the Metropolitan from 1908–1914 (sharing the podium for two seasons with Gustav Mahler), led La Scala through it's most glorious period in the 1920s, and returned to America in the 1930s, where he formed the NBC Symphony Orchestra and broadcast concerts throughout the 1940s. His return to Italy after the war was an occasion for national healing, a ritual marked, naturally, with a concert at La Scala featuring the music of Verdi and others. While the various pros and cons of Toscanini's legacy will be debated as long as there is music in America, we are greatly indebted to the man for helping to make so much "foreign" music a part of our national life.

Tatiana Troyanos (1938–1993): A great, New York–born mezzo with a striking stage presence, wide range of roles, and glorious tone and musicianship, Troyanos's untimely death from cancer left a great void in our music scene. She was particularly noted for Oktavian on Richard Strauss's *Rosenkavalier*, Countess Geschwitz in Alban Berg's *Lulu*, and Princess Eboli in Verdi's *Don Carlo*—an astounding diversity of roles and rare in our day.

Richard Tucker (1913–1975): It is said that this New Yorker only missed out on a huge international career because he liked to eat at home. Tucker had a natural warmth and feeling in his tenor voice that made him a great crowd-pleaser among New Yorkers, and he carried the Italian tenor repertory at the Met for years. Tucker never felt pressed to plumb the deeper meanings of the roles he sang, and consequently is always easy to appreciate.

Shirley Verrett (1931–): Another great American capable of jumping the boundary between mezzo and soprano, the New Orleans–born Verrett was an exciting Carmen and Norma, but will always be remembered for her laser-sharp portrayal of Verdi's Lady Macbeth.

Pauline Viardot-García (1821–1910): The youngest child of the remarkable García clan, Viardot not only possessed a deep, rich tone, but a tremendous agility. She had her greatest successes in Paris, where she settled and became a doyenne of the artistic scene, painting, composing, writing plays, and hobnobbing with all the most fabulous bohemians, including her longtime companion, Russian novelist Ivan Turgenev.

Jon Vickers (1926–): The great Canadian tenor had a glorious career in the most heroic roles of the Italian, French, German, and English repertories. He made his greatest marks in the title roles of Verdi's *Otello*, Wagner's *Tristan und Isolde*, Saint-Saëns's *Samson et Dalila*, and Britten's *Peter Grimes*.

Galina Vishnevskaya (1926–): A Russian soprano with a bright, electric sound, Vishnevskaya was a friend of composer Dmitri Shostakovich and wife of conductor Mstislav Rostropovich. Husband and wife "jumped West" in the late 1950s and resumed their careers in England and America. Vishnevskaya's memoirs, titled simply *Galina*, read like a novel of the Cold War with a diva heroine, and are not to be missed. She was an outspoken woman, and in fact once publicly insulted mezzo Elena Obrastzova for colluding with the Soviet government.

Deborah Voigt (1964–): This American soprano is one of the most exciting sopranos working today, with a powerful, focused instrument riveting audiences in Wagner, Richard Strauss, and Verdi roles.

Frederica von Stade (1945–): An American mezzo of great charm, poise, and presence, "Flicka," (as she is known to her friends and a few million fans) has riveted audiences in a variety of roles. Although she will always be known as a "pants mezzo" for her unforgettable renditions of Mozart's Cherubino in *The Marriage of Figaro* and Richard Strauss's Oktavian in *Der Rosenkavalier*, von Stade was also the heroine of Debussy's nebulous *Pelléas et Mélisande* and, more recently, Franz Lehar's *The Merry Widow*.

Leonard Warren (1911–1960): The Met mainstay baritone of the 1950s, Warren was often paired with Richard Tucker in exciting performances of the Italian repertory. He had some bad habits, some sloppy phrasing and a wandering pitch, but he could bang out the cabalettas when he had to. Most famously he died on stage in Verdi's *Forza del destino*, directly after singing the line "Morir! Tremenda cosa!" ("What a terrible thing it is to die!")

SEVEN

The Operas

Opera, of course, is a constantly evolving body of works. New operas are written every year in a variety of languages, and very old operas are exhumed from the dusty shelves even more frequently. Any opera company will try to present a variety of works within their seasons, representing new, recent, classic, and rediscovered works. However, there is no getting around the fact that there is a standard repertory that forms the core of every opera company's productions and every record company's catalogue. These are the works that show us a company's ability and a singer's ability. Few would risk hiring a singer to create a new role until he or she had passed muster in the standard works. For better or worse, the opera system revolves around the so-called classics.

Within this narrow list, a few names reappear frequently. Verdi, Wagner, Puccini, and Mozart, between them, account for over two-thirds of the operas given in America. Verdi alone carries the largest chunk. Plácido Domingo, in a recent interview, figured that 40 percent of his career as a tenor and a conductor was devoted to Verdi, and he did not think this was excessive or disproportionate in any way.

Anybody might at first assume that opera is, therefore, built around a fossilized core of museum pieces. This is not an accurate summary of the situation. A glance at the survey below will demonstrate the wide scope of the core repertory, even if a few certain composers continue to dominate it. Each of these works may well be radically reinterpreted every time they are produced or recorded. Yet they must be available, year after year, for opera to build upon its achievements. Headings for each entry are arranged: title, composer, location of premiere, date of premiere.

Aida, Giuseppe Verdi (Cairo Opera House, 1872): Verdi's grandest opera, featuring great choruses, the famous Triumphal March, and opportunities for pageantry, is also paradoxically called his most intimate. Beyond the pageantry, the opera is essentially a triangle between the title character, an Ethiopian princess enslaved by the Egyptians, the pharaoh's daughter, and the Egyptian warrior they both love. The lead soprano sings two famous arias, the fervent narrative "Ritorna vincitor!" and the plaintive "O patria mia." The tenor sings the popular and very difficult aria "Celeste Aida" only moments after the curtain rises on act I.

Andrea Chénier, Umberto Giordano (La Scala, Milan, 1896): Although this opera set in the French Revolution is not, strictly speaking, a *verismo* opera in a textual sense, the music and emotional intensity definitely place it in that category. Nobody would call the score of *Chénier* deep, but exciting singers who pack passion into the arching phrases can make it exciting. It is the story of a poet and an aristocratic girl caught in the Reign of Terror. Audiences respond to the pathos of moments such as the love duet, the tenor arias "Un dì, all'azzurro spazio" (the "Improvviso"), and "Come un bel dì di maggio," baritone's

"Nemico della Patria," and the soprano's "La mamma morta," which provided the cathartic moment in the movie *Philadelphia*.

The Ballad of Baby Doe, Douglas Moore (Central City Opera of Colorado, 1956): An easily enjoyed opera, set in the old West and telling the story of an innocent girl who goes from rags to riches and back again. *Baby Doe* uses American folk themes and an approachable style within its traditional narrative structure. Beverly Sills was particularly celebrated in the role of Baby Doe, although the opera appears to have survived even without Ms. Sills's unique talents.

Il barbiere di Siviglia (The Barber of Seville), Gioacchino Rossini (Teatro Argentina, Rome, 1816): Rossini's comic gem, which is said to have been written in two weeks, was a true fiasco on its opening night, when it was booed off the stage. Since then, however, it has remained in the public's affection, and is both Rossini's most popular and probably the world's favorite comic opera. The music seems to bubble with joy and the intrigue crucial to this famous story of Figaro, who is both a servant and a manipulator, of the aristocracy. The soprano aria "Una voce poco fa" is a staple of recitals.

Billy Budd, Benjamin Britten (Royal Opera House, Covent Garden, London, 1951): This setting of Melville's novella, about an innocent sailor who cannot recognize or combat the forces of evil, has one of opera's most sophisticated uses of the chorus. The all-male cast makes *Budd* a bit off the mainstream, but the musical deconstruction of the moral issues at stake is masterful and easy to appreciate. The lead role is for a very lyric baritone, while the good captain (lyric tenor) and evil Claggart (bass) struggle for the young man's soul.

Bluebeard's Castle, Béla Bártok (Budapest Opera, 1918): Bártok's rich sonorities, showing influence by Richard Srauss, Liszt, and

Debussy, as well as inventive features of their own, inform this grim fable of the legendary man who keeps marrying, and murdering, young women. A tour-de-force for leading bass, *Bluebeard* is a one-act opera whose main difficulty in getting staged is finding an appropriate "mate" for it.

La bohème, Giacomo Puccini (Teatro Regio, Turin, 1896): Perhaps the world's most beloved opera, *Bohème* is an ingeniously constructed, marvelously swift tale of doomed young lovers, a poet, and a girl with tuberculosis. The joyous tenor aria "Che gelida manina" has become synonymous with the joy of falling in love, while the plaintive soprano aria "Donde lieta usci" bears all the sadness of parting from love.

Boris Godunov, Modest Mussorgsky (Maryinsky Theater, St. Petersburg, 1875): This huge epic about a usurper czar in early seventeenth century Russia went through several different editions during and even after the composer's lifetime. It's almost never quite the same opera in any two productions. Whatever edition is given, the opera cannot fail to impress with its virtuoso title role for bass, the marvelous array of characters in the huge cast, and the undeniably thrilling choruses summoning both the grandeur and the anarchy of Russia.

Carmen, Georges Bizet (Opèra Comique, Paris, 1875): One of the most enduringly popular of all operas, *Carmen* is colorful and a powerful sweep of passion. The story of a free and self-determined gypsy and the young soldier destroyed by love for her is an irresistible archetypal myth. Beyond its famous arias, such as Carmen's "Habañera," the tenor's "Flower Song" ("La Fleur que tu m'avais jetée"), and the ubiquitous "Toreador Song" for the baritone, *Carmen* contains deft ensembles and sophisticated character perceptions. Nietzsche famously recommended it as the perfect antidote for the "disease" of Wagner.

Cavalleria rusticana, (Pietro Mascagni, Rome Opera, 1890): This hour-long opera was Mascagni's submission to a contest for best one-act operas. It won the contest, and changed opera forever with its straightforward story of socio-sexual codes of honor in rural Sicily. *Cavalleria*'s intermezzo is famous from concerts and even many television commercials, but the whole opera is a single arch of uncontrollable passion and a brilliant depiction of common people in the melodrama of daily life.

The Consul, Gian Carlo Menotti, Schubert Theater, Philadelphia, 1950: Menotti's lyric immediacy, his traditional narrative format, and his lack of apparent artistic agenda during a very dogmatic era made him popular with audiences for several decades. These same attributes also earned him much scorn from many quarters, which found his operas sentimental and old-fashioned. Still, there are true qualities in some of his operas and there is no reason to suspect they will be dismissed altogether in the future. His first full-length opera, *The Consul*, remains a part of the international repertory and is perhaps his most satisfying work. In addition to the expansive, Puccini-esque melody that pleases audiences and annoys experts, *The Consul* is noteworthy for a deft command of brisk recitative that unpacks the drama (about a post–World War II family attempting to immigrate to the free world) effectively.

Cosí fan tutte, Wolfgang Amadeus Mozart (Burgtheater, Vienna, 1790): The third and last collaboration between Mozart and da Ponte, *Cosí* is a sophisticated comedy with extremely dark undercurrents. So dark, in fact, that the Victorian era considered it unperformable and it languished until resurrected early in the twentieth century. This story about two brothers who decide to test their fiancées' loyalty by seducing them in disguise is still puzzling and slightly distasteful for many, but also fascinating in its ambiguity. The title means "All women do that," referring to changing their passions. Another problem presented by *Cosí* is the difficult lead role of Fiordaligi, which requires a wide range and great agility. Her aria "Come scoglio" may well be Mozart's greatest.

Dialogues of the Carmelites, Francis Poulenc (La Scala, Milan, Paris Opèra, and San Francisco Opera, 1957): One of the most popular of twentieth century operas, *Carmelites* was simultaneously premiered in three cities with the composer's wish that it be performed in the local language. Great characterizations and juicy women's roles are part of the appeal of this intense drama about a young girl in revolutionary France who must combat her fear and take holy orders, even though it will mean death on the guillotine. The finale, sometimes derided by critics for its theatricality, features a chorus of nuns marching to the guillotine. One voice at a time is eliminated by the very audible sound of the guillotine, until only one is left, and finally there is silence as the crowd disperses without music. Theatrical, perhaps, but totally effective.

Don Carlos, Giuseppe Verdi (Paris Opéra, 1867): One of the longest Italian operas, *Don Carlos* is also among the heaviest in tone. For years it was known primarily as the source of great arias for Italian singers, such as the mezzo aria "O don fatale" and the great bass aria "Ella giammai m'amo." In the last fifty years, *Don Carlo* (as it is called when given in Italian rather than the original French) has proven supremely popular when produced lavishly, conducted well, and sung by the seven great soloists required by the score. Set in the sixteenth century court of Philip II of Spain, the opera is named after the king's son, in love with his father's wife. We also meet a scheming femme fatale, a noble idealist, the Grand Inquisitor of Spain, and even the Emperor Charles V (although it might just be his ghost) in the course of events. The characters argue about issues of church and state, love, revolution, and God, and find their only common ground in their mutual longing for death. As sprawling as it is grim, *Don Carlos* is probably Verdi's most ambitious opera.

Don Giovanni, Wolfgang Amadeus Mozart (Nofritz Theater, Prague, 1787): The second of Mozart's collaborations with Lorenzo da Ponte is a serious story treated with lighthearted sophistication and even some good comedy. It was considered the "perfect" opera throughout the nineteenth century. Besides combining tone and content with perfect ease, Mozart's penetrating genius manages to depict the widest range of human activities, from the bawdy to the noble to the supernatural. It is a retelling of the old myth of Don Juan, the legendary lover of old Spain, although in the course of the evening we see that the old libertine may be losing his touch. He fails miserably with each of the four women he attempts to seduce, and faces his final ruin. A good example of *Don Giovanni*'s treasures is the "Catalogue Aria," a long list of the Don's female conquests that is simultaneously elegant and vulgar.

Elektra, Richard Strauss (Dresden Opera, 1909): The limits of tonality are explored, but never crossed, in this hour-and-a-half long shattering psychodrama based on Sophocles, with a heavy dose of Freud thrown in. The title character longs for the death of her mother and her mother's lover (who killed her much-loved father Agamemnon after his return from the Trojan War), but cannot commit the act herself and must await the return of her brother Orest. The lead role, though brief, requires a major dramatic soprano.

Eugene Onegin, Peter Ilyich Tchaikovsky (Bolshoi Theater, Moscow, 1879): All of Tchaikovsky's lyric powers are apparent in this tale of a young girl and the cad she loves. The rather long "Letter Scene," in which the girl pours out her love, is a highlight of the opera, as are the title character's narrative, the tenor's sad Farewell Aria, the rich ensembles, and the colorful choruses and dances.

L'elisir d'amore (The Elixir of Love), Gaetano Donizetti (La Scala, Milan, 1832): The undeniable grace and beauty of this comic gem have always delighted audiences with its charming story of the illiterate peasant winning the love of the prettiest girl in the village. It includes the popular tenor aria "Una furtiva lagrima."

Die Entführung aus dem Serail (The Abduction from the Seraglio), Wolfgang Amadeus Mozart, Burgtheater, Vienna, 1781: Mozart was eradicating the lines that separated "high" and "low" genres of the opera even with this early opera, written when he was twenty-three. Although a sort of vaudeville in the vernacular (German) and including dialogue, the roles require all the singing ability of the noblest operas. The story is a comedy about a young Englishwoman held captive in a harem, and her spry wiles to escape the pasha's intrigues intact and reunite with her friend and lover. The soprano aria "Marten aller Arten" requires three high Es, and shortly after she is asked to sing a low A flat. The bass role has the lowest notes written in the regular repertory.

Falstaff, Giuseppe Verdi (La Scala, Milan, 1893): The seamless action of *Otello* is refined further in *Falstaff,* Verdi's final masterpiece, based on comic episodes from Shakespeare about the fat, aging, thieving, yet somehow lovable knight. The finale to act I features nine soloists singing in three different rhythms. Musicians praise touches like this to the skies, but the real miracle of *Falstaff* is that it all appears to be unfolding in the most natural manner imaginable. There are no arias, as such, in *Falstaff,* although there are outstanding solo "narratives" such as Sir John Falstaff's melancholy "Va, vecchio John" and his coy "Quand'ero paggio del duca di Norfolk." While perhaps not as instantly lovable. as, say, *Traviata, Falstaff* provides a lifetime's worth of pleasurable exploration.

Faust, Charles Gounod (Paris Opéra, 1859): This pinnacle of French Romanticism was not a great success at its premiere, but soon carried the whole world before it. Literary purists do not appreciate an operatic setting for Goethe's masterpiece about the philosopher who sells his soul to the Devil for one more chance at youth and love, but it makes for ripping opera nonetheless. Although not as dominant as it was around the turn of the last century, *Faust* is still adored by audiences (if not by musicologists) for the lyricism of its choruses, its witty quartet, the effervescent Jewel Song, the baritone's expansive "Avant de quitter ces lieux," and the thrilling final trio.

La fanciulla del West (The Girl of the Golden West), Giacomo Puccini (Metropolitan Opera of New York, 1911): This opera, based on a David Belasco play and set in the California Gold Rush, tells of a young girl who is (chastely) loved by the miners in a grim camp, and the Mexican bandit who steals her heart. It is possibly Puccini's most masterful complete score. His use of the orchestra has been compared to both Wagner and Debussy. The vocal writing is thrilling as well, although the title role is said to be among the most difficult to cast in all opera. Even the great Wagnerian soprano Birgit Nilsson was intimidated by it. It is a sophisticated score with subtle ensemble work and few set pieces, although the brief, glorious tenor aria "Ch'ella mi creda" was one of Caruso's bestselling 78s and was sung as an anthem by Italian prisoners during World War I.

Der fliegende Holländer (The Flying Dutchman), Richard Wagner, Royal Opera House (Dresden, 1843): Wagner's youthful ghostly sea tale about a cursed sailor and the girl who must love him unconditionally in order to redeem his soul was his second success and the earliest of his operas to remain in the repertory. The title role is prized by bass baritones, and the entire score is cherished for its Gothic melodrama and its direct accessibility.

La forza del destino (The Force of Destiny), Giuseppe Verdi (Maryinsky Theater, St. Petersburg, 1862): A grand panorama of romantic passions set against mundane realities, *Forza* has puzzled as many audiences as it has thrilled. The story of an aristocratic Spanish girl, her half-Inca lover, and her revenge-bent brother, who chase each other all across Europe, is the apex of the wild Romantic imagination. Although famous for such arias as the soprano's "Madonna degli angeli" and "Pace! pace! mio dio!" the tenor's "O tu che in seno agli angeli," and the baritone's

"Urna fatale," Forza's greatest achievements are the duets between the lead characters. These include the gorgeous "Solenne in quest' ora" for tenor and baritone and an excellent extended scene between soprano and bass baritone.

La gioconda, Amilcare Ponchielli (La Scala, Milan, 1876): This most turgid of melodramatic operas has received its share of abuse over the years, not to mention outright parody. (The famous act III ballet the "Dance of the Hours" provided laughs for both *Fantasia*'s hippos in tutus and Alan Sherman's "Hello Muddah, hello Faddah"). In the hands of five exciting singers and a production with the right spirit, however, this tale of love, murder, and sky-high passions in sixteenth-century Venice can still pack a wallop. The passionate arias such as the soprano's "Suicidio!" the tenor's beautiful "Cielo e mar," and the baritone's sinister "Enzo Grimaldo, Principe di Santofior" require dramatic authenticity as well as great lungs. The frankness of the melodies and the sheer bloodlust of the libretto by Arrigo Boito clearly demonstrate this opera's paradoxical influence on the *verismo* school that came after.

Jenůfa, Leoš Janáček (Brno Opera House, 1904): *Jenůfu*, a murky tale of an unstable Moravian woman and her scheming, infanticidal stepmother, remained almost unknown until an important production in Prague in 1916 brought it to the world's attention. It languished again until around the 1960s, when it began to conquer the international circuit one city at a time. It translates the intensity and expressiveness of *verismo* opera into a distinctly non-Italian vocabulary, utilizing the orchestra in an exciting and convincing way.

Katya Kabanová, Leoš Janáček (Brno Opera House, 1921): *Katya* is Janáček's most performed opera today, even more popular than *Jenůfu*. The opera is cherished for its searing characterizations, including the lead role of a rural woman choosing to break societal strictures. Opera abounds in such women, and none are better drawn than *Katya*. This opera is also interesting for its character roles, including a bass and a mezzo or soprano role that are often taken by oldtime singers in the golden sunsets of their careers.

Lohengrin, Richard Wagner (Weimar Opera, 1850): Wagner is at his most lyrical in this medieval fable of an unknown Swan Knight and the fair princess who loves him without knowing his name. The opera is a gold mine of rich choral singing and rousing marches, with haunting solos for the two leads. The now-hackneyed "Wedding March" ("Treulich gefährt") is sung by the chorus at the beginning of act III.

Lucia di Lamermoor, Gaetano Donizetti, (Teatro San Carlo, Naples, 1835): For years, this was the only one of Donizetti's tragedies to remain in the repertory. The brilliant title role of the young woman forced to marry against her will demands spectacular abilities from the soprano, especially in the extended Mad Scene. Other well-known moments from the score include a graceful love duet, a plaintive soprano aria "Regnava nel silencio" with a notable harp introduction, the tenor's death arias, "Fra poco a me ricoverò" and "Tu, che a Dio spiegasti l'ali," and the ever-popular sextet from act II.

Lulu, Alban Berg (Zürich Opera, 1937): Berg's twelve-tone opera was not complete at the time of his death, and composer Friedrich Cerha completed act III, which was given its premiere in Paris in 1963. Needless to say, this leaves much room for various editions and endless program notes. The important thing about *Lulu*, however, is not all the erudition that invariably goes into each production, but the musicianship and dramatic authenticity of the work. In other words, *Lulu* is best judged by audiences as an opera, plain and simple. The lead role, a sexually predatory woman who meets her end at the hands of Jack the Ripper, is given to a lyric soprano. She must have good low notes, to be sure, but *Lulu* does not require a special type of singer.

Sopranos who sing *Lulu* might also sing any other lyric soprano role in the repertory.

Macbeth, Giuseppe Verdi (Teatro alla Pergola, Florence, 1847): Tired of turning out operas "by the pound" in his early years, Verdi made a great leap with this daring opera written for the intellectual crowd at Florence. This first of Verdi's settings of Shakespeare (who was not well known in Italy at that time), was revised for Paris two decades later, and the hybrid Paris version is what we usually see today. Critics have called the Witches' music "weak," but the characterizations of the two leads are magnificent and very untypical for opera. Lady Macbeth, in particular, shines in such moments as "Vieni, t'affreta!" (the "Letter Scene") and the "Sleepwalking Scene." In the latter scene, Verdi famously directed the soprano to sing certain passages "coarsely" and even "without music," although it ends on a high E flat spun out as a "thread of voice." The peasants' chorus "Patria oppressa" may be Verdi's finest set choral solo.

Madame Butterfly, Giacomo Puccini (La Scala, Milan, 1904): Puccini's setting of the David Belasco play about an innocent geisha betrayed by a callous American navy officer was a failure at its Scala premiere, but a success ever since. The title character bears almost the entire weight of the work, and must convey the full range of human experience within the course of the opera. Even in her famous solo aria, "Un bel dì" she must encapsulate all the various feelings elicited by obsessive love, from tenderness to suicidal despair.

Manon Lescaut, Giacomo Puccini (Teatro Regio, Turin, 1893): Puccini's first great success is one of the all-time great depictions of fervent young love. It is based on the Abbé Prévost's ever-popular eighteenth-century novel about a young woman devoted to luxury and the young man whose love for her almost destroys him. (Massenet used the same source for his great opera *Manon*). The act II love duet is unequaled for its passion and urgency. The tenor role demands both the amorous joy of "Donna non vidi mai" and the desperation of "Guardate! pazzo son!" The equally demanding soprano role builds to a climax in act IV's heartwrenching "Sola, perduta, abbondonata!"

Manon, Jules Massenet (Paris Opèra, 1884): Critics have always found themselves trying to justify *Manon*'s success with the public. Massenet's music and the characterizations have always been considered superficial, although everyone conceded the opera's undeniable charm. As time passed on, however, *Manon* did not disappear but continued to grow in popularity, and people have come to find unsuspected substance in the work. Audiences respond instinctively to the sensuous love duet, the lovely gavotte, and the two extremely diaphanous arias "Le rêve" and "Adieu, notre petite table" sung by the tenor and soprano, respectively.

Die Meistersinger von Nürnberg, Richard Wagner (Munich Opera, 1868): Despite its great length, huge cast and chorus, and controversial undertones, Wagner's only comedy maintains a certain "sunniness" that has kept it in the public affection since its premiere. It is the tale of a young knight in Renaissance Nuremburg who enters a song contest to win the girl he loves. The controversy is classic: Is art mostly formal rules or spontaneous expression? Between these two poles stands the remarkable character of Hans Sachs (based on a historical character) who alone can see the value of both points of view. *Meistersinger* earns every one of its nearly six hours of performance time, and it was the clear winner in a recent poll asking conductors which single score they would take with them to a desert island.

Mefistofele, Arrigo Boito (La Scala, Milan, 1867): The young Arrigo Boito, aflame with ideas from such iconoclasts as Wagner and Hegel, pounced on the opera scene with this wild, uneven experiment based on the Faust legend in 1867, and flopped. A few revisions later, the opera was a great success. Known primarily as a vehicle for a charismatic star bass, *Mefistofele* is also cherished for its magnificent, unusual choruses, its shamelessly gushing love duet, and its lyric arias "Dai prati, dai campi" and "L'altra notte in fonde al mare" for tenor and soprano respectively.

Nabucco, Giuseppe Verdi (La Scala, Milan, 1842): *Nabucco's* triumph at its premiere did not assure its immortality in opera houses. The complete opera, about love and madness in the Hebrews' Babylonian captivity, lay dormant until resurrected in Italy after World War II and around the rest of the world only within the last generation. It is now loved for the same qualities that kept it off the boards for many years; a brash and sometimes crass score. Although there is no single famous aria in *Nabucco*, the lead soprano role of Abigaille is uniquely exciting and difficult, known for frequent octave leaps and falls. Amidst all the vocal fireworks, the haunting chorus "Va pensiero" is like a dip in cool water, and always elicits at least a melancholy sigh from the audience.

Norma, Vicenzo Bellini (La Scala, Milan, 1831): Bellini's tale of a druid priestess in love with a Roman officer has been a vehicle for divas since its premiere. Her graceful hymn to the moon, "Casta diva," is a miracle of sustained sonority, while her duets with the mezzo, especially "Mira, o Norma," call for supreme agility and coloratura.

Le nozze di Figaro (The Marriage of Figaro), Wolfgang Amadeus Mozart (Burgtheater, Vienna, 1787): Based on Beaumarchais's satirical sequel to *The Barber of Seville* and set to an exquisite libretto by Lorenzo da Ponte, *Figaro* is an ingenious combination of comedy, drama, refinement, and spontaneity. Besides the marvelous ensembles, *Figaro* is known for the baritone's "Non più andrai," the mezzo's "Voi che sapete," one soprano's "Dove Sono," and another soprano's "Deh vieni, non, tardar."

Otello, Giuseppe Verdi (La Scala, Milan, 1887): This mature masterpiece, based on Shakespeare's tale of the Moorish general and his fatal jealousy, is probably the pinnacle of the art of Italian opera. Verdi, faced with changing times and tastes, did not dispense with tried-and-true forms of the genre but seemed to reinvent them for *Otello*. Thus there is every cliché of Italian opera, including a Storm Scene, a Drinking Song, an Oath Duet for tenor and baritone, and a Prayer for the soprano. Each of these, however, occurs not as a distinct and separate piece, but within a seamless context of dramatic action. The libretto by Arrigo Boito is considered a masterpiece in its own right.

I pagliacci, Ruggiero Leoncavallo (La Scala, Milan, 1892): The image of the clown who must laugh while his heart breaks, and the aria "Vesti la giubba," are operatic icons familiar to a wide audience. The opera as a whole is, however, a superb sweep of dramatic tension, delivering its powerful character study in only two brief acts.

Parsifal, Richard Wagner (Bayreuth Festival House, 1882): Although deeply mystical and loaded with pseudo-religious symbolism, *Parsifal* is written with a certain directness that renders it a powerful experience for a wide variety of fans. It is the tale of a "young fool," an innocent who must learn of life's sorrow before he can fulfill his destiny as the king of the knights of the Holy Grail. It is traditional in most cities not to applaud after the first act, which gives some indication of the reverence reserved for this work by its fans. Wagner wrote it specifically for the acoustical qualities of the Bayreuth Festival House, and intended it to be performed there exclusively. The Met managed to get a contraband copy of the score and produced *Parsifal* in New York in 1903, to the great consternation of the Wagner family and their supporters. *Parsifal* played around Europe after the Wagner family monopoly expired, but remained difficult to produce and a political issue in many places. The Third Reich, despite the Nazi's general fetishization of Wagner's work, banned it in 1940, and it did not receive a public performance in Russia until 1993.

Pelléas et Mélisande, Claude Debussy (Paris Opèra, 1902): Debussy's only complete opera was a completely new and different sort of music drama when it was premiered, and it still sounds remarkably "modern" a century later. *Pelléas* is a moody, introspective piece, a symbolist reinterpretation of an old legend about an unfathomable young girl, her aging husband, and her tragic affair with his brother. It depends on shadings of tone and the subtlest harmonies for its effect. Most surprising, it was a smash hit with the public and has remained on the boards ever since. Mezzos who want to display their psychological depth especially prize the role of Mélisande.

Peter Grimes, Benjamin Britten (Sadler's Wells Opera, London, 1945): Britten's first great operatic success, about a loner who may be murdering his apprentices and the townspeople who both create and destroy him, remains a staple of the international repertory. The lead title role is demanding but remarkably pliant, working well with any category of tenor, provided he can penetrate the character's murky exterior.

Porgy and Bess, George Gershwin (Colonial Theater, Boston, 1935): Gershwin's panorama of diverse characters in old Charleston has always commanded respect in America and has steadily increased in popularity abroad, making it one of the few American operas to do so. The opera would probably be performed more in both America and abroad except for the difficulty of the music and the large scale of the cast and chorus. Amateur and second-string companies who attempt *Porgy*, banking on the familiarity of its hits like "Summertime" and "I Got Plenty of Nuttin," usually rue the decision.

The Rake's Progress, Igor Stravinsky (Teatro la Fenice, Venice, 1951): This opera is both a parody and an homage to baroque composers such as Pergolesi, who would have been utterly mystified by it. It is loosely based on a set of engravings of the same name by Hogarth, showing a young man's fall into vice and madness amidst the strange characters of eighteenth-century London. The opera includes interesting choruses, a charismatic bass role in Nick Shadow (the Devil), a lyric coloratura soprano role, and a high-camp mezzo role for Baba the Turk, the Bearded Lady. W. H. Auden and Chester Kallman wrote the libretto in English.

Rigoletto, Giuseppe Verdi, Teatro la Fenice (Venice, 1851): A rare instance of an opera that has been popular with critics and public alike since its premiere, *Rigoletto* continues to impress audiences with its characterization of a degenerate yet noble hunchback, his innocent daughter, and an amoral nobleman. It is loaded with indisputed "hit tunes" like the ubiquitous tenor aria "La donna è mobile" and the soprano's "Caro nome," yet the overall musical-dramatic structure remains impressive.

Der Ring des Nibelung, Richard Wagner (Bayreuth Festival House, 1876): A unique achievement in opera, and perhaps in art as well, Wagner's four-part epic of gods, giants, gnomes, and heroes is more popular today then ever. *The Ring*'s many layers of meaning and interpretation make it the career goal of designers and directors as well as conductors and singers.

Roméo et Juliette, Charles Gounod (Paris Opèra, 1867): Never quite as popular as its sister opera *Faust, Roméo* nevertheless is so shamelessly lovely that it has never disappeared altogether. The coloratura soprano aria "Je veux vivre" and the heart-wrenching tenor "Ah! leve-toi soleil" are revelations in the hands of singers who can master the French style, while the ensemble "Ce jour de deuil" has recently commanded greater respect from musiclogists.

Der Rosenkevalier, Richard Strauss (Dresden Opera, 1911): Strauss's buoyant yet profound masterpiece is a bittersweet nod to the passage of time, both personal and historical. While set in baroque Vienna, and almost always produced in the splendor of that period, *Rosenkavalier* is also quintessentially Romantic and even quite modern all at the same time. The dense score is one of the most diverse, and difficult, ever written. It moves from shimmering to frollicking with every gradation in between. The characterizations are among the best in opera, and the melancholy narratives, the beautiful love scene ("The Presentation of the Rose"), and of course the monumental final trio are among *Rosenkavalier*'s most cherished treasures.

Salome, Richard Strauss (Vienna State Opera, 1905): Strauss's first major operatic success is a phenomenal blend of lyricism and depravity, featuring a twenty-minute long final monologue/ love scene by the heroine sung to the severed head of John the Baptist.

Samson et Dalila, Camille Saint-Saëns (Weimar Opera, 1877): This remarkably creative opera with a loose, almost surreal structure, has always been, championed by heroic tenors and dramatic mezzos. It imbues the biblical story of the forbidden and fatal love between the Hebrew warrior and the Philistine temptress with a thoroughly Romantic passion. The protracted love scene, including the mezzo's sensuous "Mon coeur s'oeuvre a ta voix," is one of the most irresistible in opera. Audiences are also endlessly tickled by the almost kitschy ballet toward the end of the opera, the famous "Bacchanale."

Simon Boccanegra, Giuseppe Verdi (Teatro la Fenice, Venice, 1857; revised for La Scala, Milan, 1881): Verdi and the brilliant librettist Arrigo Boito substantially reworked the composer's only mature failure into a success. The title role, about an aging doge of Genoa and his love for his long-lost daughter, is a tour de force for baritone, and includes one of Verdi's best father-daughter scenes. The "Council Chamber" scene, added for the revision, is a masterful depiction of personal issues amidst political turmoil. It is one of the very best single scenes in all opera.

Susannah, Carlisle Floyd (Tallahassee Opera, 1955): Floyd's most enduringly popular opera uses a vernacular American musical vocabulary with romantic flourishes in this tale of backwoods hypocrisy and repressed sexuality based loosely on the Apocryphal story of Susanna and the Elders. The soprano aria "Ain't It a Pretty Night" is a staple of the recital circuit.

Tannhäuser, Richard Wagner (Royal Opera House, Dresden, 1845): The tale of a medieval noble troubadour caught between good and evil ideals of Woman gives us some of Wagner's most easily enjoyable moments. These include a frenzied ballet, a beautiful prayer for the soprano, and the baritone "Morningstar Song," "O du mein holde Abendstern." The unforgettable "Pilgrims' Chorus" is both the first and last theme we hear in the work.

Tosca, Giacomo Puccini (Rome Opera, 1900): Although derided as a "shabby little shocker" by the high brows, Puccini's portrayal of a fatal love triangle during Napoleon's invasion of Italy has always thrilled audiences with its powerful characterizations and sometimes-brutal realism. The title character is an opera diva, adding another interesting dimension to the mythic meanings of the work. Tosca's great aria "Vissi d'arte" is a sort of "national anthem" for sopranos.

La traviata, Giuseppe Verdi (Teatro la Fenice, Venice, 1853): The Camille story, about the beautiful and doomed young prostitute who is actually morally superior to those around her, gets a brilliantly sensitive and remarkably modern treatment in Verdi's timeless classic. The lead role is extremely demanding, as the soprano must be capable of communicating a wide array of musical emotion, from the capricious coloratura "Sempre libera" to the haunting "Addio del passato." *Traviata* failed at its premiere, but was a success in the same city a year later. Its popularity has not wavered since.

Tristan und Isolde, Richard Wagner (Munich Opera, 1865): Wagner explores the metaphysical implications of love and death in this masterpiece, whose tonal innovations still leave musicians and audiences gasping. The two lead roles are generally considered the most difficult in all opera. Isolde, in particular, must sing beyond all human capacity throughout the evening before ending the opera with the transcendental "Liebestod," the "Love Death."

Il trovatore, Giuseppe Verdi (Teatro Apollo, Rome, 1853): In many ways, *Trovatore* is the "Uber-opera." The often-parodied opera about the mad gypsy woman who accidentally throws her own baby onto a fire is a gush of insanity, passion, and melody. The "Anvil Chorus" alone seems to be familiar to every person on earth. In the hands of great singers, arias such as the tenor's heroic "Di quella pira," the baritone's lovely "Il balen," and the mezzo's eerie "Stride la vampa" are also masterpieces of opera's ability to explore the darker regions of human emotion.

Turandot, Giacomo Puccini (La Scala, Milan, 1926): Unfinished at the time of Puccini's death in 1924, *Turandot* was completed by the composer Franco Alfano. The finale, although well done, is of course frustrating, but the opera remains popular because of its rich sonority, extraordinary choruses, and magnificently dramatic title role for soprano. It is an opera filled with myth and ritual, telling of a haughty princess in legendary China who will only give herself to the man who can answer three riddles, or die in the attempt. The Chinese fairy tale setting elicited some unique musical solutions from the composer, yet there is also some marvelous and clearly Italian music written for the commedia dell'arte characters who are also part of the panoply. The ever-popular tenor aria "Nessun dorma" begins act III of the opera.

Un ballo in maschera ("A Masked Ball"), Giuseppe Verdi (Teatro Apollo, Rome, 1859): This opera about an assassination of a king is celebrated for its refined musicality and its tight, economical drama. Act III, scene 1 begins with the popular baritone aria "Eri tu" and grows seamlessly into an ingenious quintet of conflicting agendas.

Wozzeck, Alban Berg (Berlin State Opera, 1925): Berg's once controversial opera is now considered central to the repertory, although it is still musically and dramatically shocking to many in the audience. The story, about a poor soldier who submits to medical experiments to support his wife and child, is as ghastly and as fascinating as it sounds.

Die Zauberflöte (The Magic Flute), Wolfgang Amadeus Mozart (Freihaus Theater auf der Wieden, Vienna, 1791): Like *Seraglio*, *Flute* is written in German with dialogue in between the arias and set pieces. It is a fable of love that heavily uses Masonic imagery, which is sometimes difficult for modern audiences to follow. A prince and princess must pass through various tests before they can be joined in love; while on the earthier side, a Birdman must also triumph over adversity before he can win his Birdgirl. The power of the music, such as the Queen of the Night's famous aria where the soprano is asked to sing up to a high F, is easily appreciated by audiences.

EIGHT

Opera on CD

Recordings changed the opera world. When good, full-length recordings became standard in the 1950s, many people assumed they no longer even needed to attend the theater in order to enjoy opera. The fact is that listening to opera is one experience, attending one, another. The two are in many ways only peripherally related. In fact, listening to too many studio recordings tends to ruin the experience of live theater for most fans. It is not possible to hear the same level of perfection on stage as in a studio, where in any case flubs can be altered. Still, it's undeniable that recordings make up the greatest part of the experience for most people today. In a sense, we live in a golden age of singing simply because any of us can access hundreds of different voices from the past and present at any time.

There are many other types of opera records to buy besides recordings of full-length opera. There are arias, duets, compilations, various themes (marches, choruses, etc.), and thousands of different recordings by opera singers. Lately, there has been very little an opera star would not record. You can expect to find Christmas songs, gospel songs, Broadway songs, and even some rock songs by various opera singers. The list is endless.

A recording of arias by a given singer is meant to tell us about that singer rather than about the music (let alone the opera) itself. Some, such as Maria Callas's collection *Mad Scenes from Opera*, are considered indispensable. These are choices, however, that must be left to the individual buyer with a minimum of input from "experts" and guides such as this one. If you respond to a particular singer heard on a broadcast or on a recording, for example, no amount of bad criticism should deter you from hearing more of his or her work. If you are determined to buy an "arias" recording and don't know where to begin, any cashier at a record store will be glad to direct you to his or her favorites.

The full-length recordings of the great operas, then, are the best approach—comparatively costly though it may be. One gets the work itself as well as the performers who bring it to life. Any list of "recommended recordings" is bound to be controversial at the least. The list below represents precisely thirty-one recordings, all among the "canon of greats," and all considered to be standard setting in their overall quality. These recordings would be a good starter set for anybody interested in opera, and no opera fan (except the most insanely opinionated) would be ashamed to own these. The heading for each entry indicates not just the opera and composer, of course, but the conductor, principal cast, orchestra, record label, and catalogue number.

Aida, Giuseppe Verdi; conductor, Sir Georg Solti; Leontyne Price, Jon Vickers, Robert Merrill, Rita Gorr; Orchestra and Chorus of the Rome Opera (London/Decca): Of the many classic recordings of Verdi's most large-scale opera, this one best captures the grandeur of the subject matter. Leontyne Price's celebrated interpretation of the role cuts right through the choruses and ensembles, while Vickers's heroic voice is perfect for the all-testosterone role of Radames. Merrill blends beautifully and Rita Gorr is appropriately scary. Solti's conducting is, in this case, of the "slow as the Nile" variety, but that works well for this opera of surprising complexity. The recording quality is rich and superb.

Il barbiere di Siviglia, Gioacchino Rossini; conductor, Riccardo Chailly; Marilyn Horne, Paolo Barbacini, Leo Nucci, Enzo Dara, Raquel Pierotti, Silvestro Sammaritano, Simone Alaimo, Samuel Ramey; Orchestra and Chorus of La Scala (Sony Classical): Even though many high sopranos sing the role of Rosina, it was written for a very rare bird, the mezzo coluratura. We have been blessed in our time with the artistry of Marilyn Horne, who summons both her rich tone and her light touch in this excellent recording. Leo Nucci is not to everyone's taste, but his interpretation of Figaro as a super-suave con artist is fascinating. Dara and Alaimo are lessons in Italian comic style. Even Samuel Ramey, more famous for his classic interpretations of the heaviest bass roles in opera, is fluid, idiomatic, and, best of all, quite funny.

La bohème, Giacomo Puccini; conductor, Tullio Serafin; Renata Tebaldi, Carlo Bergonzi, Ettore Bastianini, Cesare Siepi, Renato Cesari, Fernando Corena; Orchestra and Chorus of the Santa Cecilia Academy of Rome (London/Decca): This is one recording of Puccini's most beloved opera that everyone can agree on. It provided the soundtrack for the movie *Moonstruck*, and it's easy to see why. Serafin's reputation as a singers' conductor is fully in evidence. Tebaldi and Bergonzi are flowing cream, and the sheer beauty of their tonality is transcendental. Bastianini, Siepi, and Corena move from comedy to lyric grandeur effortlessly. There are many good *Bohème* recordings, but there is none better than this late-1950s classic of Italian beauty.

Carmen, Georges Bizet; conductor, Claudio Abbado; Teresa Berganza, Plácido Domingo, Ileana Cotrubas, Sherill Milnes; London Symphony Orchestra; the Ambrosian Singers (Deutsche Grammophon): While everybody has a favorite Carmen, critics and public alike agreed that Berganza's interpretation of the role was a great accomplishment. She has passion and spiritual freedom without descending into the histrionics that sometimes mar the role. Domingo was born to sing Don José. Milnes's bravado seems right on the money in this outing as the cocky Escamillo, while Cotrubas is a lovely Micaëla. Abbado's conducting is an exercise in good judgment; brisk and lyrical, rather than the alternating kitsch and mawkishnish that some conductors find right for the score.

Ernani, Giuseppe Verdi; conductor, Riccardo Muti; Mirella Freni, Plácido Domingo, Renato Bruson, Nicolai Ghiaurov; Orchestra and Chorus of La Scala (EMI): This recording demonstrates how vital early Verdi operas can be, and in fact it was partly responsible for the "all-Verdi, all the time" phenomenon of recent years. Muti is often faulted for pedantry, but he nailed this score directly, allowing the sublime Orchestra and Chorus full rein for lyric passion. The leads convey all the possibilities of Italian opera. Many neophytes have become rabid opera maniacs with one hearing of this recording. Although recorded live, the sound is excellent. Muti famously browbeat the Milan audience before the beginning of the performance, forbidding them to applaud between arias and even telling them not to cough.

Fidelio, Ludwig van Beethoven; conductor, Otto Klemperer; Jon Vickers, Christa Ludwig, Gottlob Frick, Walter Berry, Gerhard Unger, Ingeborg Hallstein; Philharmonia Orchestra and Chorus (EMI Great Recordings of the Century): This classic recording of Beethoven's always-problematic opera has only recently become available on CD. Some find the conducting too broad, others call it "metaphysical." Whatever your final opinion, Klemperer's reading reveals the full beauty of the score, whereas others often gloss over it. The lead singers are superb.

Nobody nailed this tenor role like Jon Vickers. He sings where others merely attempt to survive. Ludwig is no less impressive, and the lower men's roles intelligently and passionately delivered.

Don Giovanni, Wolfgang Amadeus Mozart; conductor, Herbert von Karajan; Anna Tomowa-Sintow, Agnes Baltsa, Kathleen Battle, Samuel Ramey, Ferruccio Furlanetto; Berlin Philharmonic Orchestra and Chorus of the Deutsche Oper Berlin (Deutsche Grammophon): Every great bass of the twentieth century has recorded this role, and archival recordings are a pleasure to listen to, but the best overall selection is Karajan's mid-eighties rendition. The lead roles are all convincing at least, excellent at best. Each singer has a specific sound, and the voices contrast well in ensembles. The sound production is brilliant, and the singers add a touch of fun to the proceedings (Baltsa is a certifiable kook). People who complain that Karajan and the Berlin Philharmonic were only good for stentorian works would be amazed by the flighty elegance of the orchestra right from the first notes.

Der fliegende Hollander (The Flying Dutchman), Richard Wagner; conductor, Antal Dorati; George London, Leonie Rysanek, Giorgio Tozzi, Karl Liebl, Richard Lewis, Rosalind Elias; Orchestra and Chorus of the Royal Opera House, Covent Garden (London/ Decca Grand Opera Series): An indisputable classic. Both leads go beyond good singing into an operatic dementia zone ideally suited to the spookiness of this gem, Wagner's earliest success to remain on the boards. Tenor Tozzi in the smaller role of Erik demonstrated the wisdom of imbuing this opera with a bit of bel canto style, something which recent scholarship has demonstrated to be within Wagner's intention. On stage, London and Rysanek created a sensation in these roles, and this recording recreates those legendary moments well.

Julius Caesar, Georg Friedrich Handel; conductor, Julius Rudel; Beverly Sills, Norman Treigle, Maureen Forrester, Beverly

Wolff; New York City Opera Orchestra and Chorus (RCA Victor Gold Seal): Sills and bass Treigle proved to the world that baroque opera can be electrifying in a 1966 New York City Opera production of this Handel gem, and their recording remains exciting today. The attention to detail, both musical and textual, sets a standard for singers approaching this difficult repertory. No one could think baroque opera was merely extravagant vocalizing after experiencing this recording. Casting a bass in the castrato role of Caesar was controversial at the time, but there are viable musical reasons for doing so and Treigle makes you think Handel must have originally conceived of the role as a bass part. The recording is in English, which was considered the best solution for Handel operas for a few years. Sills and Treigle were two of the very few singers who could sound good singing in English.

Lucia di Lamermoor, Gaetano Donizetti; conductor, Herbert von Karajan; Maria Callas, Giuseppe di Stefano, Rolando Panerai, Nicola Zaccaria. RIAS Symphony Orchestra, Berlin; Chorus of La Scala (EMI): Until recently, recordings of live performances were the domain of rabid fans, people who were willing to put up with bad sound and all the flaws of a real performance in order try to recapture a moment of brilliance from the theater. Nowadays, live-performance recordings are the rule rather than the exception. Technology has improved, and (more important) the price of renting studios has increased to the point where a studio recording is almost a rarity. However, it is a general rule that live recordings made before about 1970 were only a good buy for people devoted to the singers represented. At least one exception must be made—Callas's recording of Lucia from Berlin, made in 1955, with Giuseppe di Stefano as the hero and Karajan conducting. Karajan must be given credit for taking this opera seriously at a time when most thought of it as fluff, and he respects the score as if it were a lost Wagner manuscript. Di Stefano gives what is possibly the best performance of his brief, uneven, but often brilliant career. Nowhere is the legendary tone, perhaps the finest of any Italian tenor, as gorgeous as here. If you ever wondered what all the fuss was about Callas, this recording would explain it all. While many sopranos have sung Lucia's famous Mad Scene, with its brilliant coluratura, high notes, and roulades, as a sort of pretty parlor piece, Callas actually *goes mad* in it. But this recording explains more than Callas's reputation. It demonstrates what emotional power lurks just behind all the prettiness, musicianship, and technique. It is actually a lesson on how Italian opera works.

Macbeth, Giuseppe Verdi; conductor, Claudio Abbado; Piero Cappuccilli, Shirley Verrett, Plácido Domingo, Nicolai Ghiaurov; Orchestra and Chorus of La Scala (Deutsche Grammophon The Originals): In many ways Verdi's most unusual opera, *Macbeth* requires brains as well as musicianship to bring it off. The lead role, a baritone, must create sympathy with his voice alone, while the diva role of his Lady, sung by both mezzos and sopranos, is uniquely demented. Abbado's 1975 recording, (a studio recording made in conjunction with a now legendary production by Giorgio Strehler), with Piero Cappuccilli and Shirley Verrett in the leads is almost flawless and often thrilling. The La Scala chorus alone would make this recording worth owning.

Madame Butterfly, Giacomo Puccini; conductor, Sir John Barbirolli; Renata Scotto, Carlo Bergonzi, Anna di Stasio, Rolando Panerai, Piero di Palma; Orchestra and Chorus of the Rome Opera (EMI Classics): Renata Scotto recorded the challenging role of Puccini's most beguiling heroine at the perfect point in her career in the mid-1960s. The voice was sure, and the drama flows through the speakers. Scotto means every single word she sings, no mean accomplishment in opera, and grows audibly from naïve girl to tempestuous woman in the course of the work. She is well supported by Bergonzi as Pinkerton, one of Italian opera's few evil tenors, and Sir John Barbirolli conducting.

Manon, Jules Massenet; conductor, Julius Rudel; Beverly Sills, Nicolai Gedda, Gerard Souzay, Gabriel Bacquier; New Philharmonia Orchestra and Chorus (EMI Studio): Sills beautifully mines the full range of this most adored of French heroines, from flighty young girl to passionate temptress to tragic victim, in her most celebrated role. Her recording with a brilliant Nicolai Gedda, was unavailable for many years, and bootleg copies were traded among aficionados like Grateful Dead concert tapes. It is now commercially available and everyone who loves lyric theater should own it.

Mefistofele, Arrigo Boito; conductor, Julius Rudel; Norman Treigle, Montserrat Caballé, Plácido Domingo. London Symphony Orchestra and Chorus (EMI Classics): This is an opera that disappears from the boards periodically, only to be "rediscovered" every few years amidst great acclaim. It requires an extremely charismatic bass in the lead role as the Devil himself, and he must be, by turns, urbane, sarcastic, terrifying, and even sexy. While we can imagine what Chaliapin accomplished, and while we have more recently enjoyed Ramey in the role, Norman Treigle simply blew audiences away in the part through the early seventies. His recording remains a must. Caballé and Domingo combine ardor and lyricism in their supporting roles, and Rudel commands the all-important choruses. The lush score, once a target of derision among respectable musicians, now has an immediate appeal for people who enjoy intensity and emotional forthrightness in their entertainment.

Norma, Vicenzo Bellini; conductor, Sir Richard Bonynge; Joan Sutherland, Marilyn Horne, John Alexander, Richard Cross, Yvonne Minton; London Symphony Orchestra and Chorus (London/Decca Grand Opera Series): Sutherland's talents shine in this excellent portrayal of the role that has been called "the ultimate woman in opera." It is almost inconceivable that a human voice can be so powerful and yet so agile. Her recording with Marilyn Horne in the important mezzo role is a revelation.

Their duets are epochal. Put this on your stereo and be prepared to be floored by the power of two women singing in perfect unison.

Le nozze di Figaro (The Marriage of Figaro), Wolfgang Amadeus Mozart; conductor, Carlo Maria Giulini; Giuseppe Taddei, Anna Moffo, Eberhard Wächter, Elisabeth Schwarzkopf, Fiorenza Cossotto, Dora Gatta, Ivo Vinco, Renato Ercolani, Piero Cappuccilli; Philharmonia Orchestra and Chorus (London Classics): This early 1960s recording has both musicality and a certain comic frothiness that keep it fresh, even considered among its many later competitors. Taddei brings his command of the Italian comic opera tradition, while Wächter and Schwarzkopf are somewhat more intellectual in the German manner. In fact, this recording succeeds largely because of its combination of Italian and German elements, which is appropriate for this opera that can be seen in either light. Giulini's inherent elegance binds the various strands into a single refined whole.

Otello, Giuseppe Verdi; conductor, James Levine; Plácido Domingo, Renata Scotto, Sherrill Milnes, Paul Plishka; National Philharmonic Orchestra and Chorus, London (RCA Victor Red Label): Levine's early 1980 recording with Domingo is perhaps the best all-round recording of the opera, although Domingo continued to refine the role on stage. Still, the voice was at its most powerful when this recording was made, and his ability to blend with Milnes is uncanny. In the famous "Oath Duet," it is difficult to discern who is singing which line. Scotto has her usual blend of beautiful and unpleasant sounds, but her interpretation is beyond reproach. She approaches her final solo, quite rightly, as a Mad Scene, and the effect is of hearing someone who is already dead in some sense.

Parsifal, Richard Wagner; conductor, James Levine; Plácido Domingo, Jessye Norman, James Morris, Kurt Moll, Jan-Hendrik Rootering, Ekkehard Wlaschiha, Allan Glassman, Julien Robbins, Heidi Grant Murphy, Jane Bunnell, Paul Groves, Anthony Laciura.; Metropolitan Opera Orchestra and Chorus (Deutsche Grammophon): Domingo brought a new humanity to the sometimes hard to fathom lead role. His recording with Levine and the Met forces made many purists cringe, but it is a good entry into the unique world of Wagner's most transcendental work. Jessye Norman is appropriately enigmatic and even occasionally frightening as Kundry. Bass Kurt Moll is brilliant, making his long solos actually exciting. Levine gives one of his best performances ever conducting the Met orchestra. All the smaller roles are sung with great care and depth. The sound, an all-important consideration in this work wherein echoes and silences are part of the experience, is extraordinary. The echoing of the bells in act III alone demonstrates the care that went into this recording.

Peter Grimes, Benjamin Britten; conductor, Sir Colin Davis; Jon Vickers, Heather Harper, Jonathan Summers, Elisabeth Bainbridge, Teresa Cahill, Thomas Allen; Orchestra and Chorus of the Royal Opera, Covent Garden (Philips Duo): No English opera has had the same staying power and wide popular appeal as this dark psychological fable set in an oppressive fishing village. While Britten wrote the role for a specific counter tenor type of voice, the heroic tenor Jon Vickers demonstrated the universality of the role with his magnificent portrayal. It became his signature role, and the grandeur of his performance as a force of nature elementally at odds with his surroundings was well captured on this recording. The important smaller roles are all intelligently and passionately sung, and the chorus is magnificent.

Porgy and Bess, George Gershwin; conductor, John DeMain; Donnie-Ray Albert, Betty Lane, Larry Marshall, Wilma Shakesnider, Andrew Smith, Carol Brice, Alexander B. Smalls, Clamma Dale, Myra Merritt, Bernard Thacker, Mervin Wallace, Glover Parham, Raymond Bazemore, Shirley Baines, Phyllis

Bash, Mace, Hartwell, Richie, Cornel, Alex-Cole, Steven, Alex-Cole, Steven, Barry, Kenneth, Rowe, Hansford, Gammon, William, Ross, John B., Carrington, Alex, Hyman, Dick (RCA Victor Red Seal): Probably the greatest American opera, *Porgy* is notoriously difficult and famously uneven, presenting unique challenges to those who would take it on. In 1975, the Houston Grand Opera mounted a production widely toured around, and audiences responded rapturously. That production is well represented by their recording under conductor John DeMain. Opting for ensemble work over big-name stars proved a good choice, emphasizing the coherence of the work rather than a series of highlights, and people have never been able to speak quite as condescendingly about this thrilling opera since this recording was released.

Der Ring des Nibelungen, Richard Wagner. *Das Rheingold;* conductor, Sir Georg Solti; Vienna Philharmonic Orchestra; George London, Kirsten Flagstad, Claire Watson, Set Svanholm, Waldemar Kmentt, Eberhard Wächter, Paul Kuen, Jean Madeira, Gustav Neidlinger, Walter Kreppel, Kurt Bohme, Oda Balsborg, Hetty Plumacher, Ira Malanuik (London/Decca). *Die Walküre;* conductor, Sir Georg Solti; Vienna Philharmonic Orchestra; James King, Regine Crespin, Gottlob Frick, Hans Hotter, Birgit Nilsson, Christa Ludwig, Brigitte Fassbaender, Helga Dernesch, Berit Lindholm, Vera Schlosser, Vera Little, Helen Watts, Claudia Hellmann, Marilyn Tyler (London/Decca). *Siegfried;* conductor, Sir Georg Solti; Vienna Philharmonic Orchestra; Wolfgang Windgassen, Birgit Nilsson, Hans Hotter, Gerhard Stolze, Gustav Neidlinger, Kurt Bohme, Marga Hoffgen, Dame Joan Sutherland (London/Decca): *Götterdämmerung;* conductor, Sir Georg Solti; Vienna Philharmonic Orchestra; Wolfgang Windgassen, Birgit Nilsson, Christa Ludwig, Dietrich Fischer-Dieskau, Claire Watson, Gustav Neidlinger, Gottlob Frick, Helen Watts, Grace Hoffman, Anita Valkki, Lucia Popp, Dame Gwyneth Jones, Maureen Guy. Vienna State Opera Chorus (London/Decca): While it is admittedly cheating to list a four-set fifteen-CD collection as a single recording, Wagner's *Ring* is a single coherent work and must be approached as such. Obviously, one can start a pretty severe argument around opera people by asking which is the best *Ring* to buy, and opinions run strong on the subject. Bear in mind that all available recordings of the *Ring* are at least good. There's no way an outright lousy *Ring* can make it to the store shelves. One thing everyone can agree on is that the first complete recording of the *Ring* remains impressive, and no one would be ashamed to own it. It was made under the baton of Sir Georg Solti with a cast of stars reading like a *Who's Who* of the opera world during one of its most glorious periods in the late 1950s. Dame Joan Sutherland in the brief role of the Forest Bird in *Siegfried* is but one example of the luxuriousness of the casting. The greatness of the singers is underscored by the fact that Solti managed to imbue them each a sense of the dramatic issues at stake, and the singers actually act with their voices. There is even a book written about this epic project of recording the works, *Ring Resounding*, by producer John Culshaw (originally published in 1968, Viking, new edition 1987). *Ring Resounding* is currently out of print but easy to track down on the Internet and in some specialty book stores. It is full of interesting anecdotes and gives a good idea of the pressures involved in the task. You will want to sample several *Rings* before you buy one, but you will never regret owning this classic.

Der Rosenkavalier, Richard Strauss; conductor, Herbert von Karajan; Elisabeth Schwarzkopf, Christa Ludwig, Teresa Stich-Randall, Otto Edelmann, Eberhard Wächter, Ljuba Welitsch, Paul Kuen, Kirsten Meyer, Nicolai Gedda; Philharmonia Orchestra and Chorus (EMI): The definitive recording of this masterpiece of Viennese melancholy remains Karajan's, originally made in 1957. Schwarzkopf communicates elegance, intelligence, and humanity with every measure. Her performance is a revelation. She hovers on the verge of bitterness, but by sheer self-will, remains gracious. Even the smallest roles are well cast, and the complex ensembles make sense. Karajan's mastery of the score is apparent. The emotional range of the music, from witty to bumptious to profound, will be clear to any listener.

Salome, Richard Strauss; conductor, Sir Georg Solti; Birgit Nilsson, Gerhard Stolze, Grace Hoffmann, Eberhard Wächter, Waldemar Kmentt, Josephine Veasey, Paul Kuen, Stefan Schwer, Kurt Equiluz, Aron Gestner, Max Proebstl, Tom Krause; Vienna Philharmonic Orchestra (London/Decca): Birgit Nilsson channels nature itself in her portrayal of Oscar Wilde's demented nymphet, while the late Sir Georg Solti moves the orchestra from a sly, chamberlike quality to a thunderous tumult in the mere hour and twenty minutes of Strauss's disturbing masterpiece. The cover alone of this 1964 recording ought to scare the average, well-adjusted person.

Satyagraha, Philip Glass; conductor, Christopher Keene; Scott Reeve, Douglas Perry, Claudia Cummings, Rhonda Liss, Robert McFarland, Sheryl Woods; New York City Opera Orchestra and Chorus (CBS Masterworks): People remain strongly, even vehemently, divided about Philip Glass's work, and many good musicians frankly resent this composer's success with the public. Yet Glass can create an excellent and uniquely encompassing aural sound, and in his better works he can transcend mere ambient attractiveness and achieve dramatic tension as well. Although some of his more recent work has revealed a solid composing technique for the solo voice, his choral work has always been popular. Nowhere does it sound better than on this recording of the work *Satyagraha,* a meditation on the possibility of nonviolence as a spiritual and political goal. Christopher Keene, a rising conductor, leads the New York City Opera forces (always champions of Glass's works) in a surprisingly well-balanced performance. The finale sweeps the listener into a torrent of irresistible sound. The better your stereo system, the more you will enjoy this lush recording.

Tosca, Giacomo Puccini; conductor, Victor de Sabata: Maria Callas, Giuseppe di Stefano, Tito Gobbi; Orchestra and Chorus of La Scala (EMI Classics): It is impossible to have no reaction to Maria Callas, and Tosca was perhaps her definitive role. Buy this La Scala studio recording from 1953, conducted by De Sabata. Tenor di Stefano is in great form (and there are no voices more beautiful than his when he was "on," which was not always), and baritone Tito Gobbi conveys all the excitement he and Callas generated on stage. You may become a Callas-maniac after hearing this, or perhaps a Callas-hater (and there are plenty of both), but it is a phenomenon that must be confronted at some point in your operatic adventures.

La traviata, Giuseppe Verdi; Conductor, Sir Richard Bonynge; Dame Joan Sutherland, Luciano Pavarotti, Mateo Manuguerra, William Elvin, Ubaldo Gardini; National Philharmonic Orchestra and London Opera Chorus (Uni/London Classics): Few women can encompass all the voices needed to sing Verdi's most archetypal heroine, and no one is better than Sutherland. The coloratura alone is a phenomenon. Pavarotti is at his radiant best as Alfredo.

Tristan und Isolde, Richard Wagner; conductor, Herbert von Karajan; Helga Dernesch, Christa Ludwig, Jon Vickers, Walter Berry, Karl Riddersbusch, Bernd Weikl, Peter Schreier, Martin Vantin; Berlin Philharmonic Orchestra and Chorus (EMI Angel): Jon Vickers considered this recording to be his best ever. Dernesch does not reach the sheer musical heights of the more famous Birgit Nilsson, but her interpretation is magnificent and in many ways does equal justice to this monumental role. Karajan creates unique effects in the orchestra in this score, which is simultaneously Wagner's most cerebral and most sensual. Vickers is magnificent, both musically and dramatically. He actually seems to die in the third act. One critic called Karajan's conducting of the famous Liebestod finale "the soundtrack to *The Joy of Sex.*"

Il trovatore, Giuseppe Verdi; conductor, Herbert von Karajan; Leontyne Price, Franco Corelli, Ettore Bastianini, Giulietta Simionato, Vienna Philharmonic Orchestra and State Opera Chorus (Deutsche Grammophon): One of the most recorded operas of all times, *Trovatore* requires great lead singers and (although few people think about this) a great conductor to bring it all together. This recording has all of the requirements for a great *Trovatore* in abundance. Price ranges from lyric ease to wild whoops, each appropriate for its dramatic moment. Corelli seems to be enjoying the "trapeze act" of the role of Manrico, while Bastianini achieves something very rare: He can sound lyrical and evil at the same time. Simionato is the soul of madness, hitting phrases like she is beating off an imaginary attacker.

Turandot, Giacomo Puccini; conductor, Zubin Mehta; Dame Joan Sutherland, Luciano Pavarotti, Monsterrat Caballé, Nicolai Ghiaurov, Sir Peter Pears, Tom Krause, PierFrancesco Poli, Piero de Palma, Sabin Markov; London Philharmonic Orchestra; the John Alldis Choir (London/Decca): Sutherland was most famous for her bel canto heroines, but her voice was a Niagara of sound, and she is nothing short of awesome in this still-popular early '70s recording. Pavarotti and Caballé are no less impressive. None of these magnificent voices ever sang better than on this recording. Mehta plays the score, alternately brash and sentimental, for full cinematic value.

Vanessa, Samuel Barber; conductor, Dmitri Mitropoulos; Eleanor Steber, Nicolai Gedda, Rosalind Elias, Regina Resnik, Giorgio Tozzi; Metropolitan Opera Orchestra and Chorus (RCA Victor Gold Seal): *Vanessa* is one of the most successful American operas. Perhaps it is not as ubiquitous as it was after its premiere in 1957, but the score still reaches American audiences with its lush frankness. Some find the libretto kitschy, but since when did that stop a good opera? The Metropolitan recording made shortly after the premiere is generally agreed to be a "must have" by a wide variety of opera fans. American soprano Eleanor Steber is definitive in the role, and tenor Nicolai Gedda shows off his astounding diversity. Mezzo Rosalind Elias almost steals the show, and Giorgio Tozzi completes the flawless cast. The recording itself is rather impressive, demonstrating the rich tone and balance that could be achieved even in the supposedly primitive days of mono recording.

Wozzeck, Alban Berg; conductor, Claudio Abbado; Franz Grundheber, Hildegard Behrens, Walter Raffeiner, Philip Langridge, Heinz Zednik, Aage Haugland, Alfred Sramek; Vienna Philharmonic Orchestra and State Opera Chorus, and Vienna Boys Choir. (Deutsche Grammophon): This is a controversial recording since Grundheber and Behrens are vocally challenged by Berg's devilish music, but its clarity makes it a good first choice. Abbado understood that there are lyric as well as dissonant elements in the score, and the incomparable orchestra shimmers under his baton. Whatever the vocal shortcomings, the leads, and Behrens in particular, deliver dramatic conviction.

NINE

The Total Opera Experience

This guidebook has generally been concerned with opera as something to listen to, with just enough information about composers, terminology, and other facets of opera to provide a context for the listener. However, opera is of course much more than a listening experience. Listening to an opera at home, watching a video of a performance, and attending a live opera are actually three different experiences. Ideally, opera is an entirely unique way to experience drama, and therefore depends on what we generically call "production issues" to make it come fully alive.

Perhaps the most daunting autocrats in the opera world today are neither divas nor conductors, but directors. These are the people who decide what we will see on stage, and the designers must execute the directors' ideas. There was a time when there were no directors in opera. Singers comported themselves as they saw fit, and the chorus merely tumbled on or off the stage when they heard their musical cues. This must have been dreadful, seen by our standards, and even many composers were appalled, but audiences took it all in stride. As long as the "conventions" were followed, nobody really much cared. Realism was a late arrival in the theater. Ibsen and Chekhov only appeared later in the nineteenth century. Before them, spoken dramas were probably as stylized in their own way as operas.

Wagner took an inordinate amount of interest in the stage directions of his works. He, like many people today, was alienated by all the conventions that had accrued around opera. Why was it acceptable for a diva to "break character" and bow to applause? Why, in fact, were people even applauding when the music was theoretically trying to create a continuous action? Why did singers stand there striking glamor poses and staring fixedly at the conductor when they were supposedly addressing each other? Were they even listening to the words they were supposedly saying, or were they simply carried away by the sheer beauty of their own voices? Wagner himself rehearsed every gesture of his singers to make sure they were always trying to respond to the situation at hand and not merely being "operatic." He nailed a warning to the wall right off the stage at the Bayreuth Festival House, reminding singers never to look at the audience. Even when alone on stage, he insisted they look up or down but never straight ahead. The warning would not be amiss in the wings of our opera houses even today.

Scenic designers began to make their presence felt in a new way at about the same time. The issue, again, was realism. In the baroque era, scenic directors loved to create optical illusions for operas. The mythological and pseudo-historical nature of most baroque operas allowed scenic directors, such as the famous Bibiena brothers, to create fantastic "mindscapes" of trick perspectives and trompe l'oeil. Multitiered arcades seemed to stretch as far as the eye could see, while feather-capped castrati and divas in battleship-size skirts cavorted among the imaginary colonnades of Greece and Rome. Realism was the last reason anybody attended the opera. The nineteenth century saw a change in taste. The Romantic Era reveled in wild landscapes, spooky Gothic ruins, and idealized peasant homes. The sets may have taken liberties, but whatever was being portrayed was instantly recognizable as whatever it was meant to be.

Innovation came around the turn of the last century, as designers such as Gordon Craig and Adolphe Appia turned to the magic of electric lighting to suggest, rather than represent effects. As the operatic repertory became standardized in the 1920s, directors decided they needed to reinterpret the old warhorses. Some of the productions became classics. Nobody had said much about the psychological dimensions of Jacques Offenbach's *The Tales of Hoffmann* until the adventurous Kroll Opera of Berlin produced it as psychosexual adventure set, if anywhere, in the subconscious.

Directors assumed a more important role after World War II, largely because of the need to confront political issues in opera. The flashpoint was, of course, Wagner, and the most important director was Wagner's grandson Wieland. His triumph in forcing audiences to look anew at Wagner's operas brought him and a generation of directors into the spotlight. Suddenly, every opera director felt it was their duty to reinterpret the great works. Many of these productions have been brilliant, but the trend has led to a sort of iconoclasm for its own sake.

When attending a live opera, it is crucial to remember that you will always be seeing somebody's interpretation of an opera. Critics tend to divide productions into "traditional" and "progressive." They would do better to divide into those that successfully explore the work in question and those that fail. There are plenty of both types in both camps. How is one to discern the production from the opera itself?

One way is to ask whether the opera was enjoyable. Perhaps there were musical problems as well, but if the piece itself seemed mediocre the fault may well lie with the production. One of the advantages of having a standard repertory of operas that are commonly performed everywhere is that we can assume they each have merit. One may please us more than another, but we should be able to see why the opera ever made it to the theater in the first place. Many productions tend to obscure, rather than enhance, the opera itself. The ultimate answer lies in the score itself. By careful listening, one can easily discern whether the stage production is unpacking or smothering the music.

Another issue one must confront in a live opera is the quality of the performers, both as singers and as actors. First of all, live singing almost never reaches the vocal heights heard on studio recordings. Performances in which all the singers were in their best form are legendary. To compensate for this, there is all the excitement of a live voice, faults and all. Watching a person go through the mechanics of producing an extraordinary sound is more interesting and exciting than merely hearing the sound. There are also many problems with opera singers in terms of their physical appearance and their "acting" abilities. Some of these problems are inherent in the art form and must be accepted at face value. Wagner may have wanted his singers to look at each other, but he must have known that much of his music necessitates the singers looking squarely at the conductor so that they don't get utterly lost. It was all very good and well for Richard Strauss to make the fourteen-year-old Salome the subject of an opera, but he wrote music for her that only a woman with several decades of vocal training could even attempt. A film on the same subject could find any number of convincing young women to play the part. To say there are twelve women in the world who can successfully sing the role of Salome is extremely generous. An opera house is not going to quibble over looks and figure if they can land one of these.

Then there is acting. The cliché of the opera singer whose notion of acting is to place the back of the hand against the forehead is old and tired, yet, like many clichés, may have at least a grain of truth. The issue is similar to the case of *Salome*. Actors are many, singers fewer. Some singers are also good actors. Maria Callas, Plácido Domingo, and Teresa Stratas come to mind as opera stars who could have had great film careers had they so chosen. But these are the exceptions.

Performances on Video

Hundreds of performances are now available on video, capturing the excitement (and often the flaws and disappointments) of live theater. Almost all are at least worth a gamble; some are essential viewing. The *Live from the Met* series has contributed dozens of performances to this catalog, and any new opera produced in one of the larger houses is virtually guaranteed a television airing and subsequent video release. Many of the most exciting *Live from the Met* videos feature Plácido Domingo, who comes across well on the small screen. His performance with Renata Scotto in Puccini's *Manon Lescaut* (1981) is legendary, the two leads creating an irresistible energy as the young lovers. Scotto and Domingo triumphed again the following year in Zandonai's rarity *Francesca da Rimini*. The stunning production is helpful in orienting audiences to this still-unfamiliar work, and only Scotto and Domingo had the charisma to pull off such quirky touches as the (unsung) initial meeting of the lovers. Another remarkable performance from the Met is Wagner's *Lohengrin*, (1986). Peter Hoffmann is the radiant Swan Knight, and Eva Marton the doomed Elsa, but the best reason to rent this video is Leonie Rysanek's demented performance as the evil Ortrud. Her invocation of the pagan gods in act II marks one of the few times in recent history when a performance of a Wagner opera was interrupted by applause by a giddy audience. Beyond the Met, a performance of Verdi's *Nabucco* from the Verona Amphitheater in 1984 features the Bulgarian typhoon Ghena Dimitrova as the harpy Abigaille and a suave Renato Bruson in the title role. Watching the concentration of these two magnificent singers is helpful in following the very particular techniques that can still make this opera rock a century and a half after its tumultuous premiere. One video that all fans of Italian opera will agree is a "must-see" is Verdi's *La forza del destino*, recorded in black and white from Naples' Teatro San Carlo in 1958. This performance is so magnificent that one forgives the tacky sets and primitive acting. Renata Tebaldi, Franco Corelli, Ettore Bastianini, Boris Christoff, Oralia Dominguez, and Renato Capecchi are brilliant, and this is the definitive available performance of a romantic Italian opera.

There is another facet to acting in an opera, and here the good listener has an advantage over the mere viewer. The "acting" ideally takes place first in the voice, and later, if at all, in the body. Mozart's *The Marriage of Figaro* provides a splendid example. The neglected countess wonders at the effects time has had on her husband's love for her. In her first line, she sings "Dove sono, i bei momenti?" ("where have all the beautiful moments gone?"). By putting a bit of emotion, such as a slight vibrato, on the word "bei," ("beautiful,") she can convey a great amount of regret and melancholy. In the next verse, she asks "Dove sono, i giuramenti?" ("where are the vows?"). A good soprano will change the tone used to ask this question. Perhaps a sharp attack on the word "giuramenti" ("vows") will let us know that she is seething with anger and resentment at her husband. A stage or film actress might contort her face or use her body to convey the same message. Each uses different methods to give the same information. A soprano does it all with the subtlest modulation of the voice.

It works much the same way for sex. People who are cynical about opera wonder how fans can suspend disbelief so far as to believe that the two clumsy oafs on stage are experiencing something akin to intimacy. The answer lies in the music. A good but fat singer can stand perfectly still but "make love" to someone on stage and even to the audience. Thus the great tenor José Carreras was able to state bluntly that the statuesque Montserrat Caballé was the "sexiest woman in the world" without the slightest flippancy. People who attended performances of Wagner's *Die Walküre* with Peter Hoffmann and Leonie Rysanek in the 1980s still talk about the erotic electricity of the evening. Wagner's opera calls for a love scene that presents endless difficulties; It is between twin brother and sister. Ms. Rysanek was considerably older and tinier than the athletic Mr. Hoffmann, but their voices succeeded in sounding both like twins and like people in the midst of sexual passion. Had they looked alike as well, the scene may have simply been too much to put on stage.

Opera Movies

Throughout the twentieth century, people have commented that this opera or that one would make a great movie. In fact opera only sometimes transfers to film successfully. The inherent realism of cinema is at odds with the surrealism of opera, which relies more on symbolic suggestion than direct representation. Still, some operas have made interesting movies, and, while opera fans may carp about them, no fan would dream of missing one.

Moscow's Bolshoi Opera made a beautiful film of Tchaikovsky's *Eugene Onegin* in 1958, hiring striking actors and dubbing the voices of Galina Vishnevskaya and Tevgeny Kibkalo, among others. The approach is sumptuous realism, and the gorgeous city of St. Petersburg becomes, appropriately, a lead character in the story. The technique of sumptuous realism has been the domain of director Franco Zeffirelli in his several opera films, with varying success. The director is aided by his excellent use of color, landscapes, faces, and ability to coerce good acting out of singers. He also benefits from the prodigious talents of Plácido Domingo, who is the lead in all four of his released opera films. First came Mascagni's *Cavalleria rusticana,* (1982), filmed (beautifully) on location in Sicily. Elena Obrastzova is the demented Santuzza. This was of course followed by Leoncavallo's *I pagliacci* (1982), featuring the remarkable Teresa Stratas as Nedda. Stratas performs the title role of Zeffirelli's most successful opera film, Verdi's *La traviata* (1983). Neither she nor Domingo look like postadolescent lovers, but both are monumental and somehow totally convincing in this gorgeous film. Verdi's *Otello,* (1987), is more problematic, though still worth watching. Domingo's brilliant on-stage portrayal is only partially captured, and while Katia Ricciarelli and baritone Justino Diaz are respectively vulnerable and evil, there is much tinkering with the score to little apparent benefit.

Director Carlo Rossi applied his own version of sumptuous realism to his film of *Carmen*, (1984), starring Domingo and Julia Migenes. Domingo brings depth to the neurotic tenor role, and while Migenes is not of the legendary class of mezzos who have owned the role on stage, she comes closer than most to bringing her alive through apt characterization. Joseph

Losey's interpretation of Mozart's *Don Giovanni* (1978) balances between realism and symbolism. The story is moved to Venice and the Palladian villas of the mainland, where Ruggiero Raimondi is both fiendish and elegant while "stalked" by a ravishing Kiri te Kanawa as Donna Elvira.

Expressionism of one sort or another seems to work best for the German operas that have made their way to film. Götz Friedrich, the longtime general director of the Deutsche Oper Berlin filmed Richard Strauss's psychological nightmare *Elektra* in 1981. His grungy style became mannered on stage after many years, but was right on the money when he made this film, complete with a black-and-white set and cascades of flowing blood. Leonie Rysanek, Astrid Varnay, Caterina Ligendza, and Dietrich Fischer-Dieskau hold back nothing in this 117 minutes of pure angst. Controversial director Hans Jürgen Syberberg confused everybody with his film of Wagner's *Parsifal*, (1982). The lead character changes sex periodically, while Kundry rides a carrousel horse. Interesting, but at over four hours length, not for the faint at heart. Perhaps the most enduringly popular opera film remains Ingmar Bergman's rendition of Mozart's *Magic Flute*, (1975). Bergman opts to indulge in, rather than avoid, the "staginess" of opera, and his wonderfully creative interpretation reads like a magic puppet show. Baritone Hakan Hagegard, a much underrated actor, is excellent as the "queer birdman" Papageno. One imagines that Mozart would have been delighted.

So one must listen, first and foremost, in order to cull the pleasures of opera, even at a live performance. All this begs the question of why anyone would stage opera at all? Why not just perform it in a concert format. There is no logical answer to this, except that experience shows it is not as satisfying. To be sure, unstaged concert performances occur frequently, especially with the more obscure operas and those whose stories are considered too absurd even for the operatic stage. They can be thrilling and very satisfying in their own way, and they are especially good for displaying a singer's unique vocal attributes. Yet there is something missing as well. Wagner's notion of the "Total Work of Art" has something to it after all. The magic of visual presentation can enhance an opera rather than detract from it. However, and this is a point that many directors and designers miss, the music must always come first, or there is little point to any visual magic. Perhaps the best reason to stage an opera is that it might have an effect on the singers and inspire them to forget themselves in some sense while they interpret their characters.

There are a great many varieties of live opera experiences and venues. All have advantages and disadvantages. Attending a live opera can mean anything from a "gala benefit" at the Metropolitan in New York, complete with television cameras out front and a bevy of real or self-appointed celebrities, to picnic baskets and overalls at Wolf Trap in Vienna, Virginia. Opening night of the San Francisco Opera is almost a civic holiday, and the carnival atmosphere includes everything from white tie to costumes. Informality is the general rule at smaller theaters, and colleges and universities offer opera programs that allow the audience to experience a terrific intimacy with the singers. In any venue, the work given may be in any number of languages, including English. It may be brand-new or four hundred years old. It might be performed with a piano and a few other instruments, or with a full symphony orchestra, or with any combination of instruments, including the electrical and the synthesized. It might involve cutting-edge video installations, velvet gowns, or T-shirts and jeans. It may be about heroes of antiquity, the gods in heaven, psychological symbols, or the people next door. Opera may be a full and rich art form, but it is not a monolithic one.

The total experience of opera depends on the combined talents of many people, but we in the audience have a responsibility as well. We should assume the piece in question has some validity, since so many professional people have put so much effort into it. We may decide otherwise later on, but this is a good mindset for approaching a work. We should listen as carefully as we can, resisting the temptation to pay half-attention while waiting for something spectacular, if not very substantial, to catch our attention. We should remember that a singer may be trying to sing a phrase in a new way and judge whether he or she has accomplished this, rather than assume they are simply not as good as those we have heard on recordings (true though that may be). We should watch the onstage proceedings with an eye toward what they are attempting to say and how well they are saying it, rather than reacting immediately in either a positive or a negative way.

These are the attitudes that make opera a unique experience, one that forms a continuum from listening to music at home to the generally interesting and occasionally glorious evening of live art.

TEN

The Language of Opera

For many people, one of the main barriers to approaching the field of opera is the arcane vocabulary employed by its devotees. Besides technical terms referring to musical techniques, which tend to be in Italian, there are a host of descriptive terms that can be culled from several languages. It can be quite a problem.

The root of the problem is that language can only approximate musical meanings, and we must rely on tradition to tell us what is meant by such terms as piano, forte, and crescendo. Once enough people have understood these words, it would be absurd to try to translate them into English for the sake of appearances. All art forms have their own vocabulary, and opera is an extravagant world that has always thrived on a certain internationalism. Even a passing knowledge of opera's unique lexicon can do much to demystify this world.

Alto: (It., "high" and also "deep") One of the more confusing terms in opera. The primary meaning in opera is a woman with a low voice, below mezzo-soprano. Some say this comes from the tradition of boys' choirs in church music, where the low-voiced boys sing in roughly the same range as low-voiced grown women. Others see "alto" as a shortened version of "contralto," meaning the "opposite" or "counter of high voice." (In Italian, words often mean their own opposite, a confusing holdover from the Latin language, and actually alto can mean both "high" and "deep." Thus the Rialto, or Rio Alto, in Venice is said to refer to both the "high shore" and the "deep river" that mark the spot.) For operatic purposes, there is no true difference between an alto and a contralto. There are also some scores that call for boys' choirs (e.g., Wagner's *Parsifal*), in which case alto refers to the lower-voiced boys.

Aria: (It., "air") A solo vocal piece. It is usually set apart from the preceding and following music and can easily be sung out of context, as at a concert.

Baritone: The male singer of the middle range, above bass and below tenor. The word derives from an Old Italian term meaning "the sound of a man," and indeed the baritone voice is thought to be the most "normal" of the male registers. While there are some baritone heroes in opera, the vast majority of them are either the hero's best friend or the bad guy.

Baroque: (from Portuguese, "lumpy pearl") Scholars use the term baroque to apply to art and culture in Europe from the late sixteenth century until about 1740 at the latest. In common usage, it tends to be used for everything between the Renaissance and the French Revolution, roughly. There is no specific definition. In opera, it tends to refer for everything before Mozart (whose works are impossible to categorize).

Bass: The male singer with lowest range (and also used for low instruments, such as a bass trombone). Many men can hit low notes, but few can project them into the audience. Consequently, there used to be many different subdivisions of bass, including *buffo* (comic), *cantante* (lyric), and *profondo* (deep). These days, most basses insist on trying all varieties of roles. Religious authority figures are very often basses, as are dottering old men, very wicked intriguers, and an occasional voice from the grave.

Bass baritone: In theory, a bass baritone can sing anything in either the baritone or the bass range. It is an authoritative sound. Famous lead roles in this category include Mozart's Don Giovanni and Wagner's Flying Dutchman.

Bel canto: (It., "beautiful singing") Generally used to refer to specific style of opera popular in Italy from about 1810 until about 1850.

Cabaletta: A fiery aria that closes a scene. In baroque and bel canto opera, the cabaletta is often preceded by a slow aria, a cavatina. Both Verdi and Wagner thought the cabaletta was too formulaic, and both sought to transcend the tradition. The word itself is of unknown origin. Some think it derives from *cavallo* (It., "horse"), a highly descriptive etymology for this "galloping" sort of music.

Castrato: (It., "castrated") A male singer who was surgically altered as a boy to prevent the change of voice that accompanies puberty. The practice, usually involving a cut of the duct leading out of the testicles rather than actual removal of the testicles, grew in Italy in the seventeenth century and began to disappear before the end of the eighteenth century. There were a few castrati (pl.) in the nineteenth century, and the last of the castrati died as recently as 1922. They were also known as *evirati* ("unmanned ones").

Cavatina: A slow aria. Officially, a cavatina must be followed by a cabaletta, or else it is called in "romanza." There is, however, much fluidity in the use of these terms.

Chamber opera: Operas that are small in scale, requiring fewer instrumentalists, and theoretically ideal for smaller venues. The Baroque Era produced hundreds of operas that are said to be chamber operas. The term is used loosely, though, and many other operas are categorized as such. Richard Strauss's *Ariadne auf Naxos* is often called a chamber opera because of its small orchestra (thirty-six) and its Baroque ambience, yet it is performed at the large houses and requires voices with major heft.

Cognoscenti: (It., "those who know") The know-it-alls. The singular is cognoscente, although few cognoscenti would know this.

Coloratura: (from German Koluratur, "coloration") The agile use of many rapid notes in a scale. The word is often wrongly assumed to be Italian (although the Italian word for this is *fioritura*). Coloratura was used heavily from the Baroque period through the mid-nineteenth century, but its use has never disappeared altogether.

Commedia dell'arte: Although this term simply means "professional acting" in Italian, it has come to signify a specific, stylized form of improvisational comedy popular in Italy since the Renaissance. Harlequin and Columbine are among the stock characters used by commedia dell'arte troupes, and "Punch and Judy" shows are English relatives of the Italian archetypes. Commedia dell'arte had a great influence on the development of the opera buffa, and therefore on all subsequent opera. Pergolesi's *La serva padrona* and Rossini's *Barber of Seville* are only two of the comic operas that have been analyzed as extended versions of commedia dell'arte. For the last hundred years or so, many artists have been deeply interested in the tradition, as evidenced in the paintings of Picasso. In opera, commedia dell'arte elements have appeared in the works of Puccini (*Turandot*), Poulenc (*Les Mamelles de Tirésias*), and Korngold (*Die tote Stadt*), among many others, while Richard Strauss's *Ariadne auf Naxos* and Leoncavallo's *I pagliacci* tell the stories (in very different ways) of itinerant commedia dell'arte players.

Concertato: (It., "concerted") An elaborate ensemble with four or more vocal solos and chorus, usually used to end an act or a scene. Bel canto opera made generous use of the concertato, also known as pezzo concertato. Famous examples include the popular sextet from Donizetti's *Lucia di Lamermoor* and the finale to the third act of Verdi's *La traviata*. Reformers in the mid-nineteenth century found the device too formal and insufficiently natural. Even Rossini called the structure "the row of artichokes," referring to the lead singers standing at the footlights and caroling away without a thought to the dramatic situation. Yet there was something extremely satisfying about the form, however formulaic and unnatural it may be. Even Verdi, who also declared himself tired of the idea, used it again with great effect in his late masterpiece *Otello*.

Contralto: (It., "low") The lowest female voice, usually assigned to a scary or mysterious type of character such as Erda, the Earth Mother, in Wagner's *Ring of the Nibelung* or La Cieca, the blind woman, in Ponchielli's *La gioconda*.

Countertenor: A male singer with an ability to sing very high, but not quite the same as a falsettist. A good countertenor is rare, and a bad one is an assault on the ears. Most countertenors specialize in roles originally written for castrati, although some twentieth-century composers (most notably Benjamin Britten) have written new music for this voice.

Crescendo: (It., "growing," like the "crescent" moon) Getting louder. It can refer to a single phrase of music or a much larger segment of a score. It is possible to call the entire first act of Wagner's *Die Walküre*, for example, a single crescendo.

Diminuendo: (It., "diminishing") A musical direction, instructing a musician to go from loud to quiet. While this is a simple matter of applying less bow pressure for a violinist, it is difficult to do this elegantly with wind and brass instruments, and notoriously difficult to do well with the voice. The title character of Verdi's *Aida* has a notable moment of diminuendo when she must proceed from loud and exclamatory to quiet and introspective in two beats, changing the mood of the entire enormous Triumphal Scene with this single technique.

Dramatic: For operatic purposes, dramatic refers to a type of voice, one that is capable of great heft, volume, and tone. German operas are said (often erroneously) to require dramatic rather than lyric voices.

Diva: (It., "goddess") An honorific originally used (and subsequently much overused) for the most popular female singers. Calling someone who is not a singer a diva is not considered a compliment.

Falsetto: The "hooty" head voice men can produce above their normal range. Singing in the falsetto voice on the operatic stage will get you booed off the stage and run right out of town if it is detected as such by the audience. There are some moments in opera when the falsetto is required for comic effect, such as in Verdi's *Falstaff* and Puccini's *La bohème*.

Festival: Wagner began the whole "festival" craze in opera at Bayrueth in 1876. His notion was that his epic *Ring of the Nibelung* would be an actual communal ritual celebrating art and community, such as he imagined the ancient Athenian drama festivals. Since then, almost any two operas strung together outside of the regular season are called a festival. Some have become quite large and live up to the name, usually including activities outside the opera house (they tend to be in the summer) in a vacation atmosphere. These include Glyndebourne in England, Salzburg in Austria, Orange in France, Pesaro in Italy, Savonlinna in Finland, White Nights in St. Petersburg, Russia, and Tanglewood, Glimmerglass, Wolf Trap, Santa Fe, and Spoleto (Charleston) in America.

Forte, Fortissimo: (It., literally "strong" and "very strong") Musical directions calling for increased volume.

Gala: In the old days, a singer went to a particular city, sang a role for a few weeks, and moved on to another. If the singer proved very popular, he or she was given a gala, which was a personal benefit concert to augment salary. Today, the term is used widely, too widely perhaps, in the opera house and everywhere else. It usually refers to any performance whose ticket prices have been raised above the normal.

Gesamtkunstwerk: (Ger., "Total Work of Art") A term devised by Wagner to describe his hopes of a new style of opera that would represent the best in drama, poetry, music, dance, and production.

Grand scena: (It., "Big scene") This term has a very specific meaning in Baroque and bel canto opera. A character will enter, establish his or her position with some recitative, and sing a cavatina reflecting on the situation. After an abrupt change of situation (traditionally, a messenger delivering news and then making a hasty exit), the character will decide on a course of action, expressed in a cabaletta. Although the formula sounds restrictive, it is actually a marvelous way to demonstrate dramatic and vocal diversity, and a good grand scena is quite satisfying.

Intermezzo: (It., "in the middle") This can refer to almost anything that is "in the middle" of a larger work. Usually, it stands for a longish orchestral passage in the middle of an opera, rather than at the beginning of an act. The *verismo* operas made great use of this technique, most notably in the famous intermezzo from Mascagni's *Cavalleria rusticana*. In Baroque opera, the intermezzo was an entirely separate entertainment given between acts of a longer opera seria. Some of these intermezzi (pl.) were ballets or comic plays, but most traditionally they were comic operas written in a lighter vein than the evening's main at-traction. The same composer often wrote both. Pergolesi's *Il prigionero superbo* (1733) is now forgotten, but the "trivial" intermezzo he composed for the evening, *La serva padrona*, be-came hugely popular and is still performed.

Legato: (It., "bound together") A musical direction for voices and instruments, meaning notes should flow from one to another without a discernible break. Its opposite is staccato.

Libretto: (It., "little book") The written text of an opera. In the days before electric lighting, audiences outside of Italy were able to enjoy operas in Italian by following along with their libretti, (pl., also librettos) that is, reading the text in Italian and their own language during the course of the opera. Today, libretti are sold for those who want to read them outside of the opera house, but most in the audience today rely on in-house translations projected above the stage or somewhere else. Most people consider few libretti worthy of independent reading, but in fact they are the key to all the great operas. While their language is often famously stilted and their dramatic situations incredible, they also contain many subtleties, believe it or not. Often, one can find the answers to musical questions in the libretti. One who writes librettos is a librettist.

Leimotiv: (Ger., "leading motive") A much-abused term often used when discussing the works of Wagner (who, in fact, never used the word). A leimotiv is a musical theme associated with a character, action, or object that can be used again, either in its original or an evolved form later in the score.

Longueurs: (Fr., "the long" [times]) The boring parts. Most ope-ras have at least a few.

Lyric: This word is bandied about a great deal at the opera, even though it doesn't have much inherent meaning. To call a score lyric is to say it is easier on the ear than a harsher piece of music. Thus Wagner's *Lohengrin* is said to be more lyric than, say, Berg's *Wozzeck* (although someone somewhere would surely argue this). For voices, it connotes a pleasant tone and agility. Voice fans divide singers into lyric, spinto, and dramatic, in ascending order of strength, although there is much room for debate within each category and all opera singers, confusingly enough, are expected to sing "lyrically."

Mezza voce: (It., "half-voice") The exact meaning of this term is vague and the source of endless debate among opera people. It indicates singing at half-voice, in terms of strength. But singers insist it requires more actual physical strength than the full-voiced singing required of most operas. When it is used well, the effect is relaxing and dreamy, but singers who do it poorly are accused of "crooning" or "fudging."

Mezzo-soprano: A woman who sings in the lower-middle range, below a soprano and above a contralto. "Good girls" are rarely mezzos, although there are exceptions. Rossini was graced with very talented mezzos among his singers, and wrote lead roles for them. Mezzos make great "bad girls," however, as the French have continuously discovered in such operas as Bizet's *Carmen* and Saint-Saëns's *Samson et Dalilah*.

Orchestra: The group of instrumentalists who provide the non-vocal music of the evening. An opera orchestra can vary widely in terms of size and content. Cimarosa's *Il matrimonio segreto* (1791) can be successfully performed with a dozen instrumentalists, while Richard Strauss's *Elektra* requires over one hundred. The opera orchestra has grown steadily from Beethoven's day to our own. In addition to the standard symphony orchestra, operas often require unusual instrumentation. One might find a piano (e.g., Richard Strauss's *Ariadne auf Naxos*), an organ (e.g., Ferruccio Busoni's *Doktor Faust*), a guitar, (e.g., Rossini's *Barber of Seville* and Verdi's *Falstaff*), a harmonium (e.g.,

Strauss's *Salome*), and no end of unusual, and expensive, horns. Before Wagner's day, the orchestra played in front of the stage on the same level as the part of the audience that was not in boxes or balconies. This floor, then, is also called the orchestra in American theaters. Wagner insisted on sinking the musicians below the sight level of the audience in a pit, which is the name American theaters give to that sunken level where the musicians play. Confusingly enough, British theaters call the seating area the "pit" while the orchestra refers only to the place where the musicians sit.

Ornamentation: The extra stylization, not written in the score, that singers use to decorate a vocal line. Baroque opera composers expected singers to ornament freely, using whatever techniques they could muster. Contemporary composers prefer to write very exact instructions for singers and leave little to their choice. For the many operas written between the Baroque and Modern eras, there is much debate about what is the proper amount of ornamentation to add, and opera people are never entirely satisfied. The techniques of ornamentation include trills, *appoggiature* (little tiny notes sung around bigger notes to create a miniature trill), *rubato* (taking liberties with the time value of notes for emotional effect), and interpolated high notes.

Overture: (from the French *ouverture*, "opening") The orchestral introduction to an opera. In the concert hall, an overture can refer to any piece of music that is "about" something, such as Tchaikovsky's *1812 Overture*. Occasionally, the two meanings of the word can overlap. Beethoven's *Leonora Overture #3* is usually performed in the middle of the second act of the opera *Fidelio*.

Pants role: A male character sung by a woman, also called *en travesti* (French for "cross-dressed"). Gender has always been remarkably fluid in opera, perhaps because so much of opera explores character beneath the surface appearance. Many of the famous pants roles are written for mezzo soprano, and the character in question is supposed to be a young man or even a boy. Cherubino in Mozart's *Marriage of Figaro*, Oktavian in Richard Strauss's *Der Rosenkavalier*, and Romeo in Bellini's *I Capuletti ed I Montecchi* are all, paradoxically, young men with bustling hormones, sung by mezzos. Some pants roles were originally heroic characters written for castrati and now often (but not always) given to mezzos, such as the title roles of Gluck's *Orfeo* and Handel's *Julius Caesar*. Prince Orlofsky in Johann Strauss, Jr.'s *Die Fledermaus* is neither young nor amorous, but a mezzo in the role adds to the comedy of the great operetta. Verdi used a high, lyric, coloratura soprano, rather than a mezzo, for the role of Oscar the pageboy in *Un ballo in maschera*. In Spain, audiences have always had a difficult time with the idea of women acting as men. People are often surprised to read that José Carreras's debut role at the Teatro Liceu in Barcelona was Siebel in Gounod's *Faust*, which is sung everywhere else by mezzos.

Passaggio: (It., "passage") The break between a singer's "natural" vocal range and his or her "upper" range (which can be produced with a bit more effort). As this "narrows," the vocal cords can constrict easily and the sound can choke. This in-between area is called the passaggio. While it exists in all ranges, it is particularly noticeable in tenors, for whom the passaggio tends to be found around the E, F, and F sharp below high C (with some variation between individual singers). The best composers know how to write music for the passaggio, since notes sung in this range have an inherently emotional sound when produced by intelligent singers.

Piano, Pianissimo: (It., "soft, very soft") Musical directions, the opposites of forte and fortissimo. While orchestras have learned the art of playing music softly, it is notoriously difficult to sing well in this dynamic. The tenor voice, especially, tends to get lost when not produced with some heft. Sopranos are expected to be able to produce beautiful sounds in a piano voice, but they are aided by the nature of the female voice, which tends to float through other sounds without being pushed.

Pit: *See* Orchestra.

Pitch: The tonal value of a sound. There are two ways of measuring pitch. The first is to use any number of instruments that actually count the number of vibrations per second, or the "frequency." The second method is to rely on the opinion of supposed experts who claim to be able to discern pitch with their ears. Some singers are said to have "perfect pitch," the ability to reproduce any note at will without help from an instrument at exactly the right frequency. Others are commonly said to have pitch problems, singing just below (bad) or just above (worse) the desired note. Actually, pitch itself is a problem, and musicians of the world have had trouble agreeing on the same frequencies for centuries. For the last fifty years, international agreements, concluded with all the solemnity of peace treaties, have tried to fix the value of A just above middle C (the first note you hear when an orchestra tunes up) at 440. This means a tuning fork would vibrate back and forth 440 times in a second. Some nations have held out against this agreement, while others (especially the United States) are constantly accused of cheating. This consists of raising the pitch ever so slightly to create a more brilliant sound. In fact, pitch has crept up over the last two hundred years, which is one explanation (and a convincing one) for the dearth of high-voiced singers today.

Prelude: An orchestral introduction to an opera or an act of an opera. There is very little technical difference between a prelude to an opera and an overture, but tradition has assigned two different meanings. Overtures tend to be composed of melodies that will be heard in the course of the opera, while a prelude may have entirely separate material. Also, a prelude, theoretically, leads directly into the action while an overture is a discrete piece that may be performed in the concert hall without alterations. Of course, there is much gray zone. Wagner preferred to say prelude for his orchestral introductions simply because it sounded less conventionally operatic, and he was always eager to underscore his own remoteness from traditional opera. Thus his *Tristan und Isolde* and *Die Meistersinger von Nürnberg* are said to have preludes even though we will certainly hear the themes again. Ultimately, one must merely memorize which are which, like irregular verbs.

Prompter: People are often amazed that opera singers can remember so much music and so many details. While this is impressive, we should know that they usually have help in the form of a prompter, someone who stands under the stage with his or her head just barely poking through the floorboards and covered with a small canopy. The prompter gives cues (hand gestures) and sometimes much more, including humming notes and shouting actual words. Often, these can be heard from the audience and are quite distracting, yet seasoned opera goers accept it as a necessary evil.

Recitative: The "speech" parts of the opera, as opposed to the arias. The first opera, *Dafne* (1597), seems to have been mostly recitative. The language purists among the first opera creators wanted music only to emphasize speech, not upstage it. Melody, however, proved too powerful to resist, and the Baroque era clearly separated out the recitatives, when all the "action" took place, from the aria, which tended to reflect on the action. Wagner and Verdi blurred the lines between recitative and aria, and it became old-fashioned. As melody came into question in the twentieth century, however, using music to emphasize speech patterns once again became popular, although naturally it sounded much different than it once had. Many would say that today's operas are almost all recitative, the aria now seeming like the old-fashioned way of communicating information from the operatic stage.

Recitativo secco: (It., "dry recitative") The term for recitative in Baroque and early bel canto opera accompanied only by the harpsichord.

Recitativo accompagnato: Recitative accompanied by several instruments or even the whole orchestra. Gluck, Mozart, and Rossini all made generous use of the recitativo accompagnato.

Répétiteur: (Fr., "rehearser") The person who takes singers through rehearsals, usually at the piano. Répétition is the very descriptive French word for a rehearsal.

Ritardando: (It., "slowing") A musical direction, meaning a general slowing of the beat.

Roulade: (Fr., "a run") Although there is a specific meaning of this term referring to an ornamentation practice of splitting up a line of music into many smaller notes, the general usage refers to any "run" of difficult notes, such as those found in coloratura passages.

Soprano: The female singer of the highest range. Most, though not all, lead roles for women in opera are for sopranos. The term is also used for the highest boys' voices and occasionally for instruments (such as the soprano saxophone).

Spinto: (It., "pushed") A somewhat heavier voice than a pure lyric, though not as loud and heavy as a "dramatic." Funny, but to say a voice is a true "spinto," using the Italian word, is a great compliment, while to say it is "pushed" in plain English is a criticism.

Staccato: (It., "detached") A musical direction to separate each note from those around. In singing, this is done by stopping airflow in between notes. It is necessary to use staccato in coloratura in order to give each note its own value. The opposite of staccato is legato.

Squillo: (It., "ringing sound") The bright quality opera singers, and tenors in particular, are expected to have in their voice.

Tenor: The higher (though not highest) range of the adult male singing voice. The operatic tenor voice is a rare and fragile commodity, undeniably exciting but also prone to failure in critical moments. Thus tenors, who have had a virtual monopoly on heroic roles for about two hundred years, are almost as noted for their caprices and eccentricities as divas. In the film *All About Eve*, actress Thelma Ritter calls tenors the only people in show business more temperamental than wardrobe mistresses.

Timbre: From the Old French word for the sound of a bell, timbre (pronounced "tamber") refers to the unique harmonic quality of a voice that distinguishes it from other voices. It is common to complain that singers today lack sufficient timbre.

Trill: The rapid alternation of notes to create a single, vibrating effect. Officially, a trill is the alternation of a note with the full note directly above it, but this is not always the case in real life. A true trill (the effect can sometimes be faked) is extremely difficult to do. Many who are accustomed to hearing trills on studio recordings are disappointed when they don't hear them in live performances.

Resources for Curious Listeners

The best resource is still the music itself, but there are other resources available to the curious listener eager to learn more on the subject of opera.

Books

There are thousands of available books about every aspect of opera. Many are about composers, both biographical and critical. Richard Wagner wins the prize for most books. The Library of Congress lists over 2,200 books under his name. There are also biographies about almost all of the famous singers, headed by Maria Callas, who has over one hundred books written about her. Stage designers, conductors, and even agents have all written books about opera. Almost all of the books hold at least some interest for the reader with a general interest in opera, and he or she is sure to consume many of them over the years.

For overviews of the entire subject, however, below are listed a few books that are considered standard for all readers.

The Bumper Book of Operatic Disasters, Hugh Vickers, Michael Ffolkes: Hugh Vickers wrote two very popular small books, *Great Operatic Disasters*, and *Even Greater Operatic Disasters*, that have long been considered crucial for opera fans. Both of those books are now available in this combined volume. The anecdotal writing is accompanied by delightfully silly illustrations, yet there is genuine information in this book. For example, Vickers looks into the stories and legends that make *Tosca* (rather than, say, *Macbeth*) well known as the officially cursed opera. Great fun. Introduction by Peter Ustinov.

The New Grove Book of Operas (Abridged), Stanley Sadie, ed.: If *The New Grove Dictionary of Opera* is beyond your requirements, or your budget, you may want to "settle" for the same publishers' *Book of Operas*, coming in at a mere eight hundred pages. The information is of course of the same high quality as the complete *Dictionary*, while the formatting is handy and useful. Entries incude musical notes, historical backgrounds, and illustrations. The appendix includes an excellent "Index of Incipits," with first lines of hundreds of arias, choruses, and ensembles. An excellent resource.

The New Grove Dictionary of Opera, Stanley Sadie. ed.: While this book may not be appropriate for every household, it is considered an ultimate authority on the subject. It can usually be found in the larger public and university libraries. Very scholastic in tone, the *New Grove* makes no attempt at general readability. Instead, it is where one goes to find the information unavailable elsewhere. Virtually every known opera performed before its publication date is to be found in its pages, along with entries on performers, houses, impresarios, and so forth. The bent is, predictably, toward British performers and houses, but the research is so thorough and exhaustive that this becomes irrelevant.

The New Kobbe's Opera Book, Anthony Peattie, ed.: The classic tome of opera composers and their works has been cleverly revised and reformatted into subject matter (rather than alphabetically), making it less of a reference book and more of an interesting read. Kobbe's has been celebrated for decades as a handy resource for both experts and newcomers. While the intensely British tone can be a bit alienating to Americans, the book is a remarkably sensible compendium of crucial operatic knowledge.

100 Great Operas and Their Stories, Henry W. Simon: Operas, it cannot be stressed enough, are about more than their plots, but it is still important (and sometimes quite amusing) to read the synopses of the standard repertory operas. Simon's volume has an excellent selection, with just enough additional information to place the stories in context and provide a truly useful resource for opera listeners and attendees. Buy this book if you want to avoid the mistake of relying solely upon in-house translations to understand what is happening on stage or on a recording.

Opera Anecdotes, Ethan Mordden: Mordden must be commended for taking all the classic stories about opera and compiling them in an easy-to-digest format. With chapters on singers, composers, and even critics, broken into vignettes, Mordden's compendium delivers all the human stories that make the opera world unique. Rossini's bon mots, Wagner's bile attacks, Callas's insights (and whims), and Nellie Melba's self-dramatizations are all here and accounted for.

Opera in America: A Cultural History, John Dizikes: This award-winning (the National Book Critics Circle Award, 1993) volume is both an anecdotal and an informative look at the phenomenon of opera in America from the early nineteenth century to today. Dizikes takes nothing for granted, and his approach to the subject is as refreshing as it is eye-opening. His point of view that opera was one of the foundations of town life in the Old West, for example, challenges the whole notion of opera as a foreign art form and brings much of our national mythology into question.

Opera in Context: Essays on Historical Staging from the Late Renaissance to the Time of Puccini, Mark A. Radice, ed.: Many people know opera solely as a listening experience, whether from radio or recordings. *Opera in Context* is a valuable and fascinating book that looks at the needs of the theater, and exploring the effect actual production issues have had on specific operas. In other words, operas often sound a certain way because they need to look a certain way. The essays in Radice's anthology, written by eleven diverse scholars, examine the relationship between the physical and audio aspects of opera.

Opera 101: A Complete Guide to Learning and Loving Opera, Fred Plotkin: Plotkin analyzes the opera experience from all angles, including how to buy tickets and what to expect when attending an opera. One of the best features of this book is the author's choice to focus on eleven standard operas, with an in-depth look at how each one manages to accomplish its own goals. Plotkin takes the entire opera in each case, and his explanation of relating the parts to the whole is an object lesson in how opera works.

The Oxford Dictionary of Opera, John Warrack, Ewan West (Contributor): This reference book contains 4,500 entries, including 750 on opera composers (with bibliographies), 600 on individual operas, 900 biographies of singers, and 350 entries of specialist terms, along with hundreds covering virtually every aspect of the opera experience. It can be found in most mid-size to large libraries.

The Viking Opera Guide, Amanda Holden (editor), Nicholas Kenyon (editor), Alan Blyth (contributor): This massive (1300-plus pages) and thorough volume was originally published in 1993, and is currently out of print. It is, however, easy enough to track down via Internet sources and in libraries. Besides the thousands of encyclopedic entries on operas, composers, performers, and institutions, this clearly-written book includes marvelous photographs and a very extended guide to recordings. For those in the market for something more manageable, Viking reissued an abridged paperback version of this tome as the *Penguin Opera Guide* in 1998. *The Penguin Opera Guide* was likewise created under the superb eyes of editors Amanda Holden and Nicholas Kenyon, with further contributions by Stephen Walsh and a preface by Colin Davis. Expect the same clarity and lack of pedanticism that one finds in the larger Viking *Guide*.

Magazines

Opera magazines are around to offer in-depth articles, features, and generally excellent photographs. While much of "breaking news" once found in magazines has been relegated to the Internet, magazines are far from obsolete. In smaller cities, they can be difficult to track down, but usually available in bookstores if not on magazine stands. Probably the all-round best magazine of the opera world, *Das Opernglas*, is, unfortunately, only available in German. If you read German, or if you just want to enjoy the excellent photographs, *Das Opernglas* can be found at well-stocked foreign magazine stores. On a more local level, most of the American opera companies publish their own magazines at least quarterly that are generally only available through the company itself. Of these, Seattle Opera and Houston Grand Opera deserve special mention for interesting and informative publications. Some of the best general opera magazines are surveyed below.

American Record Guide: This bimonthly publication includes reviews of a wide range of recordings. More specifically, it includes the supplement "Musical America," dedicated to reviews of live performances. Instead of giving a few lines of review for each and every performance in the country, "Musical America" will focus in-depth on a single production. The writing, therefore, tends to avoid the operatic shorthand that is found in most reviews and that makes their language incomprehensible to all but the inner circle. An excellent resource for all fans and budding fans.

Classical Singer Magazine: From humble beginnings as a New York based newsletter, *Classical Singer Magazine* has become a major player on the music scene. It is geared, naturally, toward singers, with extensive listings of auditions, master classes, seminars, and so forth. It is worth an occasional perusal by the casual fan, however, if only as an insight into the very complicated issue of singing opera.

Gramophone: While not strictly an opera magazine, *Gramophone* is the most important and respected source of reviews and features about recordings in the classical music field. Virtually any new opera recording will get reviewed in *Gramophone*, and there are also excellent features about singers, conductors, and orchestras. *Gramophone* is published in the U.K. and is usually available in foreign-magazine stores.

Opera: This English magazine is crucial for in-depth discussions of recent performances worldwide and of currents in the opera world. *Opera* makes no attempt to reach the uninitiated. It is arch, opinionated, and steeped in the arcane terminology of this discrete world. It also tends to treat provincial British productions as more important than those of major companies in other countries, including the United States. Still, it can be a lot of fun in an English sort of way. The editorials concerning the management woes of the Royal Opera, Covent Garden over the past few years have been nothing short of a very highbrow mud fight.

Opera News: Issued biweekly by the Metropolitan Opera Guild, *Opera News* is centered around the Saturday afternoon Metropolitan Opera broadcasts during the broadcast season (December through April). There are features on the operas and the singers, accompanied by photographs of the current production. During the rest of the year, *Opera News* is comprised of feature articles about opera festivals, singers, impresarios, and other people behind the scenes. Although the magazine is definitely skewed toward events at the Met, *Opera News* does make an effort to present news of the entire opera world. There are even reviews of various performances around the world, and the reviews of Met performances are remarkably unbiased and can sometimes approach the caustic. The performers and producers who are profiled tend to be the most important people in the opera world, so anyone with an interest in opera will find this magazine indispensable.

Websites

Opera is well represented on this newest frontier. There are countless chat groups and discussion forums on opera, where opinions run high and almost any detail of the art form can become a blazing controversy. On the bright side, news about performances is now instantly available from every corner of the world. Besides the discussion groups, there are a great many websites devoted to opera. Almost every company in America, and most throughout the world, have websites, and it's possible to take an amusing world tour of opera houses through your computer. (Warning: don't expect to find casts for future performances on these websites.) There are also some very interesting websites of a more general operatic interest. Only a few can be listed here, but fans (and potential fans) are encouraged to be adventurous. Type "opera" into your favorite search engine, and watch while literally thousands of remarkably unusual sites spring up.

Classical Music Homepage (igor.rzberlin.mpg.de/cmp/classmus.html): While not a purely "operatic" resource, this website covers the operatic repertory so well that it cannot by missed by opera fans. Created by conductor Matt Boynick, it includes biographical essays, links to specific resources, and a large selection of sound bites from a huge variety of compositions.

National Public Radio (www.npr.org): Besides occasional features about opera on its news shows, National Public Radio has several programs dedicated to music and opera news, events, and performances. The website includes information on current and archived programs as well as a good deal of background material on the given subject. Sound bites of interviews and performances are often available as well.

Operabase (www.operabase.com): An astoundingly thorough, multilingual resource including news and reviews, schedules for regular seasons throughout the world (including summer festivals), an audio and video recordings database, and a large listing of further resource. Operabase even includes a handy section of maps for planning operatic odysseys.

Operissimo (www.operissimo.com): One indispensable opera resource on the web is this exhaustive compilation. Operissimo includes links to three hundred opera houses in forty-one countries, including contact information for those that do not yet have their own websites. It also includes very thorough entries on composers and performers, an on-line store for autographs and manuscripts, and news bulletins. In English, German, and Italian.

Opera America (www.operaam.org): Opera America is an extraordinary organization devoted to the general advocacy of opera. Their excellent website includes summaries of their advocacy and education programs, events, and databases. They also publish *Encore Magazine*, which is represented on the site. Although headquartered in Washington, D.C. Opera America runs and supports programs and events throughout the country, and frequently updates calendars and local links on their website.

Opera World (www.operaworld.com): A fun and informal website with lists and links for companies and international schedules. Opera World also features its own columns such as "Opera Insights," with the latest news and gossip, and "Opera Broadcast News," a free e-mail newsletter.

OperaStuff (www.operastuff.com): Another informal website, Opera-Stuff probably has the best list of links to other opera sites, in addition to some very specific lists of its own. The "Lincoln Center Area Hotels," for example, is truly useful for those planning an opera trip to the Big Apple.

Philips Music Group (www.PhilClas.Polygram.NL/index.htm): While many of the record companies operate their own websites, the Philips website must receive special recognition as the most interesting to peruse. Naturally, there are plenty of opportunities to make a purchase while on the Philips website, but there are also catalogues of performers and works, biographical essays, music backgrounds, and so forth. The website also features free e-bulletins about upcoming events.

Documentaries

There are many good film documentaries about the fascinating world of opera and the people who make it so unique. While these may appear to be aimed at the experts, in fact they are usually well suited for all opera fans and generally intended for a wide audience. Four especially fine ones are listed below.

In the Shadow of the Stars (1992): Oscar winner for best full-length documentary, it takes us backstage to look at the lives and careers of the San Francisco Opera choristers.

Maria (1987): A gripping film directed by Tony Palmer that does much to unfold the Callas phenomenon.

Tosca's Kiss (1984): An award-winning film by Daniel Schmid that takes us inside the Casa Verdi, the retirement home for musicians run by Verdi's estate. The interviews help us to understand the role opera plays in people's lives. Some of the incidental singing, even though sung by people in their 80s and 90s, is revelatory.

A Year in the Life of Plácido Domingo (1984): Shows the star covering the four corners of the earth and is, perhaps by accident, a wonderful look at the workings of the international opera scene in our time.

Index

Abbado, Claudio, 120

Abduction from the Seraglio, The
   (Mozart), 103, 148

Adams, John, 47, 52, 86

Adriana Lecouvreur, 91

Aida (Verdi), 19, 77, 78–79, 81, 82, 115,
   142, 164–165

Akhenat (Glass), 95

Albert Herring (Britten), 79

Alto, 189–190

Amahl and the Night Visitor (Menotti),
   43, 45, 100

Anderson, Marian, 43, 44, 120

Andrea Chénier (Giordano), 94–95, 142–
   143

Anna Bolena (Donizetti), 92

Anthony and Cleopatra (Barber), 86–87

Appia, Adolphe, 181

Argento, Dominick, 86

Aria (vocal solo), 11, 64–71, 190

Ariodante (Handel), 97

Armide (Gluck), 20

Artaserse (Metastasio), 54

Aspern Papers, The (Argento), 86

Aubert, Daniel, 30, 33

Bach, Johann Sebastian, 26

Ballad of Baby Doe, The (Moore), 102,
   143

Ballet, operatic element, 81–82

Un ballo in maschera (Verdi), 27, 43, 76,
   161

Balzac, Honoré, 59, 60

Barber of Seville, The (Rossini), 24, 33,
   50, 74, 108, 143, 165

Barber, Samuel, 52, 86–87

Barbiere (Paisiello), 33

Il barbiere di Siviglia (Rossini), 24, 33,
   50, 74, 108, 143, 165

Baritone, 190

Bártok, Béla, 143–144

Bartoli, Cecilia, 120–121

Bass, 190–191

Bass baritone, 191

Basso buffo, 74

Bastianini, Ettore, 183

Battle, Kathleen, 121
Bayreuth Festival, 35, 39, 42, 112, 117
Bayreuth Festival House, 28, 43–44, 180
Beecham, Sir Thomas, 96
Beethoven, Ludwig von, 26, 80–81, 87
Beggar's Opera (Gay), 118
Bel canto tradition, 27, 49–50, 66, 73, 74, 191
Bellini, Vincenzo, 50, 87–88
Berg, Alban, 59, 88–89, 110
Bergman, Ingmar, 186
Bergonzi, Carlo, 121
Berlioz, Hector, 56, 81, 89
Betrothal in a Monastery (Prokofiev), 106
Billy Budd (Britten), 79, 91, 143
Bizet, Georges, 89–90
Bjoerling, Jussi, 121
Bluebeard's Castle (Bártok), 143–144
La Bohème (Puccini), 44, 45, 63, 72, 76, 144, 165
Boito, Arrigo, 90–91
Boris Godunov (Mussorgsky), 103–104, 108, 144
Boulanger, Nadia, 102
Box office, 15
Britten, Benjamin, 79, 83, 91
Broschi, Carlo. *See* Farinelli
Bruson, Renato, 183
Bumbry, Grace, 121

Caballé, Montserrat, 122, 184
Caccini, Francesca, 11
Callas, Maria, 42, 122, 164, 182, 213
Camerata, 10, 75
Can-Can, 55
Cantalani, Alfredo, 65
Capecchi, Renato, 183
Capriccio (Strauss, R.), 83
I Capuleti ed I Montecchi (Bellini), 88
Carmen (Bizet), 29, 55, 77, 89–90, 144, 165–166, 185
Carreras, José, 122–123, 184
Caruso, Enrico, 29, 36, 123–124
Casanova (Argento), 86
Casanova, 23
Castrato, 16, 18, 24, 40, 191
Cavalleria rusticana (Mascagni), 59, 67, 82, 98, 99, 144–145, 185

La Cenerentola (Rossini), 74
Chaliapin, Feodor, 124
Chamber orchestra, 192
Charpentier, Gustave, 34
Chorus, role of, 78–79
Christoff, Boris, 183
Cilea, Francesco, 91, 183
La clemenza di Tito (Mozart), 33
Coloratura, 192
Comic duet, 73
Commedia dell'arte, 192
Consul, The (Menotti), 145
Les Contes D'Hoffmann (Offenbach), 39, 104, 181
Contralto, 193
Le Coq d'or (Rimsky-Korsakoff), 108
Corelli, Arcangelo, 17
Corelli, Franco, 124
Corigliano, John, 76–77, 92
Coronation March, 81
Così fan tutte (Mozart), 69, 145
Countertenor, 193
Craig, Gordon, 181
Crespin, Régine, 124
Il croctato in Egitto (Meyerbeer), 40
Crutchfield, Will, 55
Cunning Little Vixen, The (Janáček), 98

D'Annunzio, Gabriele, 91, 118
Da capo aria, 54
Da Ponte, Lorenzo, 22, 23, 24, 103
Dafne (Peri), 10–11, 201
La damnation de faust (Berlioz), 81
Dance music, 81
Death in Venice (Britten), 91
Death of Klinghoffer (Adams), 86
Debussy, Claude, 34, 92
Del Monaco, Mario, 124–125
Dialogues of the Carmelites (Poulenc), 105, 146
Diaz, Justin, 185
Dimitrova, Ghena, 183
Diva, 29, 194
Domingo, Plácido, 125, 141–142, 182, 183, 185, 214
Dominguez, Oralia, 183
Don Carlos (Verdi), 67, 146

Don Giovanni (Mozart), 22–24, 53, 68, 77, 146–147, 167, 185–186

Don Pasquale (Donizetti), 74

Donizetti, Gaetano, 50, 92–93

Dreigrosschenoper (Weill), 118

Drinking songs, 68

Duets, types of, 72–74

Duse, Eleanora, 91

Dvořák, Antonín, 93

Edison, Thomas, 31, 37

Einstein on the Beach (Glass), 95

Elektra (Strauss, R.), 57, 111, 147, 186

L'elisir d'amore (Donizetti), 74, 147

Die Entführung aus dem Serail (Mozart), 103, 148

Ernani (Verdi), 77, 166

Esther (Weisgall), 118

Eugene Onegin (Tchaikovsky), 65, 113–114, 147, 185

Excursion of Mr. Broucek, The (Janáček), 97

Falsetto, 18, 194

Falstaff (Verdi), 35, 71, 115, 148

La fanciulla del West (Puccini), 79, 149

Farewell arias, 65, 70–71

Farinelli, 18, 19, 119, 125–126

Farrar, Geraldine, 126

Faust (Gounod), 34, 57, 77, 96, 148–149

La favola d'Orfeo (Monteverdi), 12–13, 101–102

Fedora (Giordano), 94

Fidelio (Beethoven), 26, 76, 78, 82, 87, 166

Fiery Angel, The (Prokofiev), 105, 106

Fischer-Dieskau, Dietrich, 186

Flagstad, Kirsten, 126

Die Fledermaus (Strauss, J.), 55

Fliegende Holländer (Wagner), 50, 116, 149, 167

La forza del destino (Verdi), 68, 77, 149–150, 183

Floyd, Carlise, 93

Flying Dutchman, The (Wagner), 50, 116, 149, 167

Force of Destiny, The (Verdi), 68, 77, 149–150, 183

Four Saints in Three Acts (Thomson), 114

Francesca da Rimini (Zandonai), 60, 118, 183

Der Freishütz (von Weber), 26, 116

Frenip, Mirella, 126

Friedrich, Gstz, 186

Furtwängler, Wilhelm, 126–127

Gambler, The (Prokofiev), 105, 106

García Gutierrez, Antonio, 63

García, Manuel, 24, 127

Garden, Mary, 127

Gay, John, 118

Gershwin, George, 79, 94, 113

Gesamtkunstwerk, 5–6, 195

Ghosts of Versailles, The (Corigliano/Hoffmann), 76–77, 92

Gilbert, W. S., 55

La gioconda (Ponchielli), 60, 66, 90, 104, 150

I gioielli della Madonna (Wolf-Ferrari), 82

Giordano, Umberto, 94–95

Girl of the Golden West, The (Puccini), 79, 149

Giulio Cesare (Handel), 97, 167–168

Glass, Philip, 52, 79, 95

Glinka, Mikhail, 34

Gluck, Johann Willibald von, 20–22, 54, 95–96

Gobbi, Tito, 127–128

Goethe, Johann Wolfgang von, 57, 66

Golden Cockerel, The (Rimsky-Korsakoff), 108

Gomez, Carlos, 32

Götterdämmerung (Wagner), 70, 77, 82, 173

Gounod, Charles, 57, 96

Grand Opéra era, 25–26, 38–39

Grand Opéra tradition, 50–52, 108–109

Grossfestspielhaus, 28

Guillaume Tell (Rossini), 25, 26, 51, 78, 108–109

Hagegard, Hakan, 186

Hamlet (Thomas), 67

Handel, George Frideric, 18, 19, 68, 96–97

Hansel and Gretel (Humperdinck), 2

Herbert, Victor, 56

Heroic arias, 68

Hockney, David, 113

Hoffman, William, 76–77, 92

Hoffmann, Peter, 183, 184

Hofmannsthal, Hugo von, 63, 111

"Holy German Art," 41

Horne, Marilyn, 128

Hugo, Victor, 63

Les Huguenots (Meyerbeer), 51

Humperdinck, Engelbert, 2

Idomeneo (Mozart), 22, 54, 67

Intermezzo, 82, 83, 195–196

Iphigénie en Aulide (Gluck), 95

Iphigénie en Tauride (Gluck), 20, 21, 22, 69

L'italiana in Algeri (Rossini), 75

Janáček, Leos, 97–98

Jenůfa (Janácek), 97, 98, 150

Julius Caesar (Handel), 97, 167–168

Kallman, Chester, 113

Karajan, Herbert von, 128–129

Katerina Ismailovna (Shostakovich), 110–111

Katya Kabanová (Janácek), 98, 150–151

Khovanschina (Mussorgsky), 103, 104

Kibkalo, Tevgeny, 185

Komische Oper, 42

Korngold, Erich, 98

La Scala, 25, 30, 38–39, 41–42

Lady Macbeth of the Mtsensk District (Shoshtakovich), 37, 110, 111

Lanza, Mario, 124

Lehar, Franz, 55

Leoncavallo, Ruggero, 35, 82, 98

Levine, James, 129

Libretto, 11, 62–64, 90–91, 196

Life for the Tsar, A (Glinka), 34

Ligendza, Caterina, 186

Lind, Jenny, 31–32, 129

Liszt, Franz, 56

Live from the Met, 44, 45, 183

Lohengrin (Wagner), 56–57, 73, 151, 183

Losey, Joseph, 185–186

Love arias, 64–65, 71

Love duet, 72–73

Love for Three Oranges, The (Prokofiev), 81, 107–108

Lucia di Lamermoor (Donizetti), 66–67, 72, 76, 92–93, 151, 168–169

Lucrezia Borgia, (Donizetti), 68

Lully, Jean Baptiste, 14

Lulu (Berg), 59, 88–89, 110, 151–152

Macbeth (Verdi), 67, 68, 152, 169

MacDonald, Jeanette, 29

Mad scenes (arias), 66–67, 71

Madamé Butterfly (Puccini), 66, 73, 152, 169–170

Magic Flute, The (Mozart), 2, 55, 161, 186

Mahler, Gustav, 37, 129

Makropoulous Affair, The (Janáček), 98

Malibran, María, 24, 119, 130

Les Manelles de Tirésias (Poulenc), 105

Manon (Massenet), 99, 153, 170

Manon Lescaut (Puccini), 33, 152–153, 183

Mansaniello (Auber), 30

Marches, 81

Marriage of Figaro, The (Mozart), 22, 67, 68, 75, 184

Marton, Eva, 183

Mascagni, Pietro, 35, 99

Massenet, Jules, 33, 34, 57, 99–100

Mefistofele (Boito), 90, 91, 153–154, 170

Die Meistersinger von Nürnberg (Wagner), 67, 70, 76, 78, 117, 153

Melba, Dame Nellie, 130

Melchior, Lauritz, 130

Menotti, Giancarlo, 45, 52, 100

Merrill, Robert, 130

Merry Widow, The (Lehar), 55

Messiaen, Olivier, 100

Metropolitan Opera House, 32, 37, 39–40, 44

Meyerbeer, Giacomo, 26, 34, 51, 81, 100–101, 109

Mezza voce, 197

Mezzo-soprano, 197

Milanov, Zinka, 130

Milnes, Sherill, 131

Minimalism, 52

Moïse (Rossini), 78

Monteverdi, Claudio, 12–13, 15, 62, 101–102

Moore, Douglas, 102

Moravia, Alberto, 113

Moreschi, Alessandro, 40

Morning Song, 71

Moses und Aron (Schoenberg), 79, 109

Mother of Us All, The (Thomson), 114

Mozart, Wolfgang Amadeus, 21, 22, 23, 30, 54, 80, 102–103

Mussorgsky, Modest, 103–104

Mustafà, Domenico, 40

Muti, Riccardo, 131

Nabucco (Verdi), 30, 67, 78, 115, 154, 183

"Narratives," 69–70

Nationalism, 32, 34–35

Naturalism, 20, 53

Naughty Marietta (Herbert), 56

Neo-Romanticism, 52

Nerone (Boito), 90, 91

Nietzsche, Friedrich, 34, 90

Nilsson, Birgit, 131

Nixon in China (Adams), 69, 86

Norma (Bellini), 66, 71, 88, 170–171

Norman, Jessye, 131

Nose, The (Shostakovich), 110

La nozze di Figaro (Mozart), 54, 154, 171

Oath duet, 73

Oberon (von Weber), 26

Obrastzova, Elena, 132, 185

Of Mice and Men (Floyd), 93

Offenbach, Jacques, 55, 104

Ollivier, Emile, 25

Opera
acting, 182, 184
books, 205–209
CD recordings of, 163–178
critics, 181
definition of, 1, 7
documentaries, 213–214
experience of, 84, 181–182, 187–188
history of, 9–47
invention of, 2, 10–16
magazines, 209–211
movies of, 185–186
productions of, 179–181
useful terms, 203
videos of, 183
websites, 211–213

Opera buffa, 53

Opéra Comique, 34

Opera seria, 19–20, 53–55, 57

Operetta, 55–56

Orchestra, 197–198

Orchestral interludes, 82–83

Orfeo ed Eurydice (Gluck), 20, 22, 95

Orlando Furioso (Vivaldi), 67, 71

Orphée aux Enfers (Offenbach), 55

Otello (Verdi), 33, 41, 68, 71, 73, 78, 82, 115, 155, 171, 185

Overtures, 80–81, 198

I pagliacci (Leoncavallo), 82, 98, 155, 185

Paisiello, Giovanni, 33

Parsifal (Wagner), 29, 117, 155–156, 171–172, 186

Patti, Adelina, 132

Paul Bunyan (Britten), 74

Pavarotti, Luciano, 132

Pears, Sir Peter, 91

Les Pêcheurs de perles (Bizet), 89

Pelléas et Mélisande (Debussy), 34, 92, 156

Pergolesi, Giovanni Battista, 53

Peri, Jacopo, 10, 62

Peter Grimes (Britten), 79, 83, 91, 156, 172

Phantom of the Opera (Webber), 60

Piccinni, Niccolò, 21, 95

Picker, Tobias, 47, 52

Pinza, Enzio, 132–133

Pirandello, Luigi, 118

Plançon, Pol, 133

Polyphony, 75

Ponchielli, Amilcare, 90, 99, 104–105

Pons, Lily, 133

Ponselle, Rosa, 133–134

Porgy and Bess (Gershwin), 71, 79, 94, 156, 172–173
Poulenc, Francis, 105
Prelude, 81, 200
Price, Leontyne, 134
Prince Igor (Borodin), 108
"Prize Song," 67
Prokofiev, Sergei, 81, 105–106
La Prophète (Meyerbeer), 81, 101
Puccini, Giacomo, 33, 35, 79, 80, 106–107
I puritani (Bellini), 73

Quartets, 76
Queen of Spades (Tchaikovsky), 113
Quintets, 76–77

Rainmondi, Ruggiero, 186
Rake's Progress, The (Stravinsky), 68, 113, 156–157
Rákóczy March, 81
Ramey, Samuel, 134
"Realism," 59
Recitative, 201
Reed, Lou, 47
Reich, Steve, 52
Renaissance, 2, 27, 75
"Rescue Dramas," 62–63
Das Rheingold (Wagner), 173
Ricciarelli, Katia, 185
Rienzi (Wagner), 116
Rigoletto (Verdi), 19, 63, 70, 74, 76, 157
Rimsky-Korsakoff, Nicolai, 103, 107–108
Rinaldo (Handel), 97
Ring of the Nibelung, The (Wagner), 27–28, 34, 42, 45, 70, 77, 117, 157, 173–174
   Das Rheingold (Wagner), 173
   Die Walküre (Wagner), 70–71, 72–73, 173, 184
   Siegfried (Wagner), 73, 173
   Götterdämmerung (Wagner), 70, 77, 82, 173
Ring Resounding, 174
Rise and Fall of the City of Mahagonny, The (Weill), 117
Robert le Diable (Meyerbeer), 26, 51
Romantic movement, 22, 56–57, 66
Roméo et Juliette (Gounod), 96, 157

Der Rosenkavlier (Strauss, R.), 70, 77–78, 111–112, 157–158, 174–175
Rossi, Carlo, 185
Rossini, Gioacchino, 24–26, 75, 80, 108–109
Rusalka (Dvorák), 93
Ruslan and Ludmila (Glinka), 34
Russell, Anna, 73
Rysanek, Leonie, 134–135, 183, 184, 186

Sadko (Rimsky-Korsakoff), 108
Saint-Saëns, Camille, 109
Salome (Strauss, R.), 158, 175, 182
Samson et Dalilah (Saint-Saëns), 109, 158
San Francisco (film), 29
Satyagraha (Britten), 79, 95, 175–176
Scarlatti, Alessandro, 17
Scenas, 54
Schoenberg, Arnold, 38, 57–58, 79, 109–110
Schwartzkopf, Elisabeth, 135
Scotto, Renata, 135, 183
"Sea Interludes," 83
Semiramide (Rossini), 50, 67, 108
Serafin, Tullio, 135–136
Serialism, 38, 57–59
La serva padrona (Pergolesi), 53
Sextets, 75, 76
Shakespeare, William, 3, 63
Shaw, George Bernard, 70
Shostakovich, Dmitri, 37, 110–111
Siegfried (Wagner), 73, 173
Sills, Beverly, 136
Simionato, Giulietta, 136
Simon Boccanegra (Verdi), 90, 158–159
Six Characters in Search of an Author (Weisgall), 118
Snow Maiden, The (Rimsky-Korsakoff), 108
Solti, Sir George, 42, 174
Songs, 67–68, 71
La sonnambula (Bellini), 31, 88
Soprano, 202
Sorrows of Young Werther, The, 57, 66
Sousa, John Philip, 56
Stein, Gertrude, 114
Stevens, Risë, 136
Stratas, Teresa, 136–137, 182, 185

Strauss, Johann, Jr., 55
Strauss, Richard, 37, 57, 63, 83, 111–112, 182
Stravinsky, Igor, 68, 112–113
Suicide arias, 65–66, 70, 71
Sullivan, Arthur, 55
Susannah (Floyd), 93, 159
Sutherland, Dame Joan, 137
Sweetheart (Herbert), 56
Syberberg, Hans Jürgen, 186

Tales of Hoffmann (Offenbach), 39, 104, 181
Tannhäuser (Wagner), 51, 81–82, 159
Tchaikovsky, Peter Ilyich, 34, 113–114
Te Kanawa, Dame Kiri, 137, 186
Teatro alla Scala. *See* La Scala
Tebaldi, Renata, 41, 137, 183
Tenor, 203
Thomas, Ambroise, 67
Thomson, Virgil, 114
Tibbett, Lawrence, 137
Timbre, 203
Tosca (Puccini), 159, 176
Toscanini, Arturo, 39, 41–42, 43, 112, 138
"Total Work of Art," 5, 116, 186
Die tote Stadt (Korngold), 98
La traviata (Verdi), 59, 115, 159–160, 176, 185
Trill, 203
Trios, 77–78
Tristan und Isolde (Wagner), 28, 71, 73, 117, 160, 176
Il trovatore (Verdi), 17, 68, 82, 160, 177
Troyanos, Tatiana, 138
Les Troyens (Berlioz), 89
Tsar's Bride, The (Rimsky-Korsakoff), 108
Tucker, Richard, 138
Turandot (Puccini), 39, 73, 77, 160, 177
Turn of the Screw, The (Britten), 91

Vanessa (Barber), 86, 177–178
Varnay, Astrid, 186
"Veil Song," 67
Verdi, Giuseppe, 17, 19, 26, 27, 29–30, 90–91, 114–116
Verismo tradition, 35, 51–52, 59–60, 82, 91, 99
Verrett, Shirley, 139
Viadot-Garcia, Pauline, 139
Vickers, Jon, 91, 139
Vishnevskaya, Galina, 139, 185
Vivaldi, Antonio, 67
Vocal solo, 64–71
Vocal techniques, 2–3, 26, 27
Voight, Deborah, 139
La Voix humaine (Poulenc), 105
von Weber, Carl Maria, 26, 116
Von Stade, Frederica, 139–140
Voyage, The (Glass), 95

Wagner, Richard, 5, 26–29, 30, 34, 39, 87, 101, 116–117, 180, 182
Waits, Tom, 47
Die Walküre (Wagner), 70–71, 72–73, 173, 184
La Wally (Catalani), 65
Warren, Leonard, 140
Water Music Suite, The, 96
Webber, Andrew Lloyd, 60
Weil, Kurt, 38, 117–118
Weisgall, Hugo, 118
Wolf-Ferrari, Ermanno, 82
Wozzeck (Berg), 71, 83, 88, 89, 161, 178

Zandonai, Riccardo, 60, 118
Zarzuela, 15, 55
Die Zauberflöte (Mozart), 2, 55, 161, 186
Zeffirelli, Franco, 44, 185
Zola, Emile, 59, 60